A Nimmo

Songs and Ballads of Clydesdale

A Nimmo

Songs and Ballads of Clydesdale

ISBN/EAN: 9783744769198

Printed in Europe, USA, Canada, Australia, Japan

Cover: Foto ©Andreas Hilbeck / pixelio.de

More available books at **www.hansebooks.com**

Songs and Ballads

OF

Clydesdale.

Wtth Illustrative Notes

By A. NIMMO.

EDINBURGH AND GLASGOW: JOHN MENZIES & CO.

MDCCCLXXXII.

To Adelaide Mary Bertram of Kersewell, Carnwath.

———◆———

MADAM,

It is not that my grandfather was an old tenant of the Kersewell family ; it is not that my father was Quarter-Master in the Regiment of Cavalry commanded by the late Col. Bertram of Kersewell, and who, on returning with his comrade, Sergeant Martin, had the interesting and memorable interview with Jean Armour at the grave of Burns, as related by Gilfillan in his account of the Poet.

The deep interest you have long taken in the religious instruction of the young, and the warm sympathy you have shown for the unfortunate, the old and the imbecile, in being mainly instrumental in supporting for such a lengthened period the soup kitchen for their comfort, certainly entitles you to the gratitude of the recipients, and the public respect.

For these reasons, Madam, I take the liberty of most respectfully dedicating this volume to you, a trifling compliment, no doubt, but I had nothing better to offer.

With warmest wishes for prosperity and happiness to Mr. Bertram, yourself, and your interesting family,

I remain, MADAM,

Your much obliged and most obedient

A. NIMMO.

CARNWATH, *May,* 1882.

P.S.—It is another striking instance of the awful uncertainty of human life, that after the above lines of dedication were not only written but printed, Mrs. Bertram had an attack of illness on Thursday, the 25th of May, 1882, which closed her valuable life in a few hours. Mrs. Bertram was the daughter of John Bateman, Esq. This gentleman, many years ago, hired a small vessel at Tasmania to carry him and his two daughters to Australia ; and these three, we believe, were the first settlers in Victoria, and thus in a sense may be said to have laid the foundations of what will yet be a great and flourishing empire.

A. N.

June, 1882.

PREFACE.

PERHAPS no man in the wide region of Upper Strathclyde was more universally esteemed than the late Adam Sim, Esq., of Coulter Maynes. It is a curious circumstance, that it was only at a very *early* and a rather *late* period of our lives that we had any friendly intercourse. When a boy residing with his grandfather, Mr. John Stodart, farmer, Bank, Carnwath, I was one of the herds, and on the most intimate and familiar terms with young Mr. Sim. Even then he was beginning to show some of those traits for which he afterwards became so remarkable. The rhymes and traditions of the district, especially those respecting Wallace and the Covenanters, interested him deeply, and the finding of a small bronze figure of a pig, in a marsh at the foot of the Bank Brae, was the incident which first awakened in his mind a taste for antiquities—a taste which " grew with his growth and strengthened with his strength," until it culminated in that extraordinary collection at Coulter Maynes, which, for a private collection, I believe, was second only to that of Abbotsford. After the days of boyhood our course in life was widely divergent, but a few years before he died I received an invitation to visit him, and was most kindly received. In the course of our intercourse, he suggested that I should make a collection of " The Songs and Ballads of Clydesdale," and he would have them published. After I had a goodly number collected, his sudden death put an end to that specu- lation as far as he was concerned.

There are many very excellent people, who ridicule the

idea of any good being produced by songs, yet one distinguished statesman, who knew human nature well, said he
did not care who made the laws if he could get the making
of the songs. In this collection I have paid due attention
to the lays of the Covenanters. Many people think them
fools, rogues, or hypocrites, with no taste for literature, yet
Cleland, one of the best poets in Scotland at the time, assisted
to hunt the brave hero Claverhouse from Drumclog, and with
the single regiment of Covenanters repulsed and defeated
the repeated attacks of an army of 5,000 Highlanders at
Dunkeld. All they fought for was a free parliament and a
free assembly. And it is a curious fact, that the bulk of
our best song writers are either natives, or intimately
associated with the land of the Covenant. I need only men-
tion Ramsay, Burns, Tannahill, Campbell, Joanna Baillie,
Henry S. Riddell, &c., &c. Clydesdale is a Covenanting
district.

The present collection, instead of a compilation of the
songs of these writers, is rather meaut to show the state of
the Scottish lyre, in past and present times, among the
people of Clydesdale.

A few pieces are included which, although not written by
natives, are favourites in the district.

CONTENTS.

10 CONTENTS.

PAGE

SONGS AND BALLADS OF CLYDESDALE.

OUR AULD SCOTS SANGS.

Air—" Traveller's Return."

O WEEL I lo'e our auld Scots sangs,
    The mournfu' and the gay ;
They charmed me by a mother's knee,
    In bairnhood's happy day :
And even yet, though owre my pow
    The snaws o' age are flung,
The bluid loups joyfu' in my veins,
    Whene'er I hear them sung.

They bring the fond smile to the cheek,
    Or tear-drap to the e'e ;
They bring to mind auld cronies kind,
    Wha sung them aft wi' glee.
We seem again to hear the voice
    Of mony a lang-lost frien' ;
We seem again to grip the hand
    That lang in dust has been.

And oh, how true our auld Scots sangs,
    When nature they portray !
We think we hear the wee bit burn
    Gaun bickerin' doun the brae ;

We see the spot, though far awa',
    Where life's first breath we drew,
And a' the gowden scenes of youth
    Seem risin' to the view.

And dear I lo'e the wild war strains
    Our langsyne minstrels sung—
They rouse wi' patriotic fire
    The hearts of auld and young ;
And even the dowie dirge that wails
    Some brave but ruined band,
Inspires us wi' a warmer love
    For hame and fatherland.

Yes, leese me on our auld Scots sangs—
    The sangs of love and glee,
The sangs that tell of glorious deeds
    That made auld Scotland free.
What though they sprang frae simple bards,
    Wha kent nae rules of art !
They ever, ever yield a charm
    That lingers round the heart.

A. MACKAY.

THE BANKS O' CLYDE.

ON the grassy banks o' Clyde, bonnie lassie, O,
Oft we've roamed at eventide, bonnie lassie, O,
    'Mang the bonnie yellow broom
    When the air was all perfume
Wi' the simmer flowers in bloom, bonnie lassie, O.

Auld Tintoc looked so grand, bonnie lassie, O,
Over all the smiling land, bonnie lassie, O,
    While all the green-wood rang
    Wi' the blackbird's evening sang,
As we roamed the birks amang, bonnie lassie, O.

Happy, happy was the time! bonnie lassie, O,
When we heard the soothing chime, bonnie lassie, O,
    Of the distant village bell,
    Tolling day's departing knell,
As we trode the flowery dell, bonnie lassie, O.

When the swallows o' Clyde Stairs,[1] bonnie lassie, O,
A' were sleepin' in their lairs, bonnie lassie, O,
    And the stars in heaven so high,
    Were reflected from the sky,
In the river gliding by, bonnie lassie, O.

Then we sought the fairy bower, bonnie lassie, O ;
Where the brier and hawthorn flower, bonnie lassie, O,
    While the heaven's lovely queen,
    In all her radiant sheen,
Rose, resplendent, o'er the scene, bonnie lassie, O.

Then you'll aye be leal and true, bonnie lassie, O ;
I'll be firm and true to you, bonnie lassie, O,
    Thro' all the care and strife—
    All the ups and downs of life,
Be my true and faithful wife, bonnie lassie, O.

[1] Clyde Stairs is a high shelving bank on the right side of the river, at the point nearest Carnwath, which, in summer, is usually tenanted by a great flock of swallows.

MY LANDLADY'S NOSE.

O'ER the evils of life it's a folly to fret,
Despondence and grief never lessened them yet,
Then a fig for the world, let it come as it goes—
I'll sing to the praise of my landlady's nose!

Oh! my landlady's nose is in noble condition,
For longitude, latitude, shape, and position;
It's as round as a horn, and as red as a rose—
Success to the trunk of my landlady's nose!

To jeweller shops, your fine ladies repair,
For trinkets and nick-nacks to give them an air,
Here, living carbuncles, a score of them glows!
On the big, massy sides of my landlady's nose.

Ye wishy-wash, weak water drinkers so cold,
Come here, and the virtues of brandy behold,
Here's red-burning Etna—a mountain of snows
Would roar down in streams from my landlady's nose!

But O! when this nose, with an uplifted arm,
She grasps in the dishclout to sound an alarm,
Horns, trumpets, and drums, are mere screaming o' crows;
To the loud thunderin' twang o' my landlady's nose!

Oh! my landlady's nose unto me is a treasure,
A care-killing nostrum—a fountain of pleasure,
When I want a loud laugh, to discharge all my woes,
I only look up to my landlady's nose!   A. WILSON.

It is certainly very remarkable that all our poets, poetasters, and
balladmongers never make the least allusion to the ladies' noses; they
rave away about rosy cheeks, ruby lips, ivory teeth, dimpled chins,
alabaster brows, and eyes like stars, while the poor nose, standing alone,
yet most conspicuously, in the very centre of all these beauties, is passed
and repassed, around and around, without the least compliment or note
of recognition. And if we would only think what the greatest beauty
would be without a nose! this silence is the more culpable and inexcus-
able. We hold that Wilson, merely from the selection of this subject, is
one of our most original song writers.

SMILE ALONE ON ME.

O LASSIE, veil that rosy blush,
  And hide frae me that killin' ee ;
Or grant that other dearest wish,
  That thou wilt smile alone on me.
The infant days of pleasure took
  To wander wi' thee o'er the lea,
For early by yon purlin' brook
  I felt the magic o' thine e'e.

I gathered wild flowers frae the vale,
  I pu'd fruit's ripeness frae the tree,
And with an infant, artless tale,
  I made an offering unto thee.
With *ardent love* I view thee still,
  Tho' infant hours no longer be ;
Oh, then, thy face in pity veil,
  Or let it smile alone on me !

J. PAIRMAN, BIGGAR.

Mr. Pairman was highly esteemed by a numerous circle of friends and
acquaintances. He died suddenly at his house in Edinburgh on the 14th
December, 1843, in the 55th year of his age; his ashes repose in Biggar
Churchyard. He was a well-known portrait painter.

THE GOWD UPON CHARLIE.

IF ye'd drink ale and be cantie still,
  Sin' the breeks hae banged the kiltie,
Wale out the lads wore the white cockades,
  An' delight in a Jacobite liltie.

Then up wi' the lads wore the white cockades,
  Altho' they be scattered richt sairlie ;
There's a sough in the land, there's a heart and a hand
  That may yet pit the gowd upon Charlie !

Tho' a puir German daw's got the crap o' the wa',
  An' oor ain bonnie doo it has pookit,
We've gude falconers still, an' when they get their will
  They'll pit the richt doo in the dookit.
          Then up wi' the lads, &c.

Then keep your blue bonnet awee ere you don it,
  An' keep your claymore frae the stourin',
Ye may yet hear a horn, on a braw simmer morn,
  That may thank ye weel for the scourin'.
          Then up wi' the lads, &c.

Tho' base hireling swords and cauld-bluided words
  Hae yirded the pride o' the thistle ;
Tho' the book's in the grun, a soul's in the son
  That may yet gar auld Hanover fistle!
          Then up wi' the lads, &c.

                                        AINSLIE.

In the pilgrimage from Auld Reekie to the Land of Burns, by Edie
Ochiltree, Jinglin' Jock, and the Lang Linker, it is stated that the writer
took down this song from the singing of an auld wife at Carnwath, who
affirmed that her father had more pleasure in hearing that song sung,
when he was ill, than in any of the Psalms of David. Carnwath was
reckoned a stronghold of Jacobitism, both in 1715 and in the '45.

────────

I'LL SOON HAE A WIFE O' MY AIN.

FRAE Clyde to the banks o' sweet Earn
  I've wandered for mony a long mile,
The thochts o' my dearest lass, Ailie,
  The wearisome hours did beguile ;
The happy wae nicht that we parted
  She vowed she would constant remain ;
My heart-strings a' dirled wi' fondness,
  I kissed her and kissed her again !

It's no that her cheeks are like roses,
  Nor yet for her dark rollin' e'e ;
It's no for her sweet comely features—
  These charms are a' naething to me.
The storms o' this life may soon blast them,
  Or sickness may snatch them away,
But virtue when fixed in the bosom
  Will flourish and never decay !

Nae langer I'll spend a' my siller,
  Nae langer I'll noo lie my ain,
Nae langer I'll rin after lasses—
  I'll soon hae a wife o' my ain !
For mony a long fit I've wandered,
  And mony a nicht spent in vain,
Wi' drinkin' and dancin' and courtin'—
  But I'll soon hae a wife o' my ain !

Her mother's aye roarin' and flytin'—
  I rede ye tak' tent o' that chiel,
He'll no be that canny to live wi',
  He'll ne'er be like douce Geordie Steel !
He's courted far owre mony lasses,
  Tae slicht them, he thinks it gude fun,
He'll mak but a drucken half-marrow,
  Ye'll best rue before ye be bun'.

Tho' Geordie be laird of a housie,
  And brags o' his kye and his pelf,
And warld's wealth I be richt scant o'—
  A fig for't as lang's I've my health.
If ance I were coupled wi' Ailie,
  She'll seldom hae cause to complain ;
We'll jog on thro' life aye richt canny
  When I get a wife o' my ain.

But if that my Ailie prove faithless,
  And marry before I return,
I'll no like a coof grieve about her,
  Nor yet for ae minute I'll mourn,

But straight unto some other beauty,
Without loss o' time I will hie,
And shew to the lasses I'm careless,
Unless they're as willin' as I !

ROBERT WHITELEY, CARNWATH.

This song first appeared in Chambers' Scottish Anthology, yet, although
it is there stated to be the production of Robert, there is good reason to
believe his brother Smollet, was the author. Robert was an excellent
singer of Scottish songs, and had the merit of first introducing it to the
notice of the public, and uniformly stated that it was his own. However,
those who knew them both, were decidedly of opinion that Smollet was
the real author. One incident in his career tends to confirm this opinion—
while an apprentice to the stocking-making trade at Carnwath, he fell
deeply in love with a girl named Alison Bogle, the heroine of the song. One
night when visiting her, they quarrelled, and the mischievous girl, acting
in the character of her name, donned a white shirt over her clothes, stood
upright on the road before him when he was going home, with her arms
extended, and gave the poor fellow such a fright, and such a sweat in run-
ning from the *ghost*, that he caught a severe cold. Robert was a notorious
poacher. On one occasion he was summoned to appear before Col. Renton,
of Symington Lodge, who had got some of his snares on his lands. Holding
them up he asked : "Well, Rob, can you tell me what these are ?" Rob
took them in his hand, and looking very green, replied : "Od, I'm sure
I dinna ken, Col., if they're no some new-fashioned couples ye've gotten
for yer young dougs." "Couples for dogs, you rascal ; they are snares·
for hares," replied the Col. ; "ay, and they were set, too, by Rob
Whitley." At this stage of the interview, the report of a gun was heard,
and Rob retorted in a triumphant tone—"Say ye're no sure, Cornel, div
ye no hear that, and if I werna here, just standing in your ain room at
this precious moment, ye wad be saying, 'that's that d—— rascal
Whitley'; but suppose I do nab a bit hare noo and then, what aboot it,
Cornel, what aboot it, man ; 'The earth is the Lord's and the fulness
thereof.'" "You are quite mistaken there, Rob, quite mistaken ; all the
land hereabouts, at any rate, belongs to me and Mr. Carmichael of Eastend."
Some time after this, Rob removed to Carnwath, but continuing his
poaching habits, was at length sentenced to one month's imprisonment
in Lanark Jail. These were the days of old when matters in some respects
were taken very coolly. Rob got so far into the confidence of the jailer,
that he was allowed to go out upon his *parole* and visit his acquaintances.
One night, Rob, being treated to a little toddy by a few friends, got so
engrossed with the conversation and song singing, that it was far past
the hour when he should have returned. The Jailer said : "Rob, whatna'
a wark's this wi' ye ; I'll just tell ye plainly, sir, if ye dinna keep mair
regular hours, I'll bar ye oot a' thegither." "Friend," replied Rob ;
"I'll just tell *you*, if ye dinna keep a mair civil tongue in your head, I'll
change my lodgings ; do you really think I'm to be bothered and insulted
by a body like you; but just keep quiet, man—it's a' nae use for you and
me to cast oot; just hae patience—if once my time was out, if I dinna
send ye in twa o' the fattest hares that Liberton Muir can turn oot, my
name's no Rob Whitley." Rob died in the spring of 1836, and was buried
in Carnwath Churchyard. Both the brothers were natives of Symington.

LOCKHART'S FAREWELL TO CARNWATH.

O ! IT's hard to leave the halls where my fathers reigned of
    yore :
It's hard to be exiled and to seek a foreign shore ;
It's hard to leave the moat, so delightful aye to view—
But the hour is come at last—I must bid them all adieu !

Farewell to towering Tintoc, and lofty Coulter.Fell,
The hills of Walston and Dunsyre, the scenes I loved so well;
Tho' oceans wide may us divide, while memory is true,
I'll ne'er forget your much-loved scenes—tho' now I say adieu !

I've oft surveyed with joy, my fair domains so wide ;
Oft ranged o'er hill and valley with my staghounds by my side ;
And rambled o'er the plains where my falcons often flew—
But the hour's come at last—I must bid them all adieu !

No more I'll chase the deer, o'er the mountain and the plain ;
No more I'll steer my skiff, o'er my ain white loch again;
Nor gaze on Clyde's proud streams, rushing from the moun-
    tains blue—
The bitter hour is come—I must bid them all adieu !

No more I'll quench my thirst, at St. Mary's crystal well
Nor listen to the chime of St. Mary's auld kirk bell ;
Nor hear the bugle summons, my clansmen ever true—
For my gallant Prince's sake, I must bid them all adieu !

My sisters fair have wept, till they have no tears to shed ;
For our gallant Prince's sake my mother's heart has bled ;
My sire is far away, pierced with sorrows not a few,
Yet for Royal Charlie's sake—I can bid them all adieu !

l am hunted like the wolf, and price is on my head,
" The wee, wee German lairdie" would rejoice if I was dead;
But to him I'll ne'er submit, to honour I'll be true ;
Dear as friends and Carnwath are—I must bid them all adieu !

No! it never shall be said that the Lockhart e'er did wince
To share whatever fate has been allotted for his Prince ;
I could die for Charlie's cause, and the " red rose " yet may
    rue
The hour when Lockhart bade Carnwath—a long, a last adieu!

                                                        W. G.

The Lockhart referred to in this song was George Lockhart, younger,
of Carnwath. This gentleman and his father, George Lockhart, senior,
were both at the battle of Prestonpans, fighting gallantly on the side of
Prince Charles. As soon as victory was declared for the Prince, Mr.
Lockhart, senior, who was esteemed the best horseman in Scotland, rode
across the country in steeple chase fashion to his seat at Dryden in twenty
minutes. Being there so early it was deemed impossible he could have
been at the battle. He surrendered himself to Duncan Forbes, and
asked what he was to do, as he knew he was a suspected person, and was
ordered to go to Yorkshire, and consider that county his prison. There
he remained until the rebellion was quashed. George Lockhart, junior,
remained an officer in the Prince's army, and when the Prince left
Edinburgh for the South on Sunday, Nov. 3rd, Carnwath people being
quietly engaged in public worship, the church-door was thrown open
with great violence, and a man with a loud, stentorian voice, exclaimed—
"The rebels are comin'! the rebels are comin'!" The people started to
their feet in confusion. The minister, raising his voice, asked the
messenger, " Where are they at?" " They were at Newbigging when I
came away, and they will be at Kaimend, now." " Well, my friends,"
said the minister, "let us implore the divine protection before we
separate," which he did, and among other petitions, prayed the Lord
to put " Hooks in their noses, and bridles in their jaws, and turn them
back by the way that they came," but instead of that, the congregation
met them all in the teeth (a troop of horse) some two hundred yards
from the church-door. They took possession of Carnwath House, carried
off a great number of horses which were provided for them by Mr.
Lockhart, and about a dozen others, with their proprietors as prisoners,
to Broughton ; where they met young Mr. Lockhart, who sent them
and their horses all home again, retaining none but those which
were provided by his father. Same day Liberton congregation broke
up in great alarm, on account of the rebels being at Carnwath, so
that no collection was made for the poor. The person who alarmed
the people of Carnwath was English Jack, Mr. Bertram's footman.
After Culloden young Lockhart came to Carnwath one Saturday evening,
mounted on the Prince's horse, which was the one he rode when not
walking on foot. On the Sunday it became known that young Lockhart
was in Carnwath House, and a number of people assembled in a tumul-
tuous manner round the house. Sir Archibald Denholm, of Westshiel,
was visiting there ere going home from church, and his butler, John
Robertson, came out and asked what they wanted. One cried—" We
want the young laird!" " Weel, weel, callans," replied he, " I wad
advise ye a' to gang peaceably away hame, for there are loaded blunder-
busses lyin' on the table, that will clear the first stairfu' o' ye at ony
rate!" This intimation had the desired effect. The people went quietly

away, but on Monday morning a great crowd came down from the moor-
lands, armed with guns, scythes, and pitchforks, to apprehend young
Lockhart. But they were too late—Lockhart was gone. After leaving
Carnwath his horse cast a shoe. He went to the smith of Carstairs and
got his horse shod; and, while this was doing, walked up and down the
smiddy with a drawn sword in one hand and a loaded pistol in the
other. When mounted, at the west of Carstairs, he met the Lesmahagow
carrier. Being a powerful man, he seized the carrier by the collar, and
swore where'er he went he would go. He trailed him as far as Raven-
struther, and then threw him from him. The Jacobites had a violent
hatred of Lesmahagow people for apprehending Macdonald of Kinloch-
moidart, and taking him prisoner to Edinburgh. From thence he was
sent to Carlisle and executed. Mr. Lockhart got safe to the West
Highlands, and thence to France in the same ship with Prince Charles,
but he never saw Carnwath again. In all the acts of peace and pardon
to the adherents of the Stuarts, George Lockhart, younger of Carnwath,
was expressly mentioned by name as a person to whom no favours were
to be extended. The Prince's horse was brought back to Carnwath, and
for the Prince's sake had an easy and happy life as long as it lived.
Years rolled on, and his father getting frail, it was considered to be an
awkward matter if he should die and the heir attainted, so it was given
out that he was very ill, then that he was dead. At Paris a funeral of a
coffin filled with stones took place, word sent home that the young laird
was dead, and the next son succeeded to the estate, burdened with a
pension to his dead brother. Such is the traditional story of the people
of Carnwath.

THE FISHWIFE'S ADVICE TO HER BAIRN.

Ken the kintra, Kirsty,
    Ken it wide and weel,
Ere ye cry a codlin,
    Ere ye back a creel.

Mim be wi' the leddies,
    Words are easy spared,
Sellin' flukes and haddies,
    Bargain wi' the laird.

Cosh be wi' your kimmers,
    Whether auld or young,
But wi' flytin limmers,
    Mind your mither's tongue.

Let the auld and needy
  Ken ye hae a creel,
But the grippin' greedy
  Pit it to them weel.

Freely birl your bodle
  When the wark goes weel,
But ne'er lade your nodle
  Till ye've toomed your creel.

· Learn to blaw and blether,
    Baith wi' lad and lass ;
Gie yer tongue nae tether,
    Lang's it brings the brass.

Sae ken the kintra, Kirsty,
  Ken it wide and weel,
Ere ye cry a codlin,
  Ere ye back a creel.

AINSLIE.

It may appear to some rather superfluous that the "Fishwife's Advice to her Bairn" should appear among the songs of Clydesdale, but in that well-known song, "The Newhaven Fishwife," the heroine states in the very first stanza that her "mither cam frae Stra'ven ;" and there is an old prophecy that Carnwath will yet be a sea-port, reasons sufficient certainly for the "Fishwife's Advice to her Bairn" being enrolled among the songs of Clydesdale.

THE COVENANTER'S LAMENT.

THERE's nae Covenant noo, lassie !
  There's nae Covenant noo ;
The Solemn League and Covenant
  Are a' broken through.

There's nae Renwick noo, lassie,
  There's nae gude Cargill,
Nor holy Sabbath preachin'
  Upon the Martyrs' Hill.

It's naething but a sword, lassie !
  A bluidy, bluidy ane !
Wavin' owre puir auld Scotland
  For her rebellious sin.

Scotland's a' wrang, lassie,
  Scotland's a' wrang ;
It's neither to the hill nor dale,
  Lassie, we daur gang.

The Martyrs' Hill's forsaken
  In simmer dusk sae calm,
There's nae gath'rin' noo, lassie,
  To sing the evenin' psalm.

But the martyr's grave will rise, lassie,
  Aboon the warrior's cairn ;
An' the martyr soon will sleep, lassie,
  Aneath the wavin' fern.

                              ALLAN.

<hr />

THE MARTYRS' WIDOWS.

SIT down, sit down by your martyr's grave,
  And I will sit by mine,
And mourn for your kind and godly man,
  And I will mourn for mine.

It's wae to thee and it's wae to me,
  For oor happy days are gane,
And we maun sit wi' a tearfu' e'e
  In our bourach ha' alane.

O Scotland ! Scotland ! it's wae to thee,
  When thy lichts are ta'en awa';
And it's wae ! and its wae to a sinfu' land
  When the righteous sae maun fa'.

It was a holy covenant vow,
   We made to heaven to keep,
And it's a' for our broken covenant vow,
   That we maun sit and weep.

The gerse may be green on yon bonnie hill tap,
   And the heather sweetly bloom,
But there nae mair will we sit at e'en,
   For our hearts are in the tomb !

The hectic glow is upon my cheek,
   And the lily hue on thine,
And sune will ye sleep by your martyr's side,
   And sune will I sleep by mine !

R. ALLAN.

THE GUDEWIFE O' WILLOWDEN HA'.

THE waefu' gudewife o' the Willowden Ha'
   Was ance the beauty and pride o' the parish ;
Her daddie had died and left her his a',
   Her uncle had siller and she was his heiress.
Sic comin' and gangin', and wooin' and thrangin',
And tynin' and winnen', was ne'er i' your kennin' ;
But the laddie that carried the lassie awa',
Was Johnnie Gilfillan o' Willowden Ha'.

The lassie was bred in a braw borough toon,
   Where fouth o' gude manners she learned fu' ready ;
When a' the new fashions frae Lunnon cam' doun,
   Where a' the young misses are fine as my lady.
Wi' ribbons and ruffles, wi' feathers and muffles,
Wi' fringes and laces, and pearlins and braces,
Wi' everything bonnie and everything braw,
She dazz'lt the folks o' the Willowden Ha'.

His daddie was vauntie, his minnie was vain,
   They gied to their Johnnie the house and hadden ;
And muckle was gotten, and plenty was gaun
   For the back and the belly the day o' the waddin'.
Wi' dautin' and kissin', wi' keekin' and dressin',
Wi' jauntin' and callin', and rantin' and ballin',
The day slippit owre and the nicht flew awa,'
And a' was fu' happy at Willowden Ha.'

But wae to the wane o' the blythe hinnymoon,
   The luve o' the bonnie young leddy miscarried ;
When the daffin' was dune she gaed a' out o' tune,
   An' she thocht an unco thing noo to be marry't.
An' thinkin' and ruein', an' wishin' an' trewin',
An' greetin' an' sighin', an' sabbin' an' cryin' ;
The country was dull and the hadden was sma',
An' sair, sair she weari't o' Willowden Ha'.

Tho' Johnnie was young and had siller fu' rife,
   A braw plenish't house and weel-stocket mailin',
Yet a' wadna pleasure his gentle gudewife,
   And happiness never wad enter his dwellin'.
Sae broken and bleerie, and daizent and drearie,
And gloomin' and grievin', and daunted and driven,
He sought in the howff, whaur the drouthy loons ca',
For the peace that had fled frae Willowden Ha' !

At mornin' and e'enin', at nicht and at noon,
   They wasted, they wared, and they wrangl't wi' ither,
Till the siller, the gear, and the credit gaed dune,
   And auld uncle's penny was gien till anither.
Then waefu' and weary, and wilfu' and eerie,
Wi' poverty pressin' and a' thing distressin',
His honour, the laird, he cam' in wi' the law,
An' roupit the hadden o' Willowden Ha' !

                         LAING.

Seldom has the muse of Scottish song imparted a more important
lesson to young married people than in the story of " The Gudewife o'
Willowden Ha.' "

TO MARY FLEMING, DAUGHTER OF THE EARL OF WIGTON.

BY LOT QUEEN FOR ONE DAY AT THE COURT OF QUEEN MARY OF SCOTLAND.

A ROYAL sceptre would be thine,
Aye, Fleming in thy hand to wave,
If either worth or famous line
The prize of royal sceptre gave.

If either grace or beauty's power,
That in a noble mistress shine,
Nor any grace nor beauty's dower
Is worthier of the prize than thine.

If favour with the gods in heaven
The prayers and vows of men obtain,
The sceptre has to thee been given
By the fond vows and prayers of men.

If fickle as the changing wind,
The goddess chance our hap control,
Though deaf of years, of eyesight blind,
Devoid of understanding soul;

Yet neither deaf nor blind was she,
Nor lacked a soul to understand,
When she bestowed the realm on thee,
And gave the sceptre to thy hand;

Or if she were, the truth to tell,
If blind and deaf and void of mind,
I credit when she chose so well,
That virtue must have led the blind.

Translated from BUCHANAN by A. GIBB, Free
Church School, Carnwath.

Lady Mary Fleming was one of the Queen's Marys, and must have
been a paragon of beauty. Buchanan, being a poet, may be supposed to

have had a warm imagination, but the following prose description of her appearance on that day by the cool-headed statesman, Thomas Randolph, proves that she was no ordinary lady:—"That day it was seen, by her princely pomp, how fit a match she would be were she to contend either with Venus in beauty, Minerva in wit, or Juno in worldly wealth, having the two former by nature, and of the third so much as is contained in this realm at her command and free disposition. The treasure of Solomon, I trow, was not to be compared to that which that day hanged upon her back. Happy was it unto this realm that her reign endured no longer! Two such sights in one State, in so good accord, I believe was never seen, as to behold two worthy Queens possess, without envy, one kingdom both upon a day. My pen staggereth, my head faileth, farther to write. Their praises surmount whatsoever may be thought of them. The Queen of Beauty was that day in a gown of cloth of silver; her head, her neck, her shoulders, the rest of her whole body, so beset with stones, that more in our whole jewel house could not be found." It was part of the amusement of Mary's Court that once a-year one of her attendant ladies was chosen by lot to be for one day the Queen of Beauty; on this occasion the lot fell upon Mary Fleming, whose father's home was Boghall Castle, Biggar.

ELEGIAC BALLAD.

ALL on the grass-green margin of Clyde,
  A fair maiden disconsolate lay
Red swoll'n were her eyes with the salt trickling tear,
  And her cheek was as pale as the clay.

Withered and wan was her once red-rose lip,
  And the charms of her youth were all flown,
Like a flower that is scorched by the midsummer heat,
  Or is plucked before it be blown.

Loose on her neck hung her bonnie long hair,
  No green garland the ringlets combined;
Of her lover's false vows, and his late pledged troth,
  And misery she sang to the wind—

"Clyde! Clyde! roll on your clear crystal waves;"
  It was thus with a sigh she began;
"But roll where you will, you never will find
  Such a lovely and faithless young man.

" Beware, oh, beware ! ye fair, fair maids;
  Oh, beware ! and take warning by me,
Nor trust not a swain, though he swears to be true—
  They are false, but not lovely as he.

" It was in yon osier leaf-lined bower—
  Oh, too well I remember the place !
For my own fingers wove the green bending twigs,
  And he covered the benches with grass ;

" That he took me in his soft circling arms,
  And did fondlingly kiss me the while ;
But beware, oh, beware ! of the heart-stealing kiss,
  For men kiss where they mean to beguile ;—

" ' Eliza, to hang on thy lily-white neck,
  And to press thy fair bosom to mine
Is enough ; yes, away with that base dirty pelf,
  'Tis enough—'tis enough to be thine.

" ' Proud damsels may deck them in fine rich array,
  And every rude feature adorn,
But can riches or pride e'er attire them like thee—
  In the purple and freshness of morn.

" ' Away, foolish grandeur, I'll ne'er change my love,
  Or this kiss, this sweet kiss, be my last ;
Yes, the gods, who look down on that leaf-lined bower,
  Can witness how truly I'm blest !'

" Such, such were his words, when close to his breast
  With many a sigh he me drew ;
So kind, so sincere, and so hearty they seemed,
  That I could not but think they were true.

" How frail and how feeble a fond maid's bliss,
  Overturned by all breezes that blow !
How weak is the barrier, how narrow the line,
  That separates our love from our woe !

" Where are ye now, ye false flattering joys,
    Ye prospects of pleasures unknown ?
Like my false love, ye faithless have left me to weep,
    And with him ye to Clara have flown.

" Ah ! do not believe them, thou rash, rash maid,
    Or farewell thy composure of mind ;
They may charm for a little, but beware, ah ! beware,
    Of a poison that festers behind.

" Look, look but on me—nay, nay, never fear,
    I'm a rival you scarcely can dread ;
No roses now bloom on this pale lily cheek,
    Nor is mine the fair flock that I fed.

" Look, look yet again, and tell unto me—
    And ah ! see it be truth that you tell—
Can your fondness secure you the false wand'ring swain,
    When I'm thus but for loving too well ?

" Away, haste away, ye slow, slow hours,
    And be dipped, O yon sun in the sea—
Ah me ! but I rave, for the time is no more
    When the evening brought comfort to me.

" Sad, ever sad !—is there no kind cure,
    Not a balsam provided for woe ?
Oh, tell me, some angel ! in what happy clime
    Does the precious remedy grow ?

" Kindly remembered, thou fire-clad sprite—
    It is there, it is certainly there ;
And soon will I seek, in the cold darksome grave,
    For a balsam to love and despair ! "

From " Poems by James Græme," published in 1773 by W. Somerville,
Lanark. Græme was the fellow-student and early friend of Dr. Anderson of Edinburgh. He died on the 26th of July, 1772, at the early age
of 21. Dr. Anderson superintended the original edition, and likewise
included his friend's works, in his edition of the British Poets. There
is good reason to believe that the doctor himself was the author of this

ballad.   He states in the preface that there are a few pieces by a different
writer, which the ingenious reader would easily distinguish, from the
difference of style and subject, from the rest of the volume, and from this
statement, we believe this to be the doctor's own juvenile performance.

It is said by tradition, that the heroine of the ballad was Miss Elizabeth
Kello, daughter of a very worthy man, who bore the singular sobriquet
of "Gospel Johnnie," a Carnwath David Deans in his way.   Johnnie had
once the misfortune to lose a cow, and so much was he esteemed by
young Count Lockhart, that he saved as much from his pocket money
while a minor, as bought another cow for Johnnie.   The lovely and
faithless young man, we are happy to say, was not so bad as represented
in the text; he was gamekeeper on the Carnwath estate, and made the
love-lorn damsel a happy wife.   One of their sons, who bore his father's
name (George Ramsay), was for several years sub-editor of the *Scotsman*.
Dr. Anderson was the early friend of Thomas Campbell.   The first
edition of "The Pleasures of Hope" was inscribed to Dr. Anderson.

LINES,

BY GEORGE RAMSAY OF CARNWATH, ON SEEING TOMBSTONES STAND-ING IN THE MIDST OF A FLOWER GARDEN AT CASTLE CRAIG, THE SEAT OF SIR THOMAS G. CARMICHAEL, BART., IN THE PARISH OF KIRKURD, PEEBLESSHIRE.

OH ! who could have deemed, that those gay smelling flowers,
   To the bones of the dead were a covering ;
That bodies lay festering, under these bowers,
   Or spirits around them were hovering.

For no narrow bed, with its green, grassy mound,
   Is seen round their bones to be swelling,
Yet the grey tombstones, that are scattered around,
   Are the bounds of a cemetery telling.

And so lowly and still is this place of the dead,
   So holy, so soothing to feeling,
So charming the pall that has o'er it been spread,
   No gloom to the heart can be stealing.

Oh ! then can these flowers, as in mockery bloom,
   O'er the bodies that 'neath them are lying?
Or can they in spirit thus encircle the tomb,
   As if life with corruption was vying?

No, though to the mouldering dwellers beneath,
   They vainly their fragrance are giving—
They were placed o'er their graves, sweetest incense to breathe,
   By the kind, pious hand of the living.

And here in this flower bed, and meet is the place,
   In this flower bed so gay and imposing,
The once faithful swain, and the maid of his choice,
   Perhaps are together reposing.

Perhaps in this spot lie the bridegroom and bride,
   Who in life were so dear to each other;
The brother and sister may sleep side by side,
   The babe on the breast of its mother.

So lovely their beds who that o'er them e'er tread
   Could think of their fate to be weeping;
Or who ever mused o'er their flower spangled bed
   But envied the depth of their sleeping. ·

May mine be the spot when o'er my dark grave
   The roses I cherished when living,
The flowers that I loved all their beauties may crave,
   And all their sweet perfume be giving.

May such be the spot, in some flowery dell, where
   The larks from its turf may be springing,
Where the blackbird and mavis may love to repair
   The dirge of my rest to be singing.

Oh ! not in the dark, dripping tomb be my bed,
   Its breath all of verdure consuming,
But give me green tendrils, to wave o'er my head,
   O'er my breast let the daisy be blooming.

C

CHANGE.

WE mark it in the fleecy clouds
  That ghost-like wander by;
The brightest flower has but its hour,
  To bud, to bloom, and die;
'Tis read in old familiar things,
  As in the new and strange,
Where'er we go, whate'er we know,
  'Tis change—for ever change!

'Tis written on the tranquil waves,
  Oh! fearfully and strong;
The rivers that now calmly glide,
  In torrents gush along;
The birds that glad our summer woods,
  Have still their hour to range;
The leaves must fall—the doom of all!
  'Tis change—for ever change!

But oh! not only in the woods,
  The streams, the flowers, the trees,
Do we appear, from year to year,
  Less changed than aught of these?
Old loves we leave, old links we break,
  Old friends to us grow strange—
The saddest emblem of the heart
  Is change—for ever change!

CARNWATH FAIR IN 1770.

THE sun shines potent from the mid-day sky,
  His rays glance dazzling from the tinsled head,
The noon-tide fervour smooths the glossy hair,
  And aids the blushing of the panting maid.

The rustic gallants, with their reddening prize,
  Retire exulting from the dusty street,
Quaff the cool beer, and mixed with kisses bland,
  And forceful sighs, the tender tale repeat.

While coyly passive sits the modest fair,
  With breast wild throbbing, and dejected eye ;
Or should she kind adjust the rosy lip,
  Or yield the embrace, no envious tell-tale nigh.

On yonder board the bowl and tumbler marks
  More costly liquor and a richer miss ;
Fast by her side the brawny stripling smiles,
  Nor values sixpence while he gains a kiss.

If such the blessings of a low estate,
  Who would not joy to guide the shining share,
To whirl the flail, ingulf the delving spade,
  Or tune the reed beside the fleecy care.

Name not the biting blast the peasant bears,
  The face embrowned, the blister-swollen hand ;
A day like this rewards an age of toil !
  Softens the voice of many a rough command !

JAMES GRÆME, Carnwath.

OUR AULD GUDEMAN HAS LEFT US.

Our auld gudeman has left us—we have lost a friendly guide,
His big arm-chair is vacant noo, his staff is laid aside ;
Its aid he needs nae langer as a prop against the blast,
He is resting now in safety, his pilgrimage is past !

Our auld gudeman has left us—the venerable form
That long had stood the summer's sun, and braved the winter's
  storm,
Has yielded now to nature's call, and the angel's welcome kiss,
Hath changed his hoary winter into spring's eternal bliss !

Our auld gudeman has left us—and our eyes with tears are
    dim,
The churchyard bell, so often heard, hath called at last for him;
Full many dear ones passed away, while years still crowned
    his brow,
But God hath taken to reward His old disciple now.

Our auld gudeman has left us—tho' we fain would think him
    near,
His cautious step and kindly voice we often seem to hear;
But ah! that voice is silent now, and many a happy wean
Has sorrow felt, and blessings lost since grandpapa is gane.

Our auld gudeman has left us! nae mair auld freends he'll
    meet,
Or at the kirk on Sabbath morn amang them tak' his seat;
For he in hope o' brighter joys, by past assurance given,
Hath left the Church on earth, and joined the Church of God
    in heaven.

JAMES WATSON, DOUGLAS.

LADY GRANGE.

Air—"In Lonely Wilds."

OH! lang the Lady Grange did live
    Upon St. Kilda's rock;
But sorrow surely winna kill,
    Or else her heart had broke.
Far, far removed from kith and kin,
    And a' that life endears,
She aft looked o'er the watery waste,
    Where ne'er a ship appears.

" Oh! is it for my father's crime
    That I'm thus banished far?
Or was it ony faut o' mine
    That kindled civil war?

M'Leod and Lovat, weel I trow,
Has wrought this treacherie;
But wherefore has their cruel spite
Fa'en a' on helpless me."

And thus she mourned, fair Lady Grange,
Thus sped her life away;
The morning sun it brought no joy,
And night did close the day;
And nought was heard but the sea-birds' cry
To cheer her solitude,
Or the wild billows raging roar,
That broke o'er rocks so rude.

At length a favouring wind did bring
An auld and worthy pair,
Wha wi' the kindest charitie
Her sorrows a' did share.
They taught her pridefu' heart to bend
Aneath the chast'ning rod,
And then she kenned her prison walls
Had been a blest abode.

LADY NAIRN.

The story of Lady Grange is one of the most remarkable in Scottish history. She was the daughter of Chiesly, Laird of Kersewell, Carnwath. This gentleman being remarkable for the violence of his temper, his lady left him after being the mother of eleven children, and sued him for a separate maintenance. They agreed to submit the matter for arbitration to Sir George Lockhart, Lord President of the Court of Session, and Lord Kemnay, who decided that Chiesly was to pay £90 per annum for the support of his wife and family. Chiesly considered himself greatly injured by this decision, and vowed revenge. Some time after he watched the Lord President, and on Sunday, the 31st March, 1689, after forenoon service, went behind him on the street, and shot him in the back. Sir George fell mortally wounded, and was carried to his house in the Lawn Market, only a few yards from where he fell, and died in a few minutes. Chiesly was immediately apprehended, tried on Monday, sentenced to be executed on Wednesday, with the pistol with which he committed the murder hung round his neck, his right hand which fired the pistol to be struck off by the hangman ere he was turned over, and his body to be hung in chains. This dreadful sentence was carried into effect, at the Gallowlee between Leith and Edinburgh, on the third day after the murder; but on the very first night after the execution Chiesly's body disappeared, and it was never known what became of it until a few years ago, when Dalry House (which at the time of the murder was Chiesly's town residence) was undergoing some repairs, the workmen had occasion to lift the kitchen floor, and there found the skeleton of a man in chains, being no doubt the remains of Chiesly, whose body had been removed in the night and buried in the floor of his own house by his family. Sir George Lockhart was buried in the Greyfriars Church, with an extraordinary attendance, the Convention Parliament, which had deposed King James and elected William and Mary, being in session at the time. This is her father's crime alluded to in the text. But it was not for this she was so illegally secluded. Unfortunately for this lady, she inherited the violent temper of her father. Erskine of Grange had courted her and promised marriage, but rather seemed disposed to resile from his engagement, when Miss Chiesly told him very sternly, "Take care what you are about, sir; remember I am a daughter of Chiesly's." So Erskine, somewhat reluctantly it is believed, had to go through with the marriage for his personal safety. Mrs. Erskine was a woman of ungovernable temper. Her husband was the brother of the Earl of Mar who raised the standard of rebellion in 1715; and although he professed loyalty to the reigning house in order to retain his office, was a Jacobite at heart, and secretly abetted the efforts of his brother to overturn the Revolution Settlement. By concealing herself under a sofa in his business room, she heard the conversation of her husband with Lord Lovat and other adherents of the exiled house, and in the course of her ebullitions of temper, which were frequent and terrible, she threatened to denounce him and his friends to the Government. He was seriously afraid she would carry her threats into effect; so, consulting with her children, who were grown up, and obtaining their approval, Lord Grange had his wife seized by the emissaries of the notorious Lord Lovat on the 22nd April, 1732, and conducted from place to place by night journeys till she reached the Hebrides. She was detained in the Isle of Hisker two years, in St. Kilda seven, and in the Isle of Skye four, till her death in 1745. It is to be hoped that Lady Nairn's statement of the poor lady's temper being subdued by her secluded exile is well founded. The people of Carnwath have often seen their church arrayed in the ensigns of mourning; but surely there never was so much cause as when Sir George Lockhart, the principal heritor of the parish, was murdered on the Sunday, and Chiesly of Kersewell, another of the chief heritors, publicly executed on the following Wednesday!

JOHN FROST.

YE'VE been owre long o' coming this year, John Frost,
Wi' your snaws and your cauld icy gear, John Frost,
   And I'm ne'er a bit blate,
   Ye auld scoundrel, to say't,
That ye've nae business noo to appear, John Frost.

Tho' a dour-lookin' red-nebbit chiel, John Frost,
In your ain place I like ye fu' weel, John Frost,
  When oor callants I see,
  On your sides fu' o' glee,
And their sires at the roarin' bonspiel, John Frost.

But it's daft-like, to say naething mair, John Frost,
A' winter to skulk in your lair, John Frost,
  And now owre sweet spring
  Your cauld mantle to fling—
I'm a saint if it's even half fair, John Frost.

Wee birds 'mang the snaws whistled sweet, John Frost,
And flowers glinted fresh at oor feet, John Frost,
  And oor auld apple tree,
  Like a bride tae the e'e—
Noo the sicht o't could maist gar me greet, John Frost.

An' last week, in the auld Winterlaw, John Frost,
The nest o' the mavis I saw, John Frost,
  In the breist o' a yew,
  Wi' four eggs a' bricht blue—
Noo the deuce ye'll hae played wi' them a', John Frost.

The past was a stepmother year, John Frost,
Leavin' 'tatoes and meal baith owre dear, John Frost,
  And puir folk scant o' claes,
  Wi' toom wames and cauld taes,
And praying ye sair to forbear, John Frost.

Then tak' my advice as a frien', John Frost,
Cut your stick, and be aff trig and clean, John Frost,
  And as sure as I'm here,
  When ye come back next year,
We'll shake hands and this thraw'll be forgi'en, John Frost.

MACDONALD.

NEVER DESPAIR.

NEVER despair—let the feeble in spirit
  Bow like the willow that stoops to the blast;
Droop not in peril—'tis manhood's true merit
  Nobly to struggle and hope to the last.
When by the sunshine of fortune forsaken,
  Faint sinks the heart of the feeble with fear,
Stand like the oak of the forest unshaken—
  Never despair, boys! never despair!

Never despair—tho' adversity rages
  Fiercely and fell as the surge on the shore,
Firm as the rock on the ocean for ages,
  Stem the rude torrent till danger is o'er.
Fate with its whirlwind our joys may all sever,
  True to ourselves we have nothing to fear;
This be our hope and our anchor for ever—
  Never despair, boys! never despair!

                                    LAKE.

JEANIE DIXON.

O BONNIE Jeanie Dixon! I often mind the time,
When first we met, when we were young, in simmer's glori-
    ous prime;
The sun shone bright, the leaves were green, the lark sang
    loud and free,
And merry, merry were the hearts that danced in you and me.

O bonnie Jeanie Dixon! happy, happy were the days,
When we climbed the steeps of Arthur's Seat, and roamed
    the broomy braes,
And by the Wells o' Wearie sat, till the dews o' heaven cam
    doon,
And the stars aboon shone clear and bright, as we gaed to
    the toon.

O bonnie Jeanie Dixon ! I think I see you still—
As fair, as young, as lovely—trippin' round the Calton Hill ;
I hear the music o' thy voice, I see the witchin' smile,
The dimpled cheek and laughin' e'e, that sweetened a' my
   toil !

O bonnie Jeanie Dixon ! lang years have passed away ;
My locks were dark and glossy then, and now are thin and
   grey,
And the mists o' age are gatherin' fast around this heart o'
   mine,
Yet aye I mind the happy dreams—the dear dreams o' langsyne !

O bonnie Jeanie Dixon ! ye have passed that dreary bourne
That bounds the close of human life, and never can return !
But I will follow soon, my love, and we will meet again,
In that bright land where peace, and joy, and love for ever
   reign !

Jeanie Dixon was a most amiable and beautiful girl, a native of Collie-
burn in the parish of West Linton. She died at Glasgow, about 1844,
in the prime of life.

MORRISON'S PILLS.

Of all the wonders we have read since first the world began,
The greatest lately has appeared, and Morrison's the man ;
No longer death we need to fear, or labour under ills,
For all diseases now are cured by the Vegetable Pills !

     He says they're sure to do it,
     They're very sure to do it,
     They're safe and sure to do it,
     Are the Vegetable Pills !

If all your hair should tumble off, you need not care a fig,
Just take the Pills, 'twill grow again—you'll never need a wig;
If you're in love—your fair's unkind—despair your bosom
    fills,
She'll soon consent if you give her the Vegetable Pills!
      You'll then be sure to do it, &c.

In a battle what a charming thing for all who have to go,
That they may cut and slash away, nor loss of limb can know;
For should they lose a leg or arm, the cure is at their wills,
They'll grow again if they but take the Vegetable Pills!
      They'll find 'em sure to do it, &c.

And if they chance to lose their heads, they've nothing more
    to do—
Take twenty pills of No. 1, and forty No. 2 ;
Or if you should be cut in halves, by some sharp engine wheel,
You're whole again if you but take the Vegetable Pill!
      You'll find 'em sure to do it, &c.

If appetite be lost, the Pills restore it in a day,
Or if your appetite's too great, they'll take it quite away ;
They'll make you hot, or make you cold—do all but pay
    your bills ;
If you'd be rich, and wish for gold, take Vegetable Pills!
      They're sure to do it, &c.

The Rosslyn folks no longer now can sad mishaps forebode ;
No matter if the powder mills should happen to explode ;
Though blown to atoms, they may be united at their wills,
And every particle replaced by Vegetable Pills!
      They're sure to do it, &c.

Young married folks may now rejoice, and discord set at rest,
For if for little ones they sigh, the Pills will make them blest ;
An heir or heiress they may have, as inclination wills,
If dear mamma will only take the Vegetable Pills!
      I'm very sure they'll do it, &c.

In short, the blind may gain their sight, the dumb may find
  a tongue,
The lame may quickly run a race, the old again be young;
One dose will make them laugh or cry, and every belly fill,
In fact, if you would never die, take a Vegetable Pill!
        For the College says they'll do it, &c.

                ROBERT WILKIE, Esq., of LADYTHORN.

This exquisite *jeu d'esprit* is from the drama of "Yalla Gaiters."

LIBERTON MOOR.

THERE is a track which I never tread,
  But it fills my heart with pain;
'Tis one of the few, few places we see,
  And wish never to see again!

In the lone churchyard it is sad to stray
  Where the graves are growing green,
But still our pensiveness is shared
  With thoughts of life that has been.

But how could this waste have otherwise looked,
  Though it ne'er by men had been trod?
More desolate hardly could it appear,
  Though left and forgotten by God!

The husbandman's feeble attempts but shew
  Thy cursed soil the more;
His spirit soon fails, rude Nature prevails,
  And leaves thee, the same as before.

Vain as the haughty Persian's lash,
  On the free and unfettered main,
Which felt not the stroke, nor heeded the threat,
  But rushed to its strength again.

On the right and left, and all around,
    Lies the same unlovely scene,
And well I see thou must ever remain
    The same as thou ever hast been.

Thy birthday ode was the lapwing's shriek,
    The heath thy swaddling band;
Thy dirge shall be the curlew's cry—
    Thy shroud the barren sand.

The spring can bring no spring to thee;
    Summer to thee is a curse;
'Tis needless for winter to revel here—
    It cannot make thee worse.

If some poor wretch now would hang himself,
    This is the spot he would choose—
For here no charm would make him regret,
    To tie the unholy noose.

But, if at last, for sad relief,
    To the arms of death he would flee,
And gladly hang himself for grief,
    He must live for want of a tree!

Let me hasten away from this dreary spot,
    For my bosom swells with pain;
'Tis one of the few, few places we see,
    And wish never to see again?

                                        REV. JAMES PROUDFOOT.

When these lines were written, Liberton Moor was an open waste; it
is now enclosed, sub-divided, and adorned with plantations, where the
would-be suicide would find trees in abundance. It is curious that
Robert Chambers had similar feelings on passing through the *Lang
Whang*. "The scene,' he said, "was so desolate, it could not be recollected
without horror." On the other hand, we have heard of a Yankee who,
when he reached the summit of Achinool Hill, and saw the long treeless
expanse of the *Lang Whang* stretched out before him, clapped his hands
and exclaimed in a perfect rapture—'' Well, well! such a splendid view!
I never saw a sight like that in all my life; such a large tract of well-
cleared land!"—it was so different from the forest scenery of America.
Liberton Moor was improved while the first Sir Norman M. Lockhart was
proprietor, and that energetic gentleman, Mr. James Brown, was farmer.

IN MEMORY OF HUGH MILLER.

BORN in a cottage, schooled in cottage lore,
'Midst toilsome labour, plodding day by day,
He shamed the pride of colleges, and bore
The palm from academic halls away.

And never did strong-built Scottish frame enclose
A heart to Scotland more entirely true;
Bruce, Wallace, Burns, let Miller now repose
In patriotic fellowship with you.

A Bible-champion bold, what sceptic dared
To meet the sweep of his resistless rod,
As down into the earth he dug, and bared
The mighty footprints of the Christian's God.

He feared not the astronomer, whose flight
Soared high enough into the blue recess;
He feared not the geologist, whose sight
Dived deep enough into the dark abyss.

The paths of that abyss he downward trod,
Till Reason's lamp no more his guide would be;
And when he stumbled in the dark, O God!
Thou knowest he fell in seeking after Thee!

Go, build his monument, and build it one
Like his own genius, broad, and deep, and high;
And build it not of marble, but of stone,
The Red Sandstone of his loved Cromarty.

Yet build it not, for monuments must fall,
And columns rich with hieroglyphic lore;
Be his enduring monument the wall
Of giant rock that guards his native shore.

REV. J. PROUDFOOT.

TO ISABELLE.

O STAY not here, my fair Isabelle,
  For the dews of heaven are falling,
And the lonely craik, mid the sweet blue bells,
  To his gentle mate is calling.

The evening star burns bright on high,
  Thousands around us are rolling !
And the dulcet tones of the vesper bell
  From afar are faintly tolling.

The waterfalls and the rocky shoals
  Of the Clyde are sounding loudly,
While the moon looks down from her radiant throne
  On all the world so proudly.

The fox howls loud on the distant fell,
  The owl screams lonely and weary ;
Then stay here no longer, my fair Isabelle,
  For oh, it is cold and dreary !

PHILLIS THE FAIR.

Tune—"Robin Adair."

WHILE larks with little wing
  Fanned the pure air,
Tasting the breathing spring,
  Forth I did fare ;
Gay the sun's golden eye
Peeped o'er the mountains high :
Such thy morn ! did I cry,
  Phillis the fair.

In each bird's ceaseless song
  Glad did I share ;
While yon wild flowers among,
  Chance led me there ;

Sweet to the opening day,
    Rosebuds bent the dewy spray ;
Such thy bloom ! did I say,
    Phillis the fair.

Down in a shady' walk,
    Doves cooing were ;
I marked the cruel hawk,
    Caught in a snare ;
So kind may fortune be,
Such make his destinie,
He who would injure thee,
    Phillis the fair.

So much for namby-pamby. I may after all try my hand on it in
Scots verse,—there I always find myself most at home.

                                                BURNS.

Burns is understood to have in "Phillis the Fair," represented the
tender feelings which Clarke entertained towards Miss Philadelphia
M'Murdo, one of his pupils. This lady afterwards became Mrs. Norman
Lockhart, of Carnwath.

                                        R. CHAMBERS.

                _____

DOWN WINDING NITH I DID WANDER.

Tune—"The Muckin' o' Geordie's Byre."

ADOWN winding Nith I did wander
    To mark the sweet flowers as they spring,
Adown winding Nith I did wander,
    Of Phillis to muse and to sing.

Chorus—Awa' wi' your belles and your beauties,
    They never wi' her can compare ;
Wha ever has met wi' my Phillis,
    Has met wi' the queen o' the fair.

The daisy amused my fond fancy,
    So artless, so simple, so wild ;
Thou'rt emblem, said I, o' my Phillis !
    For she is simplicity's child.

The rosebud's the blush o' my charmer,
    Her sweet balmy lip when it's press'd;
How fair and how pure is the lily,
    But fairer and purer her breast.

Yon knot of gay flowers in the arbour,
    They ne'er wi' my Phillis can vie;
Her breath is the breath o' the woodbine,
    Its dewdrop o' diamond her eye.

Her voice is the song of the morning,
    That wakes through the green spreading grove,
When Phœbus peeps over the mountains,
    On music, and pleasure, and love.

But beauty! how frail and how fleeting—
    The bloom of a fine summer day!
While worth in the mind o' my Phillis
    Will flourish without a decay.
                                    BURNS.

Mr. Clarke begs of you to give Miss Phillis a corner in your book, as she is a particular flame of his.   She is a Miss Phillis M'Murdo, sister to "Bonnie Jean." They are both pupils of his.
                                    BURNS TO MR. THOMPSON.

"Phillis the Fair," during her happy married life, resided with her husband in Carnwath House, and there became the mother of a numerous family.   She was much admired for her beauty and personal attractions, and esteemed and beloved for her kindly sympathies for all in distress. This was the estimation in which she was held by the people of Carnwath; and the following inscription upon her tombstone in St. Mary's Aisle was the genuine expression of her husband's feelings on her untimely death after a short illness :—

THIS TABLET IS INSCRIBED BY
NORMAN LOCKHART, ESQ.,
TO RECORD, HOWEVER INADEQUATELY,
HIS DEEP SENSE OF THE MANIFOLD VIRTUES
WHICH ADORNED THE CHARACTER OF
PHILADELPHIA BARBARA M'MURDO,
HIS BELOVED WIFE;
WHO, AFTER BEING ENABLED BY DIVINE GRACE,
TO DISCHARGE IN AN ENDEARING AND EXEMPLARY MANNER
THE DUTIES OF A WIFE AND PARENT,
FELL ASLEEP IN JESUS, SEPTEMBER 5TH, 1825,
TO BE FOR EVER WITH THE LORD.

O see how soon the flowers of life decay,
How soon terrestrial pleasures fade away ;
The star of comfort, for a season given,
First shone on earth, then sets to rise in heaven.

But mourn not as of life bereft her doom,
Nor sorrowing water with thy tears her tomb ;
Redeemed by God from sin, released from pain,
To her to live was Christ, to die was gain.

ON A SPRIG OF HEATHER FROM HOME.

BY AN EMIGRANT FROM COVINGTON.

How many scenes of childhood's days
　　Pass through my mind in close review,
Though thirty years have passed, I ween,
　　Since I was where this heather grew.

Sad memories crowd around my heart,
　　Sweet heather, as I gaze on you,
Of that dear land across the sea—
　　My birth-place—where this heather grew.

The castle old, its garden wild,
　　Where still rare flowers in spring peep through
The grass that lined the half-filled moat,
　　And gowans with this heather grew.

The tales our father loved to tell
　　Of barons bold and vassals true,
Who chased the deer o'er moss and fell
　　And moorland, where this heather grew.

The dovecot, built long years ago,
　　From which at morn the pigeons flew ;
The grey old kirk, whose Sabbath bell
　　Sounds sweetly where this heather grew.

D

The stately trees, the sweetbriar hedge,
   Which o'er the air such fragrance threw ;
The blackberry copse, the school, the verge,
   The moss, where once this heather grew.

The haunted saugh, the stories told
   Of ghosts and goblins not a few ;
The witch rowan tree, 'neath which the thyme
   Bloomed sweetest where this heather grew.

The dear old Clyde, the bubbling springs,
   From which such cooling draughts we drew ;
The broomy knowes, the fairy rings
   On moors, where once this heather grew.

I think I hear the quaint old rhyme,
   Which to our childish minds seemed true,
Of Tinto, with her top of mist,
   And at whose foot the heather grew.

Full many of that kindred band,
   Who crossed with me the ocean blue,
Alas ! are laid in their cold graves,
   Far, far from where this heather grew.

Though in this land I've happy been,
   With many friends both tried and true,
My memory will forever cling
   To home, where once this heather grew.

                                 H. W.

    The writer of these lines is evidently an emigrant from Covington, the scenery of which is very well depicted, and his feelings well-expressed. Covington has sent a great number of enterprising spirits across the Atlantic—the Prentices and Purdies—and have founded no less than sixteen Covingtons in the United States.

THE DRUCKEN LAIRD OF LAMINGTON.

CAN I bear to part with thee,
Never mair thy face to see?
Can I bear to part with thee,
    Drucken Laird of Lamington?

Canty were ye owre yer kail,
Toddy jugs and jaups o' ale,
Heart aye kind and leal and hale,
    Honest Laird of Lamington.

He that swears is but so-so,
He that cheats to hell must go,
He that falls in bagnio,
    Falls in the devil's frying-pan.

Wha was't ne'er pat aith to word,
Never cringed to duke or lord,
Never sat at sinfu' board?
    The honest Laird of Lamington.

He that cheats can ne'er be just,
He that lees is no to trust,
He that drinks to drauk his dust,
    Wha can say that wrang is done?

Wha was ne'er to fraud inclined,
Never le'ed sin' he could mind,
Ane whase drouth there's few can find,—
    The drucken Laird of Lamington.

I like a man to take his glass,
Toast his friend, and bonnie lass;
He that winna is an ass—
    Deil send him ane to gallop on.

I like a man that's frank and kind,
Meets me when I hae a mind,
Sings his song and drinks me blind,
    Like the drucken Laird of Lamington.

                    J. HOGG, ETTRICK SHEPHERD.

James W. Baillie, Esq., of Culterallers, author of the "Lives of the
Baillies," is of opinion that the hero of this song is Sir William Maxwell
Baillie, son of Margaret Baillie, and heiress of Lamington, and her
husband, Sir William Maxwell. Sir William Baillie, this gentleman's
maternal grandfather, was the eighth laird in succession, and the last of
the male line of the Baillies of Lamington. The "Drucken" Laird was
knighted by James VI., and in 1612 was one of the members of Parliament for Lanarkshire. He was a great horse-racer, and had races at
Lamington, and on the public road between Lamington and Coulter, at
the Black Coal Heads. The Baillies are a very ancient family. Three
brothers, of Saxon origin, Lambinus, Robertus, and Wicius, left England
after the Norman Conquest, settled in the Upper Ward of Clydesdale,
and founded the three parishes of Lamington, Roberton, and Wiston.
This ancient family is now represented by Lord Lamington of Lamington,
who is also the descendant of the heiress of Lamington, and our great
national hero, Sir William Wallace.

TO ELIZA.

WHILE the night-bird screams, and the moonlight gleams,
    On the loch in a dazzling sheen,
At the midnight hour, in the greenwood bower,
    I muse on our parting scene.

O Eliza dear! the heart-wrung tear
    Flows afresh on this fatal eve,
Which beheld thee remove to the regions above,
    And left me alone to grieve.

The sound of thy name still thrills my frame,
    And my pulse beats quick and strong,
When as now I pace, o'er the sacred place,
    Where we met when our love was young.

And my heart still warms, when I think of the charms,
  Of thine eyes so darkly blue;
Of that rose-bud cheek, of that brow so meek,
  And that heart so kind and true.

But death's fell worm, blasts the loveliest form,
  And thine seemed of heavenly mould;
But now in the dust it sleeps with the just,
  Till time's last hour be tolled.

Thy life has been, like the opening scene,
  Of a glorious summer day;
But long ere noon, the storm's dark frown
  Veiled every shining ray.

The bright, bright beams of hope's gay dreams
  Enchant my heart no more;
For I look not for rest, till with her I love best,
  I meet on a heavenly shore!

Written in memoriam of Miss Eliza Ormiston, a beautiful young girl
of Carnwath.

—— ——

THE BONNIE BAWBEE!

WHAT a wonderfu' thing is the face of a king,
  Even on copper to see;
It pleases the child, and auld age is beguiled,
  By the aid of the bonnie bawbee!

Chorus—Then, oh! how I love the bawbee, bawbee!
  Its name is so charming to me;
  The mint or the reign, I mind not a grain,
  In pouchin' the bonnie bawbee, bawbee!

The love-stricken swain may fortune disdain,
  But oh, what a ninnie is he!
'Tis easy to prove the most lasting love
  Is love for the bonnie bawbee!

The most worthless hash, with plenty of cash,
  His neebours may find frank and free;
But from him soon they will all wheel away,
  For lack o' the bonnie bawbee!

The soldier for pay fights oft by the day;
  The lawyer fights hard for his fee;
The bustle and strife in the battle o' life
  Is all for the bonnie bawbee!

The preacher loves well his hearers to tell,
  How they should bestow charity;
Yet nae man I wist can keep in his fist,
  Such a grip o' the bonnie bawbee!

That friendship in need is friendship indeed,
  All mankind will ever agree;
But sages contend, the most worthy friend,
  Is found in the bonnie bawbee!

Yet let not this lay lead any astray,
  Of high or of humble degree,
His rank to forego, by stooping too low,
  To pick up a passing bawbee!

Yet hail to the bonnie bawbee, bawbee!
  Best emblem of true liberty, liberty!
We cannot our ain independence maintain
  Without aid o' the bonnie bawbee!

                                        TRAIN.

———

THE ICE-BOUND WAVE.

WHEN the green leaves o' simmer a' are faded and gane,
And the rich stores of autumn are swept from the plain,
Round Tintoc's high cairn, while the wintry winds rave,
Keen curlers seek the joys o' the ice-bound wave.

The warm climes o' the south, where the sun ever shines,
May boast o' their myrtles and rich laden vines ;
Tho' the choicest productions of nature they have,
Yet they never knew the joys o' the ice-bound wave.

The puir dozen'd things under tropical skies
Wad shiver in the land where the snow-wreath lies ;
But the sons of Caledonia, the free and the brave,
Have joys that kings might envy on the ice-bound wave.

On our ain White Loch, when the frost was nippin' keen,
Wi' the comrades o' my youth mony a glorious game I've seen,
And mony mae I hope to hae, before I reach the grave,
Wi' the curlers o' Carstairs on the ice-bound wave.

Now here's to Johnnie Frost, on his throne the icy pole,
May he ne'er forget to visit us, while round the seasons roll ;
And here's to a' keen curlers too, come pledge me all I crave,
Wha love the roarin' joys o' the ice-bound wave !

Written for the Carnwath Curling Club, many years ago, when Mr.
John Dymock was Secretary. The reference to Carstairs is explained
by the fact that for the previous forty years Carstairs curlers had always
defeated those of Carnwath, but at that time victory passed over to
Carnwath. The cause of the loss by Carstairs was supposed to be the
drainage, some time before, of Carstairs *Dub*, where in former times the
youths of that town were from their infancy trained in the science of
curling. After it was drained, the right hand of Carstairs lost its cunning.

TRIAL AND DEATH OF ROBERT BAILLIE, OF JERVISWOOD.

'TWAS when December's darkening scowl the face of heaven
o'ercast,
And vile men high in place were more unpitying than the
blast ;
Before their grim tribunal's front, firm and undaunted stood
That patriot chief of high renown, the noble Jerviswood.

The hand of death is on him pressed—the seal of death is
    there!
Oh, the savage of the wilderness those weak old limbs would
    spare!
Frail, frail his step, and spent his frame, and ye may plainly
    trace
The shadow of death's wing upon his pale and sunken face.
These twenty long and dreary months in the dungeon he
    hath lain—
Long days of sickness, weary nights of languishing and pain;
For him no gale hath breathed its balm, no sun hath blest
    the year,
No friendly hand to smooth his couch, nor friendly voice to
    cheer;
His lady in their lonely hall doth mournful vigils keep,
And where he sat and where he walked, his children watch
    and weep.

Yet o'er his weakness and decay, an ancient grandeur falls,
Like the majesty that lingers round some mould'ring palace
    walls;
The light of calm and noble thoughts is bright within that eye,
And purged of earthly taint, his soul prepares to mount on
    high.
Nor is he left alone: a sister faithful to him clung,
With woman's heart, with home-born love, with woman's
    look and tongue;
There in that Golgotha she sits, so tender, so benign,
Fair as the moon's sweet glimpses through the cloudy tem-
    pests shine.

The court is met, the assize are set, the robes of state look
    brave,
Yet the proudest and the lordliest there is but a tyrant's
    slave;
Blood-hirelings they, who earn their pay by foul and
    treach'rous deeds,
For swift and fell the hound must be, whom the hunter
    richly feeds.

What tho' no act of wrong e'er stained the fame of Jervis-
wood,
Shall it protect him in those times that he is wise and good ?
So wise, so good, so loved of all, though weak and worn with
care ;
Though death comes fast, he is the last whom Antichrist
would spare.
For his the bold and free-born mind, the wisdom of a sage,
The glow of youth still cherished in the sober breast of age ;
The soul of chivalry is his, and honour pure from stain,
A heart that beats for liberty, and spurns each galling chain,
Whether entwined by hands that bear the crosier or the
sword,
For he would see all nations free in Christ, who is their Lord.

And once with England's patriot band, by tyrant power
oppressed,
He had dreamt of free and happy homes in the forests of the
west ;
To breathe the uncorrupted air, to tread the fresh green sod,
And where the broad Savannah rolls in peace to worship God.
These are his crimes ! the treason this for which he now is
tried !
But though the forms of law are kept, all justice is denied.
Woe to that land, so favoured once should witness such
disgrace !
Shame that a land so powerful yet should brook a scene so
base !

Unroll your parchments black with lies, shut fast your
coward doors,
And brand the aged chief with crimes his generous heart
abhors ;
When truth avails not, well you know how to supply the
lack
With secret tales, and then with words extorted by the rack !
There is an hour for every power,—the hour of darkness
this !
Spur on ye slaves of Antichrist, or ye the goal may miss !

His strength increasing with his need, he raises bold and
   high,
And fixes on Mackenzie a clear and searching eye :
" How canst thou thus, my lord, 'gainst me such accusations
   bring,
That I have been a man of strife in plots against the King?
I hate the way of violence, the anarchist I spurn ;
Who scatters firebrands little knows where they may fall
   and burn.
In my degree I have been bold to guard the nation's right,
And keep alive within these realms the lamp of Gospel
   light.
But in my gloomy dungeon bed didst thou not visit me,
And solemnly avow that I from wicked plots was free ?
How canst thou, then, unto my charge such grievous actions
   lay,
And all thou hast so solemn said as solemnly unsay ? "

The whole assembled multitude full on Mackenzie turned,
That even his hardened countenance with shame and anger
   burned :
" True, Jerviswood, I told thee so, as my own private view :
Here I discharge the functions which to the crown are due."
" If thou hast a conscience for thyself, and another for this
   place,
I leave thee to the God of heaven, and His all-pardoning
   grace !
My lords, I add no more : proceed,—right well I know my
   doom ;
Death hath no terrors for my soul, the grave it hath no
   gloom ! "

'Tis one from old St. Giles : the blasts of midnight shake the
   hall,
Hoarse sounding like a demon's voice, which the stoutest
   hearts appal !   .
His doom is uttered : " Twelve hours hence thy traitorous
   head shall fall,
And for a terror be exposed upon the city wall ;

Thy limbs shall quartered be, and hung all mutilate and
  bare,
At Jedburgh and Lanark towns, at Glasgow and at Ayr,
That all good subjects thence may learn obedience to the
  State,
Their duty to our gracious King, and bloody treason's fate."
A horror seizes every breast—a stifled cry of dread :
" Who sheds the blood of innocence, the blood's on his own
  head."
That packed and perjured jury shrink in conscience-struck
  dismay,
And wish their hands as clear of guilt as they were yesterday.
Mackenzie's cold and flinty face is quivering like a leaf,
Whilst with quick and throbbing fingers he turns o'er and
  o'er his brief.

And the misnamed judges vainly try their rankling thoughts
  to hide
Beneath an outward painted mask of loftiness and pride.
Even she, the sweet heroic one, aye watchful at his side—
Whose courage ne'er hath blanched as yet, though sorely,
  sharply tried—
Even she is crushed beneath the weight of this last and
  deadly blow,
And sinks upon her brother's neck, o'erwhelmed in deadly
  woe.

He, he alone is calm of soul !   Powers of no mortal birth
Are gently loosening every tie that binds him to the earth ;
And inward faith gives outward force,—strong is his deep,
  dark eye,
And his brow and lip are beautiful as in the days gone by.

Meekly he rises to depart, but pauses for a space,
And looks upon his cowering foes with calm and saintly
  grace—
" The time is short, the sentence sharp—your malice I for-
  give ;
For God hath made me fit to die, as ye, my lords, to live ! "

And meekly he departs—his toils, his work, and warfare
  done—
And his martyr chariot waits him, and his triumphs are
  begun !

And twelve hours thence, upon the block his reverend head
  did fall,
And for a terror was exposed upon the city wall ;
His limbs were quartered and were hung, all mutilate and
  bare,
At Jedburgh and at Lanark town, at Glasgow and at Ayr ;
And thus through all broad Scotland these martyred relics go,
Like a fiery cross to rouse them to the tyrant's overthrow !

The ancient halls of Jerviswood are desolate and gray,
And its ancient oaks and lime trees are sinking to decay ;
These are of things that perish, and their place soon knows
  them not,
But a glory from the past illumes this consecrated spot.
To him who braves the martyr's death is deathless honour
  given,
For the faith that breeds heroic deeds is dear to earth and
  heaven,
And through all succeeding ages, amongst the wise and good,
Enshrined shall be the memory of the noble Jerviswood.

DODDS.

After the dreadful sentence upon this glorious martyr had been carried
into execution, William Leechman, a farmer at Roberton, in the parish
of Dolphinton, travelled all the way to Lanark one dark night, a distance
of 14 miles, and managed, at the risk of his life, to remove the portion
of Jerviswood's body exposed on Lanark jail, and procured for it an
honourable interment. After the Revolution, the family of Jerviswood,
as a recompense to Leechman for this mark of respect to their ancestor,
assisted him to educate his son for the Church—the well-known Dr.
William Leechman, for many years Professor of Divinity and Principal
of the University of Glasgow. Had it not been for this deed of his father,
Dr. Leechman, in all probability, would have passed through life
unnoticed and unknown. Jerviswood is in the immediate vicinity of
Lanark.

DAY DREAMS OF OTHER YEARS.

THERE are moments when my spirit wanders back to other
years,
And time long, long departed, like the present still appears ;
And I revel in the sunshine of those happy, happy hours,
When the sky of youth was cloudless, and its path was
strewn with flowers.

Oh, those days of dreamy sweetness ! Oh, those visions of
delight !
Weaving garlands for the future, making all of earth too
bright ;
They come creeping through my memory like messengers of
peace,
Telling tales of bygone blessings, bidding present sorrows
cease.

Long lost friends are gathering round me, smiling faces,
gentle forms,
All unconscious of earth's struggles, all unmindful of its
storms—
Beaming radiantly and beautiful, as in the days of youth,
When friendship was no mockery, when every thought was
truth.

Joy, illuming every bosom, made fair nature fairer still—
Mirth sported on each summer breeze, and sung on every rill ;
Beauty gleaming all around us, bright as dreams of fairy-
land—
Oh, faded now that lustre, scattered far that happy band.

Now deeply traced with sorrow is the once unclouded brow,
And eyes that sparkled joyously are dim with weeping now ;
We are tasting life in earnest—all its vain illusions gone—
And the stars that glistened o'er our path are falling one
by one.

Some are sleeping with their kindred—summer blossoms
    o'er them wave;
Some, lonely and unfriended, with the stranger found a grave;
While others now are wandering on a far and foreign shore,
And that happy, loving company shall meet—ah! never more.

But afar in memory's garden, like a consecrated spot,
The heart's first hopes are hidden, and can never be forgot;
And the light that cheered us onward, in our early, airy days,
Oft we linger in the distance to look back upon its rays.

Old Time, with hand relentless, may shed ruins o'er the earth,
May strew our path with sorrow, make a desert of our
    ' hearth—
Change may blight our fairest blossoms, shroud our clearest
    light in gloom,
But the flowery fields of early years, shall never lose their
    bloom.

                MARGARET CRAWFORD, OF CARNWATH.

NEWBIGGIN NELL.

O Newbiggin Nell, sweet Newbiggin Nell,
I ne'er saw a lassie like Newbiggin Nell!
O' a' the braw lassies that trip to the well,
There was ne'er ane to me like Newbiggin Nell.

O Newbiggin Nell is so bonnie and braw,
And Newbiggin Nell is the flower o' them a';
Our strong-lunged precentor, na' *Baitlaw* himsel',
Ne'er sung of a fairer than Newbiggin Nell!

Her breath is as sweet as the flower of the haw,
Her neck is as white as the new driven snaw,
Her cheek is as fair as the red heather bell—
O! there ne'er was a lassie like Newbiggin Nell!

There's a lad in Dunsyre, fu' campie and crouse,
That fain wad hae Nelly to keep his bit house,
But she bade him gang hame to his auld Kirkland Bell !
And no come a-courtin' to Newbiggin Nell !

The Dolphington dandie was a' fidgen fain,
To get bonnie Nell for a wife o' his ain ;
But she bade him gang back to Dolphington Dell,
And come nae mair a-courtin' to Newbiggin Nell !

O Newbiggin Nell has a dark rollin' e'e,
And kindly and sweetly she smiles upon me ;
And I'll lay my life, to an auld mason's mell,
I'm the lad that will marry sweet Newbiggin Nell !

Nell was a comely damsel in the employment of the late Mr. Ritchie,
farmer, Newbigging.

THE COVENANTERS IN CARNWATH MOOR.

THE moors and the mountains of Scotland were red,
With the blood of our best and our dearest ;
And the martyr's narrow and lonely bed,
Rose afar in the solitudes drearest.

Thick lay the mist over Clyde's lovely vale,
And slowly the morning was breaking ;
O'er the dark woods of Kersewell the stars glimmered pale,
And the blackbird her song was awaking.

Then bright rose the sun o'er the moors of Carnwath,
And the laverock was merrily singing ;
The cry of the moorcock in Falla's green Strath,
From the yelpin' Craigs echoes were ringing.

The dew glistened bright on the red heather bells,
The wild flowers in beauty were blooming ;
And far o'er the vales, and the high mountain fells,
The wild bees in thousands were humming.

The butterfly danced in the gay sunny beam,
    And wantoned from blossom to blossom ;
The speckled trout sprang from the dazzling stream,
    At the fly sailing over its bosom.

When afar in the wilds of the moors of Carnwath,
    The faithful and few met together,
Undaunted by threatenings of torture and death,
    In a valley of sweet blooming heather.

There was Denholm the bold, from the shades of Westshield,
    The cottars of lone Auchingray ;
And the stern Laird of Kersewell had met on the field,
    With his tenants around him to pray.

The preacher was Peden, the fearless and bold,
    And around him the scattered flocks gathered,
As sheep seek the home of the sheltering fold
    When a rude, stormy day has been weathered.

Aloud rose the psalm with melodious swell,
    And each heart was attuned for devotion,
When a sign from the watch on Cobbenshaw Fell,
    Shewed the ruthless dragoons were in motion.

Then fervent, though briefly, the minister prayed,
    "O God of our fathers, our safety be,
And shield us, O Lord, from his merciless raid
    Who comes to destroy us for worshipping Thee ? "

Then all sought in haste the mossy retreat,
    And the brown heather's friendly cover ;
Claverhouse soon arrived, but nothing could meet
    Save the cry of the moorfowl and plover.

But he saw from the marks on the fresh trodden heath,
    That a meeting had lately been there,
Of those whom he hunted o'er mountain and strath,
    For seeking the Saviour in prayer.

He raged and he fumed, he stormed and blasphemed,
   Disappointed at losing his prey;
And scoured every glen with his merciless men,
   To find where the fugitives lay.

Oft he passed and repassed in hot, fiery haste,
   Where in trembling concealment they lay;
But searched all in vain over mountain and plain,
   Then slowly at last rode away.

O, happy are they who the statutes obey
   Of creation's Omnipotent King;
Though destruction and wrath be around their path,
   Safety and peace He can suddenly bring.

And even though the worst on their heads should burst,
   With composure, with triumph they die;
For the Saviour they love is in heaven above,
   And their home is with Him in the sky.

This meeting was held on the farm of Woolfords. A large stone on which the preacher stood still bears the name of "Peden's Poopit." Sir William Denholm, of Westshield, was attainted, confiscated, and sentenced to be executed, as soon as he could be apprehended. He was implicated in Argyle's attempt to revolutionise the country. He concealed himself 14 days in Cranly Moss, near Westshield House, which was then occupied by a party of dragoons sent to apprehend him. He escaped to Holland; returned with William; had his estates restored, and was for many years M.P. for Lanark, and Master of the Mint. The stern Laird of Kersewell was Sir Robert Chiesly, a gentleman of considerable influence among the Covenanters. He acted as one of the agents for that body when in arms, to attempt a pacific arrangement with Charles I.

———

BUNDLE AND GO.

"FRAE the foot o' the Tintoc, where Clyde rins sae smoothly,
   And lasses and lads sing o' love a' the day,
I'm come, my dear lassie, to mak' my last offer,
   Sae mak' up your mind noo, and dinna delay.

E

I've now ta'en leave o' my comrades so loving,
    While tears of affection in plenty did flow ;
Thy glove, my love, is here as a token—
    So mak' up your mind noo, and bundle and go."

"Still true to you a season I'll tarry,
    Mair kind you'll find my daddie will grow ;
I fain would gain his blessing to marry,
    And then, my dear lad, I wad bundle and go.
But if I were to gang without tellin' my faither,
    My tocher he'd keep, sheets and blankets also ;
My mother wad rage and forever disown me,
    Yet fain, very fain wad I bundle and go."

"My mother she's gane, and the house it is eerie,
    This nicht you may rue if you answer me no ;
Ere day be grey, a stranger and weary,
    I'll mourn thy refusal to bundle and go.
But a fig for excuses ! come, kilt up your coatie ;
    Owre muirs and thro' mosses ye ken we've to go,
The Clyde we've to cross at the Lampits' auld boatie,
    So mak' up your mind noo, and bundle and go."

Love lent wings to baith, in a blink they coupled,
    With peace and with pleasure their years glide along ;
Their young sprouts are innocent, noisy, and healthy,
    And aye to please a' she lilts owre a sweet song.
His Jean now is a' his delight and his pleasure,
    Their love to each other continues to glow ;
She blesses the day she left faither and mother,
    And took his advice and did bundle and go.

                    WALTER WATSON, of Chryston.

There are many versions of the above song; but we deem it right to
enter a protest against the example which it gives to the young ladies.
For one runaway marriage which is followed by such happy results as
the above, there are ten followed by great misery. Remember the
proverb, ladies, "They who marry in haste, repent at leisure." Be
prudent, be cautious before you do what you never, never can undo !

PUIR FOLK.

SOME folk grow proud o'er bags o' gowd,
    And some are proud o' learning;
An honest puir man's worthy name
    I take delight in earning.
Slaves needna try to haud us down,
    To knaves we're unco dour folk;
We're aften wranged, but deil may care,
    We're honest folk—the puir folk.

Wi' Wallace wight we fought fu' weel,
    When lairds and lords were jinkin';
They knelt before the tyrant loon;
    We brak' his crown, I'm thinkin'.
The muckle men he bought wi' gowd,
    Syne he began to jeer folk;
But neither sword, nor gear, nor guile,
    Could turn the sturdy puir folk.

When auld King Charlie tried to bind
    Wi' airn soul and conscience,
In virtue o' his right divine
    And ither daft-like nonsense;
Wha raised at Marston such a stour
    As made the tyrants fear folk?
Wha prayed and fought wi' Pym and Noll?
    The sturdy, trusty puir folk.

And wha upon auld Scotland's hills
    Were hunted like the paitrick,
And hacked' wi' swords and shot wi' guns
    Frae Tummel's banks to Ettrick,
Because they wadna let the priest
    Aboon the conscience steer folk?
The lairds were bloodhounds to the clans;
    The martyrs were the puir folk.

We saw the corn and haud the plough ;
  We a' work for our leevin' ;
We gather nought but what we've sawn—
  A' else we reckon thievin'.
And for the loon wha fears to say
  He comes o' lowly sma' folk,
A wizen'd soul the creature has—
  Disown him a', ye puir folk.

Great sirs and mighty men o' earth,
  Ye aften sair misca' us,
And hunger, cold, and poverty
  Come after ye to thraw us ;
Yet up our hearts we try to heise
  In spite o' you and your folk :
But mind—enough as gude's a feast,
  Altho' we be but puir folk.

We thank the powers for gude and ill,
  As gratefu' folk should do, men ;
But maist ava because our sires
  Were tailors, smiths, and ploughmen.
Gude men they were, as true as steel—
  They didna rack and screw folk
Wi' empty pouches, honest hearts —
  Thank Heaven we're come o' puir folk !

Poor R. Nicoll, on him, if on any, had fallen the mantle of Burns. He
just lived long enough to show what was in him, when he was summoned
away, and all his brilliant prospects closed for ever !

SIR WILLIAM WALLACE,

THE KNIGHT OF ELLERSLIE.

THE Southron loons wrought muckle skaith,
  Unto our West countrie ;
He's ta'en the gear, but he's gat the wrath
  O' the knight o' Ellerslie.

Sir William's ta'en his sword in hand—
It was weel proved and gude;
Three waps o't round his buirdly breast,
Has cleared a Scottish rood!

Upon his lip there is a vow,
Upon his brow, a ban;
He'll learn our foemen their ain march,
If it may be learned by man.

To see him in his weeds o' peace,
Wi' the dimple on his chin,
O stood there e'er a fairer knight
A lady's love to win.

To see him in his shell o' steel,
His broadsword by his thie,
O stood there e'er a braver knight,
To save a hail countrie!

Step oot, step oot, my gallant knight!
By thysel' thou shanna stride,
Tho' white the locks lie on my brow
And my sheet o' mail hings wide.

Blaw up! there's gallant hearts in Kyle,
And the Upper Ward o' Clyde;
Blaw up, blaw up, a thousand spears
Will glitter by thy side!

There's mony vow to guard, I trow,
There's mony may through dread;
But blaw a blast, thou wight-Wallace,
And look for man and steed.

Oh! wha could bide by plough and spade,
While a Southron's in the land;
Oh! wha can lag when Wallace wight,
Has ta'en his sword in hand.

To him that does a righteous deed,
A righteous strength is given ;
And he that fights for liberty
Will be free in earth or heaven.
                                    HEW AINSLIE.

Of all the poetry of which Wallace has been the subject, the above
lines are the only ones in which a special notice of the fealty of the Upper
Ward of Clyde to Wallace is recorded ; and they were written and first
published in America, too.   At the battle of Biggar, the great hero
led the first division of the army against Edward in person ; Sir John
Graham, the second, and under him Sir Thomas Somerville of Carnwath ;
Sir Walter of Newbigging, the third, and under him were Sir John Tinto
of Crimp Cramp, and David, son of Sir Walter Newbigging.   Some
people question the truth of the battle of Biggar altogether, and say
that Edward was in Normandy at the time Blind Harry affirms the
battle took place.   But in addition to the tradition and Blind Harry's
statement, there was lately found a number of coins of Edward I. on the
very site where tradition affirmed it to have taken place.   The late Mr.
Sim of Coulter had a number of these in his possession, and they may
have been missed in the hurried retreat.   Harry may have mistaken the
date ; but that the battle of Biggar really took place there can be no
reasonable doubt.   A little runlet of water, which that day ran with
blood, still bears, from that incident, the name of *The Red Syke*.   The
day before the battle, Wallace exchanged dress with a gaberlunzie, and
in that disguise went in and deliberately inspected Edward's camp.   It
would appear that one sharp fellow had some suspicion of the *beggar*, for
tradition states that he said—

" He's crippled of a foot, and he's blin' of an e'e,
But he's as like Willie Wallace as ever I did see !"

VERSES

ON THE LATE MR. HALL, THE SECEDING MINISTER, OF ROSE STREET
EDINBURGH, GETTING A GOWN.

It is amusing, in some respects melancholy, but in all very instructive,
to mark the changes and modifications of opinions, customs, and fashions
which time is ever producing.   We have heard of a decent man in Biggar
who wore the same hat during the greater part of a life-time, and in his
latter days was wont to boast that this identical hat was twenty times in
and out of fashion.   One of the most remarkable, but least noticed of
the changes in late times, is the universal adoption of the pulpit gown
by our Presbyterian preachers.   We believe the Directory for public
worship is altogether silent upon the subject ; yet it is true that, until
comparatively recent times, pulpit gowns were unknown.   The Rev.
George Mark, who died in 1816, was, for nearly forty years minister of
Carnwath, and had generally half-a-dozen ministers assisting at the
Sacrament, yet neither he, nor they, ever donned the gown.   The first
minister of Carnwath who did so was the late Rev. Mr. Walker who was

in lucted in 1817. It will appear from the following lines that Mr. Hall, of Rose Street, seems to have been the first minister of the Secession who wore the gown. The lines are very curious, as shewing the feelings and prejudices of the time, and the estimation in which the writer held the Secession. We believe a copy of this piece is very rare; it appears never to have been printed in any other form previously than on a broadside.

"Vanity of vanities, saith the preacher, all is vanity."

HA, ha! Seceders! brag nae mair
O' your pretended zeal and care;
You ha'e o' pride as large a share
          As ither folk.
Your priests wear bands and *pouthered hair*,
          And sic vain troke!

And now your vanity to crown,
Your great gun, Hall, has got a gown;
Which cleeds him a' baith up and down,
          And by the same,
A clatter's raised through a' the town
          Nought to his fame.

Oh! what wad Ralph and Eben say,
Had they been leevin' at this day,
To see him clad in sic array,
          Wi' gown and bands?
They wad exclaim (as weel they may),
          Oh, sinfu' lands!

Now pastors (wha should plainly show
The way in which we ought to go)
Are buskèd up like ony beau,
          For play or ball,
The truth o' which we see and know,
          As witness Hall!

But ministers should lead the way,
Wi' humble lives and plain array,
And no like actors in a play,
          Wi' braw *dressed hair!*
And a' their tassels vain and gay,
          To mak us stare.

A gude grey plaid o' Maggie's mak
Would better far become his back,
When he gaed to the kirk to crack
                O' holy things,
Than bands and gowns, like Popish pack,
                Wi' belts and strings !

Sic trappin's do but ill adorn
The mean proud hearts by whom they're worn,
But aff their backs they should be torn,
                Wi' just disdain,
For meekness is man's uniform
                In his mean frame.

Harm in the gown tho' there were nane,
Yet surely he is much to blame
When o' his hearers mony a ane
                By it's offended;
He might hae lettin it alane,
                For weel he kenn'd it.

It wad hae been some sma' excuse,
An' what we couldna weel refuse,
Had he ne'er read the dismal waes
                In Holy Scripture,
And a' the ills which them pursues
                Wha breed a rupture.

But he his vanity to feed,
Doth scatter them he ought to lead,
And unto such his help as need,
                To clear the way,
He proves a stumbling-block indeed
                By his array.

This conduct of the Reverend Hall
Is widely different from Paul,
Who, rather than offend at all,
                Did aft decline,
From eating flesh at nature's call,
                Or drinking wine.

Our Saviour lowly was and meek,
Whose great example a' should seek,
Laid down His life for elect sheep,
      While Mr. Hall
His idiot gown resolves to keep,
      Spite of them all !

Sic stiffness in a Popish priest,
Or those who at religion jest,
Might be excused (or we at best
      Made less to wonder),
But in a minister of Christ,
      'Tis a great blunder.

Some o' his folks are to be pitied,
For, waesucks ! they are sadly cheated,
After collections aft repeated,
      This mony a day ;
An' ither burdens on them heapèd,
      To offend them sae.

If I were them, I wad be clear
To stop him o' his vain career ;
Speak bauldly out, and dinna fear
      Though he may brag ;
Tell him your conscience canna bear
      That Romish rag !

And no about his testimony blast,
For now he is conforming fast ;
He first wore bands, and now that's past—
      He wears a gown !
Reading comes next, and then at last
      His zeal fa's down !

QUOTHQUAN.

I SING of Tinto and the Upper Ward,
Whose pleasing scenes demand our due regard ;
And richly would my muse deserve the ban,
Did she o'erlook the village of Quothquan.
A straggling clachan ! houses here and there,
With no attempt at order anywhere,
And yet a place, as clearly may be seen,
Where larger population once had been ;
For there a ruined church attracts the eye,
Enclosed within an ancient cemetery,
Whose frequent graves and tombstones clearly show
What multitudes of dead must lie below.

I take a special interest in Quothquan,
From a remembrance of a worthy man,
A native of the place, a man of mark—
John Thorburn—long the village patriarch.
Blest with the higher attributes of mind,
He was sagacious, simple, social, kind,
With touch of the romantic, yet withal
Solid, exact, and intellectual ;
Or if the epithet you would prefer,
He was a thorough-born philosopher.

None ever knew the man, who had a doubt
He was our Scottish Socrates throughout ;
The two in many things how much the same,
And yet with what diversity of fame ;
But had the two been in each other's place,
Each would have acted with becoming grace.

Had Socrates been native of Quothquan,
And worthy John the Athenian,
The Greek his humble part had well sustained,
And John the fatal hemlock would have drained ;
Yes, drained it to the very dregs had he
Believed he died for truth and verity.

But to the Scottish sage one praise is due
Which neither Greek nor Roman ever knew
He was a Bible Christian to the core,
Deep read and deeply skilled in saving lore ;
But here his type is no old heathen sage,
A nobler type he had in later age—
That type he found in the apostle Paul,
Like whom he made the cross his all in all.

Till eighty years of age the worthy man
Seemed quite a part and parcel of Quothquan—
A plant indigenous, sprung from the ground,
Like any of the aged trees around ;
Nor did I deem uprooted more could be
Of that old man than of the olden tree ;
And yet he was uprooted at the last,
And far from Clyde his future lot was cast.

That day he left Quothquan no cheek was dry,
Loud sobbed the young, the old stood silent by,
All grieved to think the place should never more
Resume the blythsome look it had before.
Ah ! how he strove his feelings to repress,
To hide his own and lessen their distress.

Right cheerfully he went on board the ship
Without complaint expressed by look or lip ;
And when a long and stormy voyage threw
A damp and discontent among the crew,
His happy, hopeful look served to illume
Their sinking spirits and dispel the gloom.

When ten long years of residence abroad
Saw him, like Enoch, walking with his God,
When no Canadian heats nor wintry snows
Could sour his mind or spirits discompose ;
When loving and beloved by all around,
'Mong strangers he a second home had found,
How like himself came on the closing scene—
The tree decaying, yet the leaf still green.

Death came at last; the venerable sage
Sunk to his rest at ninety years of age—
So gently sunk, that failure of the breath
Seemed a translation more than hand of death.
Light lie the earth upon that godly man,
Far from the Law and village of Quothquan!

Rev. JAMES PROUDFOOT.

In the seventeenth century, Quothquan and Liberton parishes were
united at the instance of the Earl of Carnwath. The communicants in
the two parishes at that time did not exceed 900. Liberton got the communion plate of the former parish under the obligation to return it,
should Quothquan ever again become a distinct parish. In 1812, Liberton
Church was rebuilt, and the heritors resolved to put Quothquan bell on
the new church, but it disappeared, and was not found till a new bell
was got for Liberton. Quothquan folk hid their bell in the Clyde, and
fished it up after all danger of losing it was gone.

SONG OF THE OLD CARNWATH CHURCH BELL

Ding, dong! ding, dong!
Warning the people to church to throng,
To join in prayer and grateful song;
Time flies—man dies!
Leave earthly things and seek the skies!
Ding, dong! ding, dong!

Heard far—heard near,
I've sounded this warning loud and clear,
From week to week, from year to year;
Men have come—men have gone,
But still I'm giving the same old tone—
Ding, dong! ding, dong!

Bridal chime—funeral knell!
Of changeful man's estate I tell;
Two hundred years the auld kirk bell
Strife I've seen, and change I ween,
Yet dream'd not that such for me had been,
In my ding, dong! ding dong!

But love cools—like's change ;
They cast me aside, and a new bell arrange,
In their bran-new church—and then, oh, strange !
    Aside thus flung—(ah, how stung !)
New friends flocked around, and again me hung.
But now in a Free Church—vigorous, young—
    Ding, dong ! ding, dong !

    Blessings abound
To the friends in need I thus have found ;
Theirs to enjoy the truths I sound
        O'er moss—o'er fen,
O'er moorland and woody glen—
" Peace on earth, good-will to men,"
    In my ding, dong ! ding, dong !

These lines were written on the occasion of the old Bell of Carnwath
being transferred to the Free Church, in the spring of 1870.   It had rung
a solemn knell at the funeral of no fewer than five generations of the
people, six Lairds of Carnwath, and many a merry peal for the victories
of Nelson and Wellington.   Recast in 1880, with the ministers' names
carved upon it—Rev. James Walker, D.D., and George G. M'Leod,
minister of the Free Church : it was tolled all night by Willie Spence
when the news of Waterloo came to Carnwath, although saddened by
the fact that George M'Call, whose father and mother lived next door,
had fallen on the field.

NETHAN WATER.

No poet in his dream has had Nethan for his theme,
    Nor sounded his praise in a song ;
Yet not the less his praise deserves the richest lays,
    As he gracefully sweeps along.

His course is quickly run—ended ere well begun—
    Yet on his wooded banks around,
From Cummer to the Clyde, rich gems on every side
    Of both nature and art abound.

From 'mong heather and broom, near Stockbriggs' Gothic hall,
   He starts on his winding career;
Soon joined by Logan's flood sweeps thro' Auchlochan wood,
   As he bounds along bright and clear.

Passing Birkwood's lofty towers, 'mong bonnie woods and
   bowers,
   He enters consecrated ground;
Where St. Machate's monk told beads and mumbled Popish
   creeds,
   While old Nethan murmured around.

Ah! these were happy times when rung the vesper chimes,
   And a monk kept the conscience clear;
When for every sin and shame that tongue of man can name
   Forgiveness could be purchased here!

To follow Nethan down and leave this holy ground,
   Passing Auchty's stately old halls,
Sometimes o'er tiny linn he leaps with little din,
   And sometimes he listlessly crawls.

See Kerse so lovely stand 'mid trees on terrace grand,
   Enriching the western side;
Old Nethan's spirits rise as on and on he plies,
   Like the rush of the high spring tide.

What gorge is this ahead by some ancient earthquake made,
   With a gem on its shoulder high?
The wonder of the time—"a romance in stone and lime"—
   The work of skilful hand and eye?

More rapid on his path he tumbles through the strath
   Beneath a mimic rainbow's span,
Quite a gossamer affair, suspended in mid-air
   By the wonderful skill of man.

On classic ground once more: the pride of Nethan's shore,
   To old Tillietudlem, all hail!
Ah! the wizard hand is cold the witching tale that told—
   Wail, Scotland!   Old Scotland, wail!

Pause, dear old Nethan ; pause—don't rush into the jaws
  Of that huge glen gaping wide !
Thou won't ! then fare thee well, thy bygone tale I'll tell,
  Since thou'rt met and married to the Clyde.

S. R., Abbey Green, November, 1870.

THE WESTSIDEWOOD.

The Westsidewood ! O the Westsidewood !
The sweet shady groves o' the Westsidewood !
How the wild woods ring when the blackbirds sing
Among the shady groves o' the Westsidewood.

There are sweet, rosy flowers at the Westsidewood,
There are sweet cosie bowers at the Westsidewood,
And the sun shines bright o'er the mornin' clud,
On the bonnie, bonnie braes o' the Westsidewood.

O the grass grows green at the Westsidewood,
And lovely is the scene at the Westsidewood ;
How the butterfly skims, and the wild bee hums,
O'er the bonnie, bonnie braes o' the Westsidewood.

O ! splendid is the view from the Westsidewood,
Auld Tintoc looks so blue from the Westsidewood ;
And the lofty Coulter Fell, the monarch o' Clydedale,
Looks down from the heavens on the Westsidewood !

There are douce, decent men at Westsidewood,
And that the lasses ken, at the Westsidewood ;
There's Tam, and there's Dan—the very wale o' men—
A credit and an honour to the Westsidewood !

There are lassies young and braw at the Westsidewood,
That ding the parish a', at the Westsidewood,
And this soft heart o' mine, plays aye thud ! thud ! thud !
When I see the bonnie lassies at the Westsidewood.

Here's a health to the Laird o' the Westsidewood,
Lang may he tread the swaird o' the Westsidewood,
Aye the friend o' the poor, to ill-doers stiff and dour—
Lang, lang may he be at the Westsidewood.

Westsidewood, the seat of John Wilson, Esq., M.D., is delightfully
situated on the right bank of the Dippool, nearly in the centre of the
parish of Carnwath.   Dr. Wilson was a much respected gentleman, and
for many years administered the affairs of the Parish as Chairman of
the Parochial Board, and in the most satisfactory manner to all concerned.

SONG ON THE CATTLE DISEASE.

At Ormotherly Church, in Yorkshire, in the cattle plague of 1747, a
psalm, composed by the Clerk, was sung.   The first four stanzas contained an account of the cattle that died, and a list of the farmers who
suffered.   The remaining verses were as follows :—

No Christian's bull nor cow, they say,
  But takes it out of hand ;
And we no cattle soon will have
  At all within this land.

The doctors, tho' they all have spoke
  Like learned gentlemen,
And told us how the entrails look
  Of cattle dead and green—

Yet they can nothing do at all,
  With all their learning's store ;
So Heaven drive out this plague away
  And vex us not no more !

This was so well received by the congregation that it was desired again
by the whole assembly, except five farmers, who wept, declaring it was
too moving.   The minister on going out, said to his clerk, "Why, John,
what psalm is that we had to-day?   It is not one of David's."   "Na,
sir, na," quoth John, in great pride of heart, "David ne'er made yan
like it since he were born; this is yan of my ain!"

THE LASSIE'S WARDROBE.

The whimsicality of this song is greatly enhanced by the consideration that it was written by an old unmarried lady, as a kind of burlesque of her own habits and history, and was frequently sung by herself with great glee.

Air—The Laird o' Cockpen.

THERE lived a lass by yon burn braes,
And she was weel provided wi' claes ;
She had three mutches, a' but twa,
And nae bonnie lad wad tak' her awa'.

Tak' her awa', tak' her awa',
Nae bonnie lad wad tak' her awa' ;
She had three mutches a' but twa,
Yet nae bonnie lad wad tak' her awa'.

She had a gown, it was at the makin',
But it wantit a fore-breadth, it wantit the backin' ;
It wantit the sleeves, the linings an' a',
And nae bonnie lad wad tak' her awa'.

Tak' her awa', &c.

She had twa stockin's, they were at the knittin',
They wantit the legs, they wantit the fitten ;
They wantit the heads, the heels an' a'—
And nae bonnie lad wad tak' her awa'.

Tak' her awa', &c.

She had a shawl, it was just like a riddle,
It wadna' been the waur o' the thread and the needle,
For the middle was holed, the border awa',
And nae bonnie lad wad tak' her awa'.

Tak' her awa', &c.

She had a purse to keep her siller,
Wi' it she thought to catch the miller ;
But she tint the purse, the siller an' a',
And nae bonnie lad wad tak' her awa'.

Tak' her awa', &c.

F

She had a kist to keep her claes,
It might ha'e served her a' her days,
But like a gouk she gied it awa',
And nae bonnie lad wad tak' her awa'.
    Tak' her awa, &c.

And now she lives in a wee bit garret,
Without a friend, but a cat and a parrot,
For her father is dead, her mother an' a',
And nae bonnie lad has ta'en her awa'.
    Ta'en her awa', &c.

And what can she do, but live her lane,
Since a' her hopes o' marriage are gane;
For she's auld, she's bauld, she's wrinkled an' a',
And nae bonnie lad will tak' her awa'.
    Tak' her awa', &c.

Now listen, fair damsels, to my lays,
Ye wha are proud o' your braw claes;
For if ye're no guid as weel as braw,
O nae bonnie lad will tak' ye awa'.

        Tak' ye awa', tak' ye awa',
        If ye're no guid as weel as braw,
        Nae bonnie lad will tak' ye awa',
        O nae bonnie lad will tak' ye awa'.
                                    ANON.

LINES ON QUOTHQUAN LAW.

THE Tweed pours its waters afar
    Down the links of yon wild, winding glen,
And the mountains look up to the stars,
    Round the haunt and the dwellings of men.

But Tintoc rears higher his crest,
  And guards a far lovelier tide,
Where the power of his shadow is cast
  O'er the fair spreading vale of the Clyde.

And yet, tho' so stately his form,
  His features look weary and wan,
And convey to the heart not a charm,
  Like the bonnie green hill of Quothquan.

The kind and true-hearted dwell there,
  And bliss to the soul can restore—
Health smiles in the young, sunny fair,
  And wit in the locks that are hoar.

Where'er in this world I roam,
  The leal to my heart shall be dear,
And when far away from my home,
  I'll think on the home I found there.

Oh! here may true bliss still abide,
  While the breezes of nature shall fan
The fair spreading vale of the Clyde,
  And the bonnie green hill of Quothquan.
                          H. SCOTT RIDDELL.

THE CAMERONIAN'S DREAM.

In a dream of the night, I was wafted away
To the muirlands of mist where the martyrs lay ;
Where Cameron's sword and his Bible are seen
Engraved on the stone where the heather grows green.

'Twas a dream of those ages of darkness and blood,
When the minister's home was the mountain and wood ;
In Wellwood's dark valley the Standard of Zion
All bloody and torn 'mong the heather was lying.

'Twas morning, and summer's young sun from the east
Lay in lovely repose on the green mountain's breast;
On Wardlaw and Cairntable, the clear shining dew
Glistened sheen 'mong the heath-bell and mountain flowers
    blue.

And far up in heaven, in a white, sunny cloud,
The song of the lark was melodious and loud;
And in Glenmuir's wild solitudes, lengthened and deep,
Were the whistling of plovers and bleating of sheep.

And Wellwood's sweet valley breathed music and gladness,
The fresh meadow blooms hung in beauty and redness;
Its daughters were happy to hail the returning,
And drink the delights of July's sweet morning.

But, ah! there were hearts cherished far other feelings—
Illumed by the light of prophetic revealings—
Who drank from the scenery of beauty but sorrow,
For they knew that their blood would bedew it to-morrow.

'Twas the few faithful ones, who with Cameron were lying
Concealed 'mong the mist where the heathfowl were crying;
For the horsemen of Earslhall around them were hovering,
And their bridle reins rung through the thin misty covering.

Their faces grew pale, and their swords were unsheathed,
But the vengeance that darkened their brow was unbreathed;
With eyes raised to heaven, in calm resignation,
They sung their last song to the God of Salvation.

The hills with the sweet mournful music was ringing,
The curlew and plover in concert were singing;
But the melody died 'mid derision and laughter,
As the host of ungodly rushed on to the slaughter.

Though in mist and in darkness and fire they were shrouded,
Yet the souls of the righteous were calm and unclouded;
Their dark eyes flashed lightning, as proud and unbending
They stood like the rock which the thunder is rending.

The muskets were flashing, the blue swords were gleaming,
The helmets were cleft, and the red blood was streaming,
The heavens grew black, and the thunder was rolling,
As in Wellwood's dark muirlands the mighty were falling.

When the righteous had fallen, and the combat was ended,
A chariot of fire through the dark cloud descended;
The drivers were angels on horses of whiteness,
And its burning wheels turned upon axles of brightness.

A seraph unfolded its door bright and shining,
All dazzling like gold of the seventh refining;
And the souls that came forth out of great tribulation
Have mounted the chariot and steeds of salvation.

On the arch of the rainbow the chariot is gliding,
Through the path of the thunder the horsemen are riding;
Glide swiftly, bright spirits! the prize is before ye—
A crown never fading, a kingdom of glory!

The author of these lines, James Hyslop, was in his youth a shepherd
in the vicinity of Airsmoss, where the battle was fought which he has
described so beautifully in his "Dream." It was first published in the
Edinburgh Magazine for February, 1821. Subsequently he was appointed
schoolmaster on board a war vessel. While acting in this capacity on
board the *Tweed* man-of-war, he, along with others, made a visit to
the island of St. Jago and slept all night on shore. The whole party were
seized with fever, which in no fewer than six cases proved fatal (including
Hyslop), after twelve days' illness. He died on the 4th of December,
1827, in his 29th year.

MORTALITY.

O why should the spirit of mortal be proud?
Like a fast flitting meteor, a fast flying cloud,
A flash of the lightning, a break of the wave—
He passes from life to his rest in the grave!

The leaves of the oak and the willow shall fade!
Be scattered around and together be laid;
And the young and the old, and the low and the high,
Shall moulder to dust and together shall lie.

The child that a mother attended and loved,
The mother, that infant's affection that proved,
The husband, that mother and infant that blest,
Each—all are away to their dwelling of rest :

The maid on whose cheek, on whose brow, in whose eye,
Shone beauty and pleasure—her triumphs are by ;
And the memory of those that beloved her and praised,
Are alike from the minds of the living erased.

The hand of the king that the sceptre hath borne,
The brow of the priest that the mitre hath worn,
The eye of the sage, and the heart of the brave,
Are hidden and lost in the depths of the grave.

The peasant, whose lot was to sow and to reap;
The herdsman, who climbed with his goats to the steep ;
The beggar that wandered in search of his bread,
All have faded away like the grass which we tread.

The saint that enjoyed the communion of heaven,
The sinner that dared to remain unforgiven,
The wise and the foolish, the guilty and just,
Have quietly mingled their bones in the dust.

So the multitude goes—like the flower and the weed
That wither away to let others succeed ;
So the multitude comes—even these we behold
To repeat every tale that hath often been told.

For we are the same things that our fathers have been,
We see the same sights that our fathers have seen,
We drink the same stream, we feel the same sun,
And we run the same course that our fathers have run.

The thoughts we are thinking our fathers would think,
The death we are shrinking from they too would shrink,
To the life we are clinging to they too would cling,
But it speeds from the earth like a bird on the wing !

They loved—but their story we cannot unfold ;
They scorned—but the heart of the haughty is cold ;
They grieved—but no wail from their slumbers may come ;
They joyed—but the voice of their gladness is dumb.

For they died—ay, they died! and we things that are now,
Who walk on the turf that lies over their brow,
Who make in their dwellings a transient abode,
Meet the changes they met in their pilgrimage road.

Yea, hope and despondency, pleasure and pain,
Are mingled together like sunshine and rain ;
And the smile and the tear, and the song and the dirge,
Still follow each other like surge upon surge.

'Tis the wink of an eye, 'tis the draught of a breath,
From the blossom of health to the paleness of death,
From the gilded saloon to the bier and the shroud—
O why should the spirit of mortal be proud ?

WILLIAM KNOX.

These lines having been found in manuscript among the papers of the
late Abraham Lincoln, President of the United States, were published in
America as the work of the great Liberator of the American slaves ; it is so
far creditable to Lincoln's taste that he appreciated them so much as to
copy them with his own hand.   But there can be no doubt respecting
the authorship.   They first appeared in 1825, in a volume of lyrics,
entitled the "Harp of Zion."   Knox was a native of Lilliesleaf, Roxburgh-
shire, where he was educated.   He was for some time a farmer, and died
at Edinburgh in 1825 at the age of 36.   He published several volumes of
sacred poetry.   Many of his pieces are exquisitely beautiful.   It is
worthy of notice, that Lincoln admired them so much that he was in the
habit of often quoting and reciting them, both in public and private.
He made inquiry for the author, and on being informed he was dead, sent
a donation of £10 to the poet's father.

KATIE GLASGOW.

O BONNIE Katie Glasgow ! how are ye fennin' now,
Has fleetin' time nae shadow cast upon your sunny brow,
And is your e'e as sparkling bright, your heart as free o' cares,
As we were a' that happy nicht when I was at Carstairs.

O bonnie Katie Glasgow! ye were handsome, young, and fair,
Love danced amang the ringlets o' your rich and glossy hair;
And youth and love and beauty, and happy hearts were theirs,
Who formed the merry company when I was at Carstairs.

O bonnie Katie Glasgow! I've wandered far and wide,
O'er deserts wild, o'er mountains high, o'er ocean's foaming
    tide,
And joined in luxury's festive scenes where wealth and
    splendour glares,
But ne'er forgot that happy nicht when I was at Carstairs.

I've seen the Highland maidens bloom, sweet flowers amang
    the hills,
I've seen the factory beauties stream in hundreds frae the mills,
And the ruddy dark-eyed Clydesdale maids at Clydesdale
    merry fairs,
But ne'er forgot that happy nicht when I was at Carstairs.

I've seen the city ladies shine, the noblest of the land,
So proudly pacing Princes Street in silks and satins grand,
But all the city's beauties, all the pride of Edinbro's squares,
Could ne'er efface that happy nicht when I was at Carstairs.

O bonnie Katie Glasgow! I often mind you still,
Though you have lang forgotten me, forget I never will;
For deeply carved on memory's page, my heart again declares—
I'll ne'er forget that happy nicht when 1 was at Carstairs.

Katie was a native of Carstairs, and became the wife of a farmer at
Dolphinton.

A CRACK OWRE A CHAPPIN IN AMERICA,

WI' JOHN PRENTICE, LATE OF COVINGTON MAINS, BY HEW AINSLIE.

LET's tell auld tales o' far awa'
    While stretchin' out oor legs;
An' though oor drink's no usquebaugh,
    'Twill serve to weet our craigs.

Wake up, ye spirits of the past
That haunted life's braw morn ;
An' if a girnin' ghaist looks in,
We'll lay him wi' a horn.

Ay, let our youngsters kick the mools,
They're geared for life's braw race ;
The gowd an' siller's at the dools,
High honours, post an' place.

But stoutest tree e'er stood on lan'
At last comes to the grun',
An' biggest blether e'er was blawn,
What ends it but in *win'* ?

We ken hoo things are handled here,
Howe'er we puff or pech ;
So, savin' win' to cool oor kail,
Let's toom anither quaich.

It's richt bee-like to fill the byke,
An' keep things het at hame,
But weary on your niggard drone
That never prees the kame.

Gloomin' at a' things in his grip,
Blin' onward fares Sir Greed,
Nor recks the coof some slippery loof
Will sune skail a' abreed.

It's lang been said what's crossed the craig
Can ne'er be testamented ;
An' sages hint that what is tint
Is twice tint when lamented.

But saws o' age an' counsels sage
Are no' aye owre weel ta'en ;
So here we'll quat—haud in your cup—
Here's tae ye, Jock, again.

Mr. Prentice was the son of Archibald Prentice, farmer in Covington

Mains, with whom Burns spent the night, and was hospitably entertained with a large company of Mr. Prentice's friends, on his first journey to Edinburgh. John succeeded his father as the farmer of Covington Mains, but ultimately went to the United States, where he made the acquaintance of Ainslie.

A PRAYER.

O Thou! who rulest and reignest on high;
Far above yon glorious sun and sky—
Where angels, archangels, and cherubims stand,
All reverently veiled, and await Thy command—
With ransomed millions round that dazzling throne,
Which no mortal eye ever gazed upon—
All in shining robes and with harps of gold,
Rejoicing safe in the heavenly fold.
Great Creator of all! Thy glories we sing,
Immortal! Eternal! Omnipotent King!
O! look not upon us in wrathful frown,
But for Jesus' sake, look in mercy down!

We are wandering in sorrow and darkness here,
With many a doubt, and many a fear,
And temptations and trials on every hand,
While fighting our way to the better land :
For the angels of darkness around us throng,
Numerous and terrible, subtle and strong,
And we are all weakness, all guilt and sin,
Polluted without, and polluted within ;
Yet, look not upon us in wrathful frown,
But, for Jesus' sake, look in mercy down!

Our sins, we confess, are in number more
Than the stars of heaven, or the sands on the shore,
For Thy holy precepts were all forgot,
Thy warnings and threatenings remembered not;
'Gainst light and knowledge both we have sinned,
And the blessed Jesus, the sinner's friend ;

And we are all ruined, all lost and undone,
Yet we plead for the sake of Thine only Son—
O ! look not upon us in wrathful frown,
But, for Jesus' sake, look in mercy down !

O fill our hearts with Thy Holy Spirit,
And clothe us all with the Saviour's merit ;
And wash our souls in that precious blood
That streamed from the Cross in a crimson flood ;
And lead and guide us in the narrow way
That leads to the light of eternal day ;
And when life is o'er, and our dust in the tomb,
May our souls rejoice in the heavenly home—
Now hear us, O God ! not in wrathful frown !
But, for Jesus' sake, look in mercy down !

———

CARNWATH KIRKYARD.

O ! WHAT a quiet spot is Carnwath kirkyard,
What a dear spot to me is Carnwath kirkyard ;
Thousands of thousands below the green sward,
Are a' sleepin' sound in Carnwath kirkyard !

My father, my mother, and my sweet sisters three,
All so peacefully sleep by yon auld ash tree ;
In the storms and the tempests o' this life they shared
Now, they're a' sleepin' sound in Carnwath kirkyard !

The rich and the poor, the young and the old,
The sweet modest maiden, the termagent scold,
The teacher, the preacher, the lady, the laird,
Are a' sleepin' sound in Carnwath kirkyard !

The child of a day, who never saw the sun,
And him who had seen a whole century run ;
The soldier, the sailor—who a' dangers dared—
Are now sleepin' sound in Carnwath kirkyard !

The Bertrams of Kersewell sleep silent and sound,
Within the old wall that encloses them round ;
And Denholm the bold, who the tyrants' wrath dared,
Has been long laid to rest in Carnwath kirkyard !

The Somervilles sleep in their old Gothic aisle ;
Our old Earls, too, in the same holy pile :
But Carnwath Lockhart now is the owner and guard
Of the old Norman aisle in Carnwath kirkyard.

Wise sages, great statesmen, old barons so grand,
Great parliament members, proud peers of the land,
Life's journey all over, their mission declared,
Are a' sleepin' sound in Carnwath kirkyard.

Yet the dust is but here, all the spirits have gone
Before the great Judge on the great white throne ;
Every thought of each heart before him was bared,
That is now but a clod in Carnwath kirkyard.

Is your purse fu' o' gold, your heart fu' o' pride,
And health in your veins in high gushing tide ?
Yet remember how short your life may be spared—
How soon you may rest in the auld kirkyard !

Then prepare ! O prepare ! for the fast comin' time,
When life's journey's over, we leave this cold clime,
And face the great judge ; have our sentence declared ;
And our bones laid to rest in the auld kirkyard.

THE COVENANTERS' HYMN.

WHEN the orb of morn enlightens
    Hill and mountain, mead and dell,
When the dim horizon brightens
    And the serried clouds dispel,

And the sunflower eastward bending,
  Its fidelity to prove—
Be thy gratitude ascending
  Unto Him whose name is Love.

When the evening star is beaming
  In the coronet of heaven,
And the lake and river gleaming
  With the ruddy hues of even;
When a thousand notes are blending
  In the forest and the grove—
Be thy gratitude ascending
  Unto Him whose name is Love.

When the stars appear in millions
  In the portals of the west,
Bespangling the pavilions
  Where the blessed are at rest;
When the milky way is glowing
  In the cope of heaven above—
Let thy gratitude be flowing
  Unto Him whose name is Love.

ANON.

JOHN COPLAND'S SHOP.

A CARNWATH DITTY

JOHN COPLAND's shop! O John Copland's shop!
It's waesome to look at John Copland's shop!
For the roof is clean gone, and in spite o' the prop,
The wa's tumblin' doon o' John Copland's shop!

John Copland lang was a lang-headed man,
And a' the wise men o' the toon to him ran
When vexed wi' hard questions; there still was a hope
They wad a' be cleared up in John Copland's shop!

For Adam and Davie were sure to be there
In simmer and winter, be't foul or be't fair;
And the souter, the tailor—naethin' could them stop
From attendin' the meetin's in Copland's shop.

The laird and the landlord, and bold Jamie Vere,
The merchant, the cooper, a' gathered in there;
For a' things that could excite fear or hope,
Were canvassed and settled in Copland's shop.

Now the shop is a ruin, deserted and lone,
The wise men who met there all scattered and gone;
Time's merciless scythe has put a full stop
To the far-famed meetin's in Copland's shop.

Ah! these were the men, ay, and that was the time,
And the shop was the place of knowledge sublime!
In the darkness of ignorance no one need grope
Who attended the meetin's in Copland's shop!

The debates were long, the debates they were loud,
The orators eloquent, fiery, and proud;
Many a figure sublime and beautiful trope
Were born and buried in Copland's shop.

Oh! for the days and the men o' langsyne,
And oh! for their wisdom and eloquence fine;
Our best smiddy meetin's noo never can cope
Wi' the meetin's langsyne in John Copland's shop!

MORRIS'S SMIDDY.

A CARNWATH DITTY.

O COME to the meetin' in Morris's smiddy,
Come a' to the meetin' in Morris's smiddy;
Your heart wad beat high, your head wad be giddy,
If you heard the debates in Morris's smiddy.

When Weir mounts the rostrum wi' auld Fleming's head,
And lectures on bumps and the dark bloody deed,
And shews you the loon that should swing in a widdy,
Ye wad a' mind the lecture in Morris's smiddy.

In the Parliament houses, in Lunnon so grand,
Meet the greatest o' men that we hae in the land;
But Palmerston, Russell, Gladstone and Dizzy,
Wad a' meet wi' their match in Morris's smiddy.
We have great Scottish preachers of world-wide fame—
Caird, Candlish, and Guthrie—mony mae we could name—
But the deepest divine ever sat in a study,
Could ne'er match the Dungeons in Morris's smiddy.

Your great men of science—Locke, Newton, and Bacon—
Have often been found to be greatly mistaken;
In truth little better than poor Irish Biddy,
Is a fact often proved in Morris's smiddy.
Great questions of state, of science and law,
Are discussed every night where the bellowses blaw;
Of wisdom and wit, if ye want a subsidy,
Then come to the meetin's in Morris's smiddy.

Or wad ye rather hear about Calvin and Knox,
Election, Freewill, and a' sic stumblin'-blocks,
Morisonians, Arminians, or Presbyters steady,
Then come to the meetin's in Morris's smiddy;
For a' that has been in this world thae ken,
A' that has been *prentit* or written wi' pen,
Frae the heaven's aboon to earth's centre, they're ready
To explain every mystery in Morris's smiddy!

In country villages tradesmen's shops are the gathering places where assemble those who are fond of discussing the public news or the local gossip of the district. In John Copland's shop all the ups and downs of the Reform Bill of 1832, with the merits and demerits of the principal statesmen supporting and opposing that great measure, were freely discussed. After that came the Voluntary controversy, then the Non-Intrusion controversy, culminating in the Disruption. After the desertion and downfall of Copland's shop the party migrated to Morris's smiddy, where their debates were conducted with great spirit and eloquence. The principal speakers were James Weir, John Copland,

Thomas Capells, David Aitken, Walter Watson, John Dymock, David
Girdwood, James Brown, Adam Tennant, Andrew Anderson, William
Gibson, &c., but alas! alas! with one or two exceptions, they are all now
beneath the sod, and the meetings are closed for ever.

LANARK MILLS.

ADIEU! romantic banks of Clyde
   Where oft I've spent the joyful day ;
Now weary wandering on thy side
   I hear the plaintive, joyless lay.
In other lands I'm doomed to rove—
   The thought with grief my bosom fills ;
Why am I forced to leave my love
   And wander far from Lanark Mills ?

Can I forget the ecstatic hours,
   When ('scaped the village evening din)
I met my lass 'midst Braxfield's bowers,
   Or near the falls of Corra Linn !
While close I clasped her to my breast
   (The idea still my bosom fills !)
I thought myself completely blest
   By all the lads of Lanark Mills.

Deceitful, dear, delusive dream,
   Thou'rt fled—alas ! I know not where ;
And vanished is each blissful gleam,
   And left behind a load of care.
Adieu ! dear winding banks of Clyde,
   A long farewell, ye rising hills ;
No more I'll wander on your side,
   Though still my heart's at Lanark Mills.

While Tintoc stands the pride of hills,
   While Clyde's dark stream rolls to the sea,
So long, my dear loved Lanark Mills,
   May Heaven's best blessing smile on thee.

· A last adieu ! my Mary, dear,
The briny tear my eye distils ;
While reason's powers continue clear,
I'll think of thee and Lanark Mills.

STUART LEWIS.

Stuart Lewis was the son of an Innkeeper at Ecclefechan ; his father died bankrupt when he was quite young. He learned the tailor trade and commenced business at Chester, but was unfortunate. He set up at Ecclefechan, where he married. He tried the hawking trade, then enlisted into the Hopeton Fencibles. This regiment being disbanded, he was entrusted by a merchant with the sale of goods, but being robbed, like the " Wee Wifeckie," when under the influence of the " Drappikie," this employment came to an end. He next became an umbrella maker in Manchester, then tried various occupations, but was unfortunate in them all. He finally tried, what Burns says, in one of his epistles to a friend, is " *The last o't, the warst o't, is only but to beg !*" In his wanderings he was accompanied by his wife, who, although a severe sufferer on account of his follies, always retained for him the most devoted attachment. On her death in Edinburgh, in 1817, he became almost insane, roamed wildly through the country, seldom remaining more than one night in the same place. Falling accidentally into the Nith, which induced a fever, he died at Ruthwell in 1818. His is a very sad history, and is another melancholy instance of the evil effects of strong drink.

THE WEE, WEE GERMAN LAIRDIE.

Oh, wha the deil have we got for a king,
But a wee, wee German Lairdie !
An' when we gaed for to fetch him hame,
He was delvin his kail yardie ;
Sheuchan kail and layin' leeks,
But the hose, and but the breeks,
Up his beggar duds he cleeks—
The wee, wee German Lairdie.

And he's set down in oor Gudeman's chair,
The wee, wee German Lairdie !
And he's brought fouth o' foreign trash,
And dibbled them in his yardie ;

G

He's pu'd the rose o' English loons,
And brak the harp o' Irish clowns,
But oor Scots thistle will jag his thumbs—
This wee, wee German Lairdie.

Come up amang the Hieland hills,
    Thou wee, wee German Lairdie,
And see how Charlie's lang-kail thrive,
    They dibbled in our yardie ;
And if a stock ye daur to pu',
Or haud the yokin' o' the plough,
We'll break your sceptre owre your mou',
    Thou wee bit German Lairdie !

Our hills are high, our glens are steep,
    No fittin' for a yardie,
And our Norlan thristles winna pu,
    Thou wee, wee German Lairdie !
And we've the trenchin' blades o' wear,
Wad rob ye o' your German gear,
And pass ye neath the claymore's shear,
    Wee feckless German Lairdie !

He'll ride nae mair on ait-straw sunks,
    For gawen his German hurdies ;
But he sits on our gude king's throne,
    Amang the English lordies.
Auld Scotland, thou'rt owre cauld a hole,
    For nursin' siccan vermin ;
But the very dogs in England's court,
    They bark and yowl in German !   ANON.

The author of this merciless satire is unknown ; but, according to tradition, it was a great favourite at Carnwath House after the accession of
George I. to the British throne. George Lockhart, the Laird of Carnwath, was a decided Jacobite ; in 1715 he raised a troop of horse for the
service of the Pretender, was imprisoned for a considerable time in
Edinburgh Castle on suspicion, a measure which in all probability saved
both his head and his estate. He had a groom, who was an excellent
singer, who frequently made the stable ring with the "Wee, wee German
Lairdie." It is not unlikely that Lockhart himself was the author; his
works show that he was a writer of no mean power, both in poetry and
prose.

THE FLOWER OF ABBEY GREEN.

'Tis sweet when owre Glendevon's towers,
  The sun pours forth his golden rays ;
'Tis sweet in Birkwood's bonnie bowers,
  To hear the linnet's thrilling lays ;
'Tis sweet to wander owre the braes,
  O'erhanging Nethan's winding stream,
For there the Queen of Beauty strays—
  The lovely Queen of Abbey Green.

Sweet is the rose upon the brier,
  And sweet the blossom on the thorn,
And sweet the laverock's sang so clear,
  Far up amang the cluds at morn ;
And to the exile sad, forlorn,
  Sweet hame is ever dear, I ween ;
But sweeter, dearer far to me,
  'S the lovely Flower of Abbey Green.

Then tell nae me of beauties rare,
  Beneath yon distant eastern skies,
Wi' her they never can compare,
  They'd pale beneath her sparkling eyes ;
For such a flower did never rise,
  Since Eve in Paradise was Queen !
A' nature's sweets she does comprise—
  The lovely Flower of Abbey Green.

Her form is of the finest mould,
  Beauty sits throned upon her brow ;
I wadna gie a smile frae her
  For a' that monarchs can bestow.
Had I the wealth of Mexico,
  And all the power of Albion's Queen,
I'd part with all, without one throe,
  For the lovely Flower of Abbey Green.
                                    W. G.

BONNIE ANNIE GRAY.

O BONNIE Annie Gray, I must bid you now adieu!
My steed stands waiting on the mead, to bear me far from you;
But where I stray, by night or day, I will remember still
The lovely rose I left behind at Castle Somerville.

O bonnie Annie Gray, the bugle sounds to arms,
And I maun go to meet the foe, and share in war's alarms;
But midst the strife of battle wild, and trumpets sounding
    shrill,
I'll ne'er forget the lovely Rose of Castle Somerville.

I have loved thee, Annie Gray, with a pure and fervent love,
And neither time nor distance can my passion e'er remove.
Oh! every danger I could meet, and combat every ill,
Tae shield frae harm the lovely Rose of Castle Somerville.

It may be, Annie Gray, that a soldier's death I'll die
Upon the field of battle red, beneath an Indian sky;
But even then, I'll love thee, Anne, for death can never chill
The love I have for my sweet Rose of Castle Somerville.

O bonnie Annie Gray, though I leave auld Scotland's isle,
I'll ne'er forget that jewelled eye, that sweet bewitching smile,
That silver voice, so sweet and clear, which my heart's core
    can thrill;
I'll see and hear, though far away, from Castle Somerville.

O bonnie Annie Gray, let me kiss away that tear,
Which like a gem, lies on that cheek so lovely and so clear,
For something whispers in my ear that soon return I will!
And my sweet rose will be my bride, at Castle Somerville!

W. G.

Castle Somerville was an old residence of the Somerville family, in the
town of Carnwath. The Free Church Manse is built upon a part of the
property, and is now Castle Somerville. The old buildings were taken
down in the present century.

CARNWATH LASSES.

O BEAUTY blooms bright in this village of ours !
What heart hath not felt its enlivening powers ?
By mountain, by meadow, by streamlet, or strath,
Nae lassies ye'll find like the fair of Carnwath !

Our Jennies are handsome, our Jeanies are rare,
Wi' our Matties sae meek there's nane to compare ;
Where the sun looks in glory adown from his path,
He shines on nae lassies like ours in Carnwath !

Our Gracies might grace any meeting of beauty,
Our Marys might wile even a sentry frae duty ;
The sailor mair danger ne'er met at Cape Wrath
Than to catch but a glimpse o' the fair o' Carnwath.

Our Beenies are bonnie, our Bells they are braw,
Our Maggies hae mony a heart stown awa' ;
Elsewhere, ilka rose a thorn in it hath,
But nane sic ye'll find in the flowers o' Carnwath.

Our Nannies are neat, our Nellies nae less,
Mair kind than our Katies ne'er keeked in a glass ;
Auld Fame, clean thy trumpet and gie it full breath
In honour and praise o' the fair o' Carnwath !

Our Betties are beauties, our Fannies are fair,
Wi' our Mennies sae modest there's nane to compare ;
Go tell it in Askelon, publish't in Gath—
We'll match the wide world wi' the fair o' Carnwath !

A. NICOL.

The author of the above was for many years schoolmaster of Carnwath.
He was a gentleman of high talent, and wrote many pieces, but we
believe this was the only one which ever appeared in print.

THE LADS OF CARNWATH.

O WHERE will ye find sic braw lads as our ain,
You may search every island that gems the wide main,
You may search every mountain, and range ilka strath,
But ye'll never find lads like the lads o' Carnwath !

We've Adams—nane braver in battle e'er fell,
And for pleasing the lasses our Andrews excel ;
Nae brawer chaps ever trod over the heath,
Than the Adams and Andrews we have in Carnwath.

Douce chiels are our Davies, and if there's a faut
It's blateness ; but gie them a wee drap o' maut,
Then they'll laugh at a' danger, and even face death,
To mak braw lasses wives in toon o' Carnwath.

Our Johnnies are jolly, a' braw buirdly men,
And weel they can wield baith the sword and the pen ;
Frae the Yankees' far west, to the gates o' Somnauth,
Ye'll find none like the Johnnies we have in Carnwath.

Our Major is michty in science and arts ;
He has been at the moon, and a' thae foreign parts ;
He has travelled the planets, and the far milky path ;
But could never find lads like the lads o' Carnwath.

So great is his genius, just oot o' mere fun,
A year or twa back he invented a gun
Of such terrible power—he could stand at Carnwath
And knock down his foe on the peak of Cape Wrath.

Our Maurice is meek, as a Moses should be,
While he gets his ain way ; but just cross him a wee,
He'll drive a' afore him, as wind drives the chaff—
Beware o' the Maurice we hae in Carnwath.

Our Robins are rare, and our Tams are a treat,
And our Gudgets a budget of humour and wit;
Sublime are their sallies, and mony's the laugh,
Of the Gudgets and Robins we hae in Carnwath.

Our Watties are witty, our Willies are wise,
Their inventions have gien mony a ane a surprise;
" Ever onward" 's their motto—they tread glory's path,
And fresh laurels have heaped on the toon o' Carnwath.

And auld Mysie Broon, at the head o' the toon,
Has very near seen a hale century wheel roun';
And auld Mysie says she can gie her great aith,
That she never saw lads like the lads o' Carnwath.

W. G.

KATIE CORE O' COULTER.

Tune—" Roy's Wife."

KEN ye Katie Core o' Coulter?
Ken ye Katie Core o' Coulter?
Nane can dance, or laugh, or sing,
Sae weel as Katie Core o' Coulter.

Hey for Katie Core o' Coulter!
Hey for Katie Core o' Coulter!
Nane can dance, or laugh, or sing,
Sae weel as Katie Core o' Coulter.

Our Katie's faither was a laird,
Katie was his only daughter;
Rowth o' gear an' lan's had she,
An' mony mony braw lads sought her.

Hey for Katie Core o' Coulter, &c.

Katie had been rale weel schuled,
For she had a first-rate tutor;
An' she wasna to be fuled,
Na! troth she lookit weel about her.
 Hey for Katie Core o' Coulter, &c.

Kate could discourse on kirk an' State,
She ne'er met ane that could confute her;
The minister had to retreat,
Whene'er he met wi' Kate o' Coulter.
 Hey for Katie Core o' Coulter, &c.

'Mang a' the belles o' Biggar toun,
'Mang a' the beauties roun' about her,
Kate stood the foremost o' them a',
Sae fair was Katie Core o' Coulter.
 Hey for Katie Core o' Coulter, &c.

An' scores o' wooers cam' an' swore
They couldna' live an hour without her;
Kate leuch, and pat them to the door,
An' tell't them no to dee in Coulter!
 Hey for Katie Core o' Coulter, &c.

A Hielan' laird, choke fu' o' pride,
Tried to come round her wi' his butter;
She kick't the breekless creature out,
An' tumbled him into the gutter.
 Hey for Katie Core o' Coulter, &c.

A gallant youth fresh frae Carnwath,
Cam' next—he was a pressing suitor,
He whispered something in her lug,
An' gained fair Katie Core o' Coulter.
 Hey for Katie Core o' Coulter, &c.

W. G.

DAVIE'S LEFT BANKMAINS.

O DULL and dreary is our hame,
　Which ance was blythe and gay,
And sorrow's ta'en the place o' joy
　Since Davie gaed away;
I ne'er kenned what it was to love,
　Ne'er felt its witherin' pains,
Nor what it was to sigh and pine
　Till Davie left Bankmains!

A' nature has put mournin' on,
　The sun is dull and gray,
The very grass is no sae green
　Since Davie gaed away;
The stars by nicht are no sae bricht,
　An' cheerless are the plains,
The flowers have never raised their heads
　Since Davie left Bankmains!

The neebours gibe an' taunt me now,
　I'm pale and wan, they say;
The roses noo have left my cheeks
　Since Davie gaed away.
My mother winna haud her tongue,
　But mair and mair complains
That a' my spirit's sunk and gane
　Since Davie's left Bankmains.

They took me to the dance yestreen
　To drive away dull care,
But ah! it had nae charms for me,
　For Davie wasna there.
The doctor's brought me —gude kens what!
　Puir body, he's nae brains;
The best thing he could bring to me
　Is Davie to Bankmains!　　　W. G.

Bankmains was a small hamlet of four families within half a mile
south of Carnwath; the houses are now all razed from the foundation.
It was a most beautiful dwelling place.

COVIN'TON MANSE.

KEN ye the lassie o' Covin'ton manse?
The sweet, bonnie lassie o' Covin'ton manse?
Your een they wad glisten, your heart it wad dance,
If ye met wi' the lassie o' Covin'ton manse!

Her cheek is as fair as the red heather bell
That blooms in rich clusters on Covin'ton fell;
Her teeth like the pearls frae the far Isle o' France,
And her lips like the cherries at Covin'ton manse!

Love sits in her ringlets so glossy and rare—
Wi' her smiles an' her dimples there's nought to compare;
And wha can resist the love-thrilling glance
Of the bonnie, sweet lassie o' Covin'ton manse?

There are weavers and tailors and souters an' a',
And merchants and farmers sae braid and sae braw
Gang rappin' and tappin', but I ween they've nae chance
To speed wi' the lassie at Covin'ton manse.

For this very day the Post cam' to oor door
Wi' a valentine kind frae the lass I adore;
And I'll owre Clyde again, tho' the door ye should rance,
To see bonnie Jeanie at Covin'ton manse.

Gude health, an' gude nicht to you, friends, ane an' a';
Wi' my plaid and my staff I'm aff and awa';
Drink to my success, for I think there's a chance
Ye'll soon hear of a waddin' at Covin'ton manse!

ON THE SKULLS OF MY ANCESTORS

BEING TURNED OUT OF AN OPENED GRAVE, FEB. 28, 1788.

THESE ghastly skulls ! these naked bones !
  Were my relations dear ;
My parents and their little ones
  Do all lie mingled here.

Long have they dwelt among the dead,
  And now they are not known ;
I view the skulls but cannot read
  The owner's name thereon.

What havoc there is made in death !
  It makes relations vain ;
And nothing but a heaven-born faith
  Can make them rise again.

Dear skulls ! were you the honoured heads
  That lately called me son ;
On whom the meanest reptile crawls
  And yet no injury done ?

Where are the eyes that looked on me,
  The face that on me smiled,
The lips that poured out sympathy,
  The arms that hugged their child ?

Where is the breast that glowed with love,
  The heart that throbbed with care,
The affections that in concert strove
  With tenderest feelings there ?

The soul is fled—and naked dust
  No passions can display ;
What are they now ? the same I must
  When I put off my clay.

'Tis thirty years since they were seen,
  And O ! how strange to tell !
We meet, and not a word between,
  But soon must take farewell.

Like theirs, in future years, my bones
  Round the grave's mouth may lie,
While at the grave, perhaps my sons
  Attend, and think as I.

My parents' skulls before me lie,
  And to me seem to say—
" In view of vast eternity,
  Improve your every day.

" Death has dissolved the tenderest tie,
  In worlds of spirits we dwell,
And no concern, or grief, or joy,
  On your account we feel."

How soon my tender little ones
  Shall cease to be my care !
My eyeless skull and naked bones
  Can't form a wish or prayer.

Let Jesus be when I am gone
  Their Father, Judge, and Friend;
Widows may trust on Him alone,
  Orphans on Him depend.

                    DR. MEIKLE, CARNWATH.

———

THE HIGHLAND HOST.

    Lieutenant-Col. Cleland, of the Cameronian Regiment, wrote a poem
in Hudibrastic style, on the invasion of the Highland Host among the
Covenanters of the western counties, in 1678.   Sir Walter Scott and
Dr. M'Crie, both admit his works show considerable talent, and although

neither song nor ballad, yet being a Clydesdale author and containing
a most amusing and graphic description of the Highland Host and their
doings, a sample of the work is worthy of a place in our collection. This
is his account (page 4) of

THE HIGHLAND ARMY.

SOME might have judged they were the creatures
Called selphies, whose customs and features,
Paracelsus doth decry,
In his occult philosophy,
Or fauns, or brownies, if ye will,
Or Satyrs, come from Atlas Hill.
But those who were their chief commanders,
As such, who bore the pirnie standards,
Who led the van, and drove the rear,
Were richt weel mounted in their gear;
With brogues, trews, and pirnie plaids,
With gude blue bonnets on their heads,
Which on the one side had a flype,
Adorned with a tobacco pipe;
With dirk, and snapwork, and snuff mill;
A bag, which they with onions fill;
And their strict observers say,
A tup horn filled with usquebae;
A slashed out coat, beneath her plaids;
A targe of timber, nails, and hides;
With a long two-handed sword.
In nothing they're accounted sharp,
Except in bagpipe and in harp.

At page 34 he represents them as exhibiting—

More different postures
Than sewed on hangings, beds, or bolsters;
More various actings, modes, and stances,
Than's read in poems or romances.
Pipes were playing, drums were beating,
Some sneeshin from their fellows getting;
Trumpets sounding, skenes were glancing,
Some were " Tonald Cowper" dancing.

The inhabitants of Clydesdale, who had signed the bond of the Anti-Covenanters, are thus characterised :—

The Clydesdale bonders, as ye ken,
Are scarcely reckoned amongst men ;
The tumid Earl, Papist Haggs,
An Atheist Jew, to save his bags,
Bidla, with Towcorse and Woodhall,
John Thomson's man—plague on them all !

Cleland seems to have had as much respect for the rivers of Scotland as Burns himself. On this subject he says—

There's as much virtue, sauce, and pith
In Annan, on the water of Nith,
Which slips so quietly by Dumfries,
As any water in all Greece ;
For there, and several other places,
About mill-dams and green brae faces,
Both eldritch elves and brownies stayed,
And green-gowned fairies danced and played.
When old John Knox and other some
Began to plott the bags of Rome,
They suddenly took to their heels,
And did no more frequent these fields.

The rapacity of the Highland Host, who were let loose upon the poor Covenanters of the West in order to induce them to adopt the religion of a *gentleman*, is thus described :—

They dirk our tenants, shame our wives,
And we're in hazard of our lives ;
They plunder horse, and them they laden
With coverings, blankets, sheets, and plaiden,
With hodden gray and worsted stuff ;
They sell our tongs for locks of snuff ;
They take our coulters and our socks,
And from our doors they pull the locks ;
They leave us neither shools nor spades,
And take away our iron in lades ;
They break our ploughs, even when they're working ;
We dare not hinder them for dirking.

My Lords! they so harass and wrong us,
There's scarce a pair of shoes among us,
And for blue bonnets they leave none
That they can get their clauts upon ;
If any dare refuse to give them,
They dirk them, strip them, and so leave them ;
They ripe for arms, but all they find
Is arms with them—leave nought behind !

CURLING ON CARNWATH LOCH IN 1766.

FRETTED to atoms by the poignant air,
Frigid and hyperborean flies the snow
In many a vortex of monades ; wind-winged,
Hostile to noses, dripping oft
A crystal humour, which as oft is wiped
From the blue lip wide-gashed ; the hanging sleeve
That covers all the wrist—uncovered else,
The peasant's only handkerchief, I wot,
Is glossed with blue brown ice.   But reckless still
Of cold or drifted snow, that might appal
The city coxcomb, armed with besoms pour
The village youngsters forth, jocund and loud,
And cover all the Loch ; with many a tug
The ponderous stone, that all the summer lay
Unoccupied along its oozy side,
Now to the mud fast frozen, scarcely yields
The wished-for victory to the brawny youth
Who, braggart of his strength, a circling crowd
Has drawn around him to avouch the feat.
Short is his triumph—fortune so decrees,
Applause is changed to ridicule ; at once
The loosened stone gives way, supine he falls
And prints his members on the pliant snow.

The goals are marked out, the centre each
Of a large random circle.   Distance scores

Are drawn between—the dread of weakly arms.
Firm on his crambits stands the steady youth
Who leads the game; low o'er the weighty stone
He bends incumbent, and with nicest eye
Surveys the furthest goal, and in his mind
Measures the distance; careful to bestow
Just force enough, then balanced in his hand
He flings it on direct; it glides along
Its course murmuring, while plying hard before,
Full many a besom sweeps away the snow
Or icicle that might obstruct its course.

But cease my muse! what numbers can describe
The various game?   Say, canst thou paint the blush
Impurpled deep, that veils the stripling's cheek,
When wandering wide, neglects the rink,
And stops midway?   His opponent is glad,
Yet fears a similar fate, while every mouth
Cries—" Off the Hogg !" and Tinto joins the cry.
Or couldst thou follow the experienced player
Through all the mysteries of his art,
Or teach the undisciplined how to wick, to guard,
Or ride full out, the stone that blocks the pass?

The bonspiel o'er, hungry and cold they hie
To the next alehouse, where the game is played
Again, and yet again, over the jug,
Until some hoary hero—haply he
Whose sage direction won the doubtful day;
To his attentive juniors tediously talks
Of former times ;—of mony a bonspiel gained
Against opposing parishes ; and shots—
To human likelihood secure, yet stormed :
With liquor on the table, he portrays
The situation of each stone.   Convinced
Of their superior skill, all join and hail
Their grandsires steadier of surer hand.

                                        JAMES GRAEME.

These lines are interesting, as being we believe, the earliest descriptive

poem on our great national game of curling. It is somewhat remarkable
that Thompson, although a Scotchman and no doubt well acquainted with
the game, while describing winter makes no allusion to curling. When
these lines were written, Burns would only be some 10 or 11 years old.
Graeme was dead years before Burns began to sing, and all that he says
upon the subject are these lines in Tam Sampson's elegy.

> When winter muffles up his cloak,
> And binds the mire like ony rock ;
> When to the loch the curlers flock
>   Wi' gleesome speed,
> Wha will they station at the cock?—
>   Tam Sampson's deid.
>
> He was the king o' a' the core,
> To guard, or draw, or wick a bore,
> Or up the rink like Jehu roar,
>   In time o' need.
> But now he lags on death's hog score—
>   Tam Sampson's deid.

LAMINGTON.

I WITH a friend, some thirty years agone,
Occasion had to visit Lamington ;
That friend a painter was, whose practised eye
Caught all expressions of the earth and sky.
Well, as the antique village came in sight
He started with a look of high delight,
And with uplifted hands and kindling eyes,
He thus expressed his pleasure and surprise :—

"Oh ! what a sight—than all conception more—
What I have dreamt, but never saw before ;
These charming cottages so finely grouped,
With such old-fashioned windows, quaintly looped,
All unprofaned by slate or glaring tile,
In simple thatch they wear a sober smile ;
How picturesque these long and slanting lums,
From which the smoke so beautifully comes.

"In what a graceful harmony are joined
Peat stacks before, with stacks of hay behind,

H

All interspersed with young and joyous squads
Of ragged children and barefooted lads.
No wonder that yon mountain stream delights
To mix its murmurs with such sounds and sights ;
No wonder that these stately, tow'ring trees
Rejoice to overshadow scenes like these.
Oh ! such a sight might fire the dullest brain,
And make my humble self a Claude Lorraine."

So spake that painter, while his ardent eye
Showed feeling nothing short of ecstasy ;
That painter's eye in death hath long been dim,
Long, long that painter's hand hath ceased to limn ;
But fancy how indignant he had been
Could he these Gothic ravages have seen,—
These mountains, bearing not a trace,
Not one memorial of the dear old place.
Oh ! tis enough to mar his long, last sleep,
And cause his very marrow bones to creep,
That his loved village, now beloved in vain,
Should, like a dream, have perished from the plain.

Thou modern village, loath were I to say
What might in me a prejudice betray ;
But yet, if all my feelings must be told,
Far less I love thee than I loved the old.
These model houses, ranged in order due,
Delight me not, so stiff they look and new ;
And then their upstart and pretentious air
Is more than my endurance well can bear.

Lord of the manor, justly dost thou claim
For all thy deeds a philanthropic aim ;
They all are meant to aid, we do confess,
To aid the growth of health and happiness.
All this is granted—freely granted—yet
We linger o'er the past with fond regret ;
What boots the pedantry of wood and stone,
When the romance and poetry are gone !

Alas ! a hundred years shall not restore
The painter's village, gone for evermore !

It is a curious fact that the same changes which are here lamented
were carried into effect much about the same time by the late Henry
Monteith, Esq., in the village of Carstairs, and by the late Norman
Lockhart, Esq., in Carnwath ; peat-stacks and dunghills being banished
out of sight, old thatched houses put down, and neat, new slate-roofed
ones erected instead.

———

THE MERRY MAIDS O' SCOTLAND.

YE merry maids o' Scotland,
  Dear lasses o' langsyne,
How turns o' some auld melody
  Will bring ye to my mind.
Wi' your daffin' and your laughin'
  Frae glint o' day to gloam,
When corn was whitenin' on the lea
  And hay was on the holm.

At Martinmas and Whitsunday,
  At bridal or at fair,
Wi' Sunday braws, like drifted snaws,
  Ye wore a doucer air ;
But smirks around your rosy lips,
  Wi' glintin's o' the e'e,
Tauld aye how soon a canty tune
  Could wake ye into glee.

When dreary days o' winter
  Were scalin' sleet and snaw,
Your fresh unfrosted merriment
  Sent simmer through the ha' ;
Your kind gude een, and winsome mien,
  Wad thaw the plowman chiel,
While merry sang the lee night lang
  Was chorused wi' your wheel.

I'm far awa', I'm lang awa',
   An' muckle's cum atween,
The night we reelit at the ha'
   Or link'd it on the green ;
But sooth, e'en yet, wi' canty lilt,
   Ye're a' afore my min',
Dear merry maids o' Scotland,
   Sweet lasses o' langsyne.

                              AINSLIE.

POVERTY PARTS GOOD COMPANY.

When white was my o'erlay as foam o' the linn,
And siller was clinkin' my pouches within,
When my lambkins were bleatin', on meadow and brae,
As I gaed to my love in new cleadin so gay,
         Kind was she, and my friends were free,
         But poverty parts gude company !

How swift passed the minutes and hours of delight,
When piper played cheerily, and cruisie burned bright,
And linked in my hand was the maiden so dear,
As she footed the floor in her holiday gear !
         Woe is me, and can it then be
         That poverty parts sic company ?

We met at the fair, we met at the kirk ;
We met i' the sunshine, we met i' the mirk ;
And the sound o' her voice, and the blinks o' her e'en,
The cheerin' and life o' my bosom hae been.
         Leaves frae the tree at Martinmas flee,
         And poverty parts gude company !

Whenever I gaed the blythe lasses smiled sweet,
And mothers and aunties were mair than discreet,
While kebbuck and bicker were set on the board
But noo they gang by me, and never a word !
         Sae let it be, for the worldly and slee
         Wi' poverty keep nae company !

At bridal and infare I've braced me wi' pride ;
The broose I hae won, and a kiss o' the bride ;
And loud was the laughter good fellows amang,
As I uttered my jest or chorused my sang.
      Dowie to dree are jestin' and glee,
      When poverty parts gude company !

But the hope of my love is a cure for its smart,
And the spaewife has told me to keep up my heart,
For wi' my last saxpence her loof I hae crossed,
And the bliss that is fated can never be lost.
      Though cruelly we may every day see,
      How poverty parts gude company !
                   JOANNA BAILLIE.

HOOLY AND FAIRLY.

AH ! neebours, what had I ado for to marry ?
My wife she drinks possets and wine o' Canary,
And ca's me a niggardly thraw-gabbit carlie ;
Oh, gin my wife wad drink hooly and fairly !
      Hooly and fairly, hooly and fairly,
      Oh, gin my wife wad drink hooly and fairly !

She sups wi' her kimmers on dainties enow,
Aye bowin' and smilin' and wipin' her mou,
While I sit aside, and am helpit but sparely ;
Oh, gin my wife wad feast hooly and fairly !
      Hooly and fairly, hooly and fairly,
      Oh, gin my wife wad feast hooly and fairly !

To fairs and to bridals, and preachin's and a',
She gangs sae licht-headed, sae buskit an' braw ;
Her ribbons and mantles they gar me gang barely ;
Oh, gin my wife wad spend hooly and fairly !
      Hooly and fairly, hooly and fairly,
      Oh, gin my wife wad spend hooly and fairly !

I' the kirk sic commotion last Sabbath she made,
Wi' bobs and red roses and breast-knots o'erlaid,
The dominie sticket the psalm very nearly ;
Oh, gin my wife wad dress hooly and fairly !
    Hooly and fairly, hooly and fairly,
    Oh, gin my wife wad dress hooly and fairly !

She's warrin' and flytin' frae mornin' till e'en,
An' if ye gainsay her her e'en glows sae keen,
Then tongue, neive, and cudgel shall lay on ye sairly;
Oh, gin my wife wad strike hooly and fairly !
    Hooly and fairly, hooly and fairly,
    Oh, gin my wife wad strike hooly and fairly !

When tired wi' her cantrips she lies in her bed,
The wark a' negleckit, the house ill upred,
While a' our gude neebours are stirrin' richt early ;
Oh, gin my wife wad work timely and fairly !
    Timely and fairly, timely and fairly,
    Oh, gin my wife wad work timely and fairly !

A word o' gude counsel or grace she'll hear none,
She bardies the elders, and mocks at Mess John,
While back in his teeth his ain text she flings rarely ;
Oh, gin my wife wad speak hooly and fairly !
    Hooly and fairly, hooly and fairly,
    Oh, gin my wife wad speak hooly and fairly !

I wish I were single, I wish I were freed,
I wish I were doited, I wish I were deid,
Or she in the mools to torment me nae mairly ;
What dost avail to cry hooly and fairly ?
    Hooly and fairly, hooly and fairly,
    Wastin' my breath cryin' hooly and fairly !

                          JOANNA BAILLIE.

OUR NATIVE HILLS.

THE EMIGRANT'S SONG.

OH ! swiftly bounds our gallant bark
  Across the ocean drear ;
While manly cheeks are pale wi' grief,
  And wet wi' sorrow's tears.
The flowers that spring upon the Clyde
  Will bloom for us in vain ;
Nae mair wi' lichtsome step we'll climb
  To Tintoc Tap again.

In Clydesdale's glens our fathers sleep,
  Where mony a thistle waves ;
And roses fair and gowans meek
  Bloom o'er their lowly graves.
But we maun dree a sadder fate,
  Far owre the stormy main ;
We long may look, but never see
  Our native hills again.

Yet mid the forests of the west,
  When starnies light the sky,
We'll gather round the ingle-side
  And sing o' days gone by ;
And sunny blinks o' joy will come
  To soothe us when alane,
And oft in nightly dreams we'll climb
  Our native hills again.
                                        LITTLE.

THE DAYS WHEN WE WERE YOUNG.

THE happy days of yore !
  Will they ever come again
To shed a gleam of joy on us,
  And win the heart from pain ?

Or will they only come in dreams,
    When nicht's black curtains hung?
Yet even then 'tis sweet to mind
    The days when we were young.

For memory, wi' its mystic power,
    Brings early scenes to view,
Again we roam among the hills
    Sae wet wi' mornin' dew.
Again we climb the broomy knowes,
    And sing wi' prattlin' tongue,
For we had nae cares to fash us
    In the days when we were young.

How oft, when we were callants,
    Hae we sought the river's shore,
And launched wi' glee our tiny boats,
    And heard the billows roar?
And oft among the glancin' waves
    In daring sport we've sprung,
And swam till we were wearied,
    In the days when we were young.

In winter, round the ingle-side,
    We've read wi' kindlin' e'e,
How Wallace wight, and Bruce the bold,
    Oft made the Southrons flee;
Or listened to some bonnie sang,
    By bonnie lassie sung,
Oh! love and happiness were ours,
    In the days when we were young.

Oh! his maun be a waefu' heart
    That has nae sunny gleams,
Of by-gone joys in early days,
    Though it be but in dreams;
Wha thinks nae o' his mother's arms
    Sae aft around him flung,
To shield him safe frae earthly harms
    In days when he was young?

Wha thinks nae o' his sisters fair
That toddled out and in,
And ran about the braes wi' him,
And played wi' meikle din ;
And his maun be a barren heart,
Where love has never sprung,
Wha thinks nae o' the days gone by,—
The days when he was young.

LITTLE.

James Little was born at Glasgow in 1821, the son of a respectable shoemaker, who claimed through his maternal grandmother, the title and estates of the last Marquis of Annandale. He was trained to his father's business ; some time after, enlisted as a private soldier, and after eight years' service bought himself off, and resumed his original trade in his native city. Several of his songs have been published, with music, in the "Lyric Gems of Scotland."

LANGSYNE WHEN A LADDIE.

How blest were the days o' langsyne when a laddie !
Alane by a bush wi' my dog and my plaidie,
Nae fop was sae happy tho' dressed e'er so gaudy—
O sweet were the days o' langsyne when a laddie !
Whiles croonin' my sonnet amang the whin bushes,
Whiles whistlin' wi' glee as I pu'd the green rushes ;
The whim o' the moment kept me aye frae sorrow,
What I wanted at night was in prospect to-morrow.

The nest o' the lintie I fondly explored,
And plunderin' bykes was the game I adored ;
My pleasures did vary as I was unsteady,
Yet I always found something that pleased when a laddie.
The boy with great pleasure the butterfly chases ;
When manhood approaches the maid he embraces :
But view him at once baith the husband and daddie,
He fondly looks back to the days when a laddie !

When childhood was over, my prospects were greater,
I tried to be happy ; but alas, foolish creature !
The sports of my youth were my sweetest employment ;
Much sweetness in prospect embitters enjoyment !
But now I'm grown auld, and wi' cares I'm perplexed ;
How numerous the woes are by which I am vexed !
Since tentin' the kye wi' my staff, dog, and plaidie :
How changed are the days since langsyne when a laddie !

AFFLECK.

BIGGAR AULD CROSS KNOWE.

How shifting are the scenes of time !
    Had I a tongue to cry,
In accents loud I would proclaim
    My grief to passers by ;
My sides are pierced with pointed steel—
    Let hearts with feeling glow ;
This the fate—the mournful state,
    Of Biggar Auld Cross Knowe.

I've been the place of rendezvous,
    At mid-day, nicht, and morn,
A blest retreat for ages past—
    What thousands I have borne !
I'm heavy-laden, grown with years,
    Nae grass grows on my pow ;
Let youth a moral lesson learn
    Frae Biggar Auld Cross Knowe.

I've been the haunt on market days,
    The haunt o' mony a fair—
The lads and lasses, men and wives,
    To me wad a' repair.
And blythesome bairnies on my side,
    With pleasures they wad row,
While worn-out age wad station keep
    On Biggar Auld Cross Knowe.

Ye living forms who at me gaze,
  You'll mix with kindred clay ;
And all of me will soon be laid
  Upon the king's high-way.
The braw Tontine will tak' my place,
  To stand while it can dow ;
But never, never will it stand
  As Biggar Auld Cross Knowe.

I've served my time—I must depart ;
  Yet why should I repine ?
Vain mortals, view your coming fate,
  It may be seen in mine.
Before old age shall press you sore
  Still wiser may you grow ;
Lay this to heart—you must depart
  Like Biggar Auld Cross Knowe.

                              AFFLECK.

THE GRAY BROTHER.

THE Pope he was saying the high, high mass,
  All on St. Peter's day,
With the power to him given by the saints in heaven
  To wash men's sins away.

The Pope he was saying the blessèd mass,
  And the people kneeled around,
And from each man's soul his sins did pass
  As he kissed the holy ground.

And all among the crowded throng
  Was still both limb and tongue,
While through vaulted roof and aisles aloof
  The holy accents rung.

At the holiest word he quivered for fear
  And faltered in the sound,
And when he would the chalice rear,
  He dropped it to the ground.

" The breath of one of evil deed
  Pollutes our sacred day ;
He has no portion in our creed,
  No part in what I say.

" A being whom no blessed word
  To ghostly peace can bring ;
A wretch at whose approach abhorred
  Recoils each holy thing.

" Up, up, unhappy ! haste, arise !
  My adjuration fear !
I charge thee not to stop my voice,
  Nor longer tarry here !"

Amid them all a pilgrim kneeled
  In gown of sackcloth gray,
Far journeying from his native field,
  He first saw Rome that day.

For forty days and nights so drear
  I ween he had not spoke,
And save with bread and water clear
  His fast he ne'er had broke.

Amid the penitential flock
None seemed more bent to pray,
But when the Holy Father spoke,
  He rose and went his way.

Again unto his native land
  His weary course he drew,
To Lothian's fair and fertile strand
  And Pentland's mountains blue.

His unblest seat, his native seat,
  Mid Esk's fair woods regain ;
Through woods more fair no stream more sweet
  Rolls to the eastern main.

And lords to meet the pilgrim came,
  And vassals bent the knee,
For all mid Scotland's chiefs of fame
  Was none more famed than he.

And boldly for his country still
  In battle he had stood ;
Ay, even when on the banks of Till
  Her noblest poured their blood.

Sweet are the paths, O passing sweet !
  By Esk's fair streams that run
O'er airy steep, through copsewood deep,
  Impervious to the sun.

There the rapt poet's step may rove,
  And yield the muse the day ;
There Beauty led by timid Love
  May shun the tell-tale ray.

From that fair dome where suit is paid
  By blast of bugle free, [1]
To Achindinny's hazel glade [2]
  And haunted Woodhouselee. [3]

Who knows not Melville's beechy grove, [4]
  And Roslin's rocky glen ; [5]
Dalkeith, which all the virtues love, [6]
  And classic Hawthornden ? [7]

[1] Barony of Pennycuik is held by the proprietor being bound to wind three blasts of a horn when the king hunts on the Borough Muir.
[2] Auchindinny, situated on the Esk below Pennycuik.
[3] Haunted Woodhouselee—see notes to Cadzow Castle.
[4] Melville Castle, seat of Lord Melville, near Lasswade.
[5] Ruins of Roslin Castle.
[6] Dalkeith, residence of the Duke of Buccleuch.
[7] Hawthornden, the residence of the poet Drummond.

Yet never a path from day to day
    The pilgrim's footsteps range,
Save but the solitary way
    To Burndale's ruined grange.

A woeful place was this I ween,
    As sorrow could desire;
For nodding to the fall was each crumbling wall,
    And the roof was scathed with fire.

It fell upon a summer's eve,
    While on Carnethy's head
The last faint gleams of the sun's low beams
    Had streaked the gray with red;

And the convent bell did the vesper tell
    Newbattle's oaks among;
And mingled with the solemn knell
    Our Ladye's evening song:

The heavy knell, the choir's faint swell,
    Came slowly down the wind,
And on the pilgrim's ear they fell
    As his wonted path he did find.

Deep sunk in thought, I ween, he was,
    Nor ever raised his eye,
Until he came to that dreary place,
    Which did all in ruins lie:

He gazed on the walls so scathed with fire,
    With many a bitter groan—
And there was aware of a Gray Friar
    Resting him on a stone.

" Now Christ thee save," said the Gray Brother,
    " Some pilgrim thou seem'st to be ; "
But in sore amaze did Lord Albert gaze
    Nor answer again made he.

"O come ye from east, or come ye from west,
Or bring relics from over the sea?
Or come ye from the shrine of St. James the divine,
Or St. John of Beverley?"

"I come not from the shrine of St. James the divine,
Nor bring relics from over the sea;
I bring but a curse from our Father the Pope,
Which for ever will cling to me."

"Now, woeful pilgrim, say not so!
But kneel thee down to me,
And shrive thee so clean of thy deadly sin,
That absolved thou mayest be."

"And who art thou, thou Gray Brother,
That I should shrive to thee,
When he, to whom are given the keys of earth and heaven
Has no power to pardon me?"

"O I am sent from a distant clime
Five thousand miles away,
And all to absolve a foul, foul crime
Done here 'twixt night and day."

The pilgrim kneeled him on the sand,
And thus began his say—
When on his neck an ice-cold hand
Did that Gray Brother lay.

.　　　.　　　.　　　.　　　.

SIR W. SCOTT.

The "Gray Brother" is founded upon a sad story given in the "Memorie of the Somervilles." Instead of going to Rome, Sir John Herring, the pilgrim, fled to Lord Somerville in Couthally Castle, and was there concealed until he made his peace with the Church. He had set fire to a house and burnt two licentious monks, one of whom had seduced his daughter. He was proprietor of Kersewell, Carnwath; they were of Newbattle Abbey. The place where this tragedy took place was near Gilmerton, and still bears the name of Burntdale. Sir John had to give up a good slice of his estate, to pay for masses for the repose of the souls of those he had sent so summarily out of the world. Lord Somerville married a daughter of this Sir John Herring, which marriage brought the lands of Drum into the Somerville family.

VERSES.

William Lithgow, the celebrated Lanark traveller, while standing sentry on a dark stormy night, on ship-board, in a creek of one of the islands of Greece, where the ship had taken refuge on being pursued by Turkish galliots, composed a poem of which the subjoined verses are a part.

WOULD God I might but live,
    To see my native soil;
Twice happy is my happy wish
    To end this endless toil.
Yet still when I record
    The pleasant banks of Clyde,
Where orchards, castles, towns, and woods,
    Are planted by his side;
And chiefly Lanark thou,
    Thy country's lowest lamp,
In which this bruised body now
    Did first receive the stamp.

        .   .   .   .   .

To thee sweet Scotland, first,
    My birth and breath I leave,
To heaven my soul, my heart King James,
    My corpse to lie in grave.
My staff to pilgrims I,
    And pen to poets send,
My hair-cloth robe, and half-spent goods,
    To wandering wights I lend.

        .   .   .   .   .

These trophies I erect
    While memory remains,
An epitomical epitaph
    On Lithgow's restless pains.
My will's inclosed with love,
    My love with earthly bliss,
My bliss in substance doth consist
    To crave no more but this.

Thou first, is, was, and last,
    Eternal of thy grace;
Protect, prolong Great Britain's King,
    His son, and royal race.

Lithgow is believed to be the only person who endured all the tortures of the Inquisition and escaped alive. It is little to the credit of the natives of Lanark that no memorial of him exists in their beautiful cemetery.

THE BOWER O' CLYDE.

ON fair Clydeside there wonnit ane dame,—
    Ane dame of wondrous courtesie;
An' bonnie was the kindly flame
    That streamit frae her saft blue e'e.

Her saft blue e'e, 'mid the hinney dew,
    That meltit to its tender licht,
Was bonnier far than the purest starne
    That sails thro' the dark blue hevin at nicht.

If ony could look and safely see
    Her dimplit cheek and her bonnie red mou,
Nor seek to sip the dew frae her lip,
    A lifeless lump was he, I trow.

But it wad hae saftened the dullest wight,
    If ae moment that wight micht see
Her bonny breast o' the purest snaw,
    That heavit wi' love sae tenderlie.

Oh! dear, dear, was this bonny dame,
    Dear, dear, was she to me;
Oh my heart was tane, and my sense was gane,
    At ae blink o' her bonny blue e'e!

And sair, an' saft I pleadit my love,
    Though still she hardly wad seem to hear,
An' wad cauldly blame the words o' flame
    That I breathit sae warmly in her ear.

I

Yet aye as she turned her frae my look,
  There was kindness beamit in her e'e ;
And aye as she drew back her lily han',
  I fand that it tremblit tenderlie.

But the time sune cam'—the waesome time,
  When I maun pass awa' frae my dear ;
An' oh ! that thocht, how often it brocht
  The deep-heavit sigh, and tho cauld bitter tear.

Then I socht my love, her cauld heart to move,
  Wi' my tears, an' my sighs, an' my prayers,
As I gaed by her side doun the banks o' the Clyde,
  An' the hours stole awa' unawares.

'Twas a still summer nicht, at the fa' o' the licht,
  At the gloamin's soft an' shadowy hour,
As we wander'd alane till the daylicht was gane,
  An' we cam' tae a sweet simmer bower.

The mune was up i' the clear blue sky,—
  The mune an' her single wee star ;
The win's gaed gently whisperin' by,
  There was stillness near an' far.

Alane we sat i' the green simmer bower,
  I told her a' that was kind an' dear ;
An' she didna blame the words o' flame
  That I breathit sae warmly in her ear.

She listened to the love-sang warm,
  Her breast it throbbit an' heavit high ;
She could hear nae mair, but her gentle arm
  She leant upon mine wi' a tender sigh.

Then warmly I prest wi' my burnin' lips
  Ae kiss on her bonny red mou',
An' often I prest her form to my breast,
  An' fondly an' warmly I vowed to be true.

An' oh ! that hour, that hallow't hour,
   My fond heart will never forget ;
Though drear is the dule I hae suffered sin syne,
   That hour gars my heart beat, beat warmly yet.

The parting time cam', an' the parting time past,
   An' it past without the saut tear ;
An' awa' to anither an' far awa' land
   I gaed, an' I left my ain dear.

I gaed, an' though ither an' brichter maids
   Wad smile wi' fond love in their e'e ;
I but thocht o' the sweet green bower by the Clyde,
   An' that was enough for me.

HUNTER.

THE TWA BROTHERS.

" Oh ! will ye gang to the schule, billie,
   Or will ye gang to the ba' ;
Or gang to the wood a-warslin,
   To see whilk o' us maun fa' ? "

" I winna gang to the schule, billie,
   Nor will I gang to the ba' ;
But I'll gang to the wood a-warslin,
   And there it's you maun fa'."

They warsled up, they warsled down,
   Till John fell to the ground ;
And there was a knife in Willie's pouch
   Gied him a deadly wound.

" O billie, lift me on your back ;
   Tak me to yon wallie fair,
And wash the blude frae aff my wound,
   And it will blude nae mair."

He's liftet him up upon his back,
    Ta'en him to yon wallie fair,
And washed the blude frae aff his wound,
    But aye it bled the mair.

" O billie, tak aff my Holland sark,
    And rive't frae gair to gair,
And stap it in my bluidy wound,
    An' syne it will blude nae mair."

He has ta'en aff his Holland sark,
    And riven't frae gair to gair,
And stap't it in to the bluidy wound,
    But aye it bled mair and mair.

" O brother dear ! tak me on your back,
    Tak me to yon kirkyard,
And dig a grave baith wide and deep,
    And lay my body there.

" Ye'll lay my arrows at my head,
    My bent bow at my feet,
My sword and buckler by my side,
    As I was wont to sleep.

" When ye gang hame to our faither dear,
    He'll speir for his son John ;
Say ye left him at Carnwath schule,
    Learnin' the schule alone.

" And when ye gang hame to your sister fair,
    She'll speir for her brother John ;
Ye'll say ye left him at the White Loch,
    But ye fear he'll never come hame.

" When ye gang hame to my true love,
    She'll speir for her loved John ;
Say that ye left him at Carnwath Fair,
    But ye fear he's dead and gone."

Sae Willie has buried his brother dear
  Beneath the sod so green,
And when the doleful task was done,
  It's homeward he has gone.

Oh, heavy, heavy was his heart,
  As to the door he cam ;
But when he reached his faither's chair,
  He grew baith pale and wan.

" What blude is that upon your brow,
  My dear son, tell to me ? "
" It's but the blude o' my gude grey steed,
  He wadna ride wi' me."

" Oh, thy steed's blude was never so red,
  Nor ever so dear to me ! "
" Then it's the blude o' my dear brother ;
  Oh, dule and woe is me ! "

" Now, whatna death will ye dee, Willie;
  Now, Willie, come tell to me ? "
" Ye'll put me in an oarless boat,
  And I'll gae sail the sea."

" And when will ye come hame, Willie;
  Dear Willie, come tell to me ? "
" When the sun and mune dance on Carnwath Green,
  And that will never be ! "

He turned himsel' right round about,
  And his heart it burst in three.
" My ae best son is dead and gone,
  And my t'other ane I'll ne'er see ! "

This ballad refers to a tragical event in the noble family of Somerville,
which is thus detailed in the " Memorie of the Somervilles :"—This year
(1589), in the month of July, there fell out a sad accident, as a farther
warning that God was displeased with the family. The Lord Somerville,
having come from Cowthally early in the morning; in regard the weather
was hot, he had ridden hard to be at the Drum by 10 o'clock, which

having done he laid him down to rest.   (Drum is about four miles south
from Edinburgh, and was then in the possession of the Somervilles.)
The servant with his horses; William, Master of Somerville, and John
his brother, went with the horses to ane shott of land, called the Pretty
Shott, directly opposite the front of the house, where there was some
meadow ground for grazing the horses, and willows to shadow them from
the heat.   They had not long continued in this place when the Master of
Somerville, after some little rest, awakening from his sleep, and finding
the pistols that lay hard by him wet with dew, began to rub and dry
them, when unhappily one of them went off the ratch.   Being lying upon
his knee, and the muzzle turned sideways, the ball struck his brother
John directly in the head and killed him outright; so his sorrowful
brother never had one word from him, albeit he begged it with many
tears !   The Master of Somerville, who thus accidentally occasioned his
brother's death, in about three years after followed him to the tomb.
He died at Cowthally in January, 1592, about the 27th year of his age,
and was buried in the aisle of Carnwath ; and with him perished all
hope and expectation of the house of Cowthally.   It was no less truly
than prophetically spoken by a devout gentleman, William Inglis of
Eastshiel, who was himself as well his predecessors great lovers and followers of the Lords Somerville—employed by them for the most part as
their Bailie in the Barony of Carnwath ;—this good gentleman, as the
corpse passed the outer gate of Cowthally, struck upon his breast, and
cried out in the hearing of many, "This day the head is as clean taken
off the house of Cowthally, as you would strike off the head of a sybba ;"
and indeed so it proved, for from that day all things went cross.

WILLIE AND MAY MARGARET.

WILLIE stands at his stable door,
    And clappin' at his steed,
And lookin' owre his white fingers
    His nose began to bleed.

" Gie corn unto my horse, mother,
    Gie meat unto my man,
For I maun gang to Margaret's bower
    Before the nicht comes on."

" O stay at hame, my dear son Willie,
    The win' blaws cauld and dour,
The nicht will be baith mirk and late
    Before you reach her door."

" O though the nicht were never sae dark,
  Or the win' blew never sae cauld,
I will be in my Margaret's bower
  Before twa hours be tauld."

" O gin ye gang to May Margaret
  Without the leave o' me,
Clyde's water's wide and deep enough—
  My malison drown thee."

" The gude steed that I ride upon
  Cost me thrice thritty pound,
And I'll put trust in his swift feet
  To bear me safe to land."

He mounted on his gude swift steed,
  And fast he rode awa',
But ere he cam' to Clyde's waters
  Fu' loud the win' did blaw.

As he rode owre yon hie, hie hill,
  And down yon dowie den,
The roar that was in Clyde's waters
  Wad feared a hundred men.

" O roarin' Clyde, ye roar owre loud,
  Your stream is wondrous strang ;
Mak' me your wreck as I come back,
  But spare me as I gang."

So he has swam the Clyde water,
  Though it was wide and deep,
And he cam' to May Margaret's door
  When all were fast asleep.

Oh, he's gane round and round about,
  And tirled at the pin ;
But doors were steekit and windows barred,
  And none wad let him in.

" Oh ! open the door to me, Margaret,
    Oh ! open, and let me in,
For my boots are fu' o' Clyde waters,
    And frozen to the brim."

" Oh, wha is this at my bower door,
    That calls me by my name ? "
" It's your first love, your ain sweet Willie,
    This nicht newly come hame."

" I hae few lovers thereout, thereout,
    As few ha'e I therein ;
The ae best lover that ever I had
    Was here just late yestreen."

" Oh, gin ye winna open the door,
    Nor yet be kind to me,
Now tell me o' some oot chamber
    Where I this nicht may be."

" Ye canna win in this nicht, Willie,
    Nor here ye canna be,
For I've nae chambers out nor in,
    Nor ane but barely three ;

" The tane o' them is fu' o' corn,
    The tither is fu' o' hay,
The tither is fu' o' merry young men—
    They winna remove till day."

" O fare ye weel, then, May Margaret,
    Sin' better mayna be ;
I have won my mother's malison,
    Comin' this nicht to thee."

He's mounted on his coal-black steed,
    Oh, but his heart was wae !
But ere he came to the Clyde's waters
    'Twas half up owre the brae.

As he rode up yon hie, hie hill,
  And down yon dowie den,
The roar that was in Clyde's waters
  Wad feared a hunder men !

When he cam' to Clyde's water
  'Twas flowin' to the brim,
The rushin' that was in Clyde's waters
  Took Willie's cane frae him.

He leaned him owre his saddle bow,
  To catch his cane again ;
The rushin' that was in Clyde's waters,
  Took Willie's hat frae him.

He leaned him owre his saddle bow
  To catch his hat thro' force,
The rushing that was in Clyde's waters
  Took Willie frae his horse.

His brother stood upon the bank,
  Said—" Fye, man? will ye droon?
Ye'll turn ye to your hie horse head,
  And learn ye how to soom."

" How can I turn my hie horse head
  And learn me how to soom?
I've gotten my mother's malison
  It's here that I maun droon?"

The very hour sweet William sank
  Into the pot so deep,
Up-wakened his sweet May Margaret
  Out o' her drowsy sleep.

" Come here, come here, my mother dear,
  And rede this dreary dream ;
I dreamed my love was at oor yett,
  And nane wad let him in."

"Lie still, lie still, my May Margaret,
    Lie still and take your rest;
Sin' your true love was at oor yetts
    It's but twa quarters past."

Nimbly, nimbly rose she up,
    And nimbly put she on,
And the higher that the Lady cried,
    The louder blew the win'.

The first step that she steppit in,
    She steppit to the kute,
"Ohone, alas!" said that ladye fair,
    "This water is wondrous deep!"

The neist step that she waded in,
    She waded to the knee;
The deepest pot in Clyde's waters
    She got sweet William in.

"You've had a cruel mother, Willie,
    And I have had another;
But we will sleep in Clyde's waters,
    Like sister and like brother."

This ballad first appeared in Jameson's popular ballads and songs.
There are different versions both of it and the "Twa Brothers." From
the description of "Roarin' Clyde," it would appear the locality of this
ballad must be somewhere between Carnwath and Hyndford Bridge, where
the shoals make a great noise in the river. There are many sad cases of
drowning connected with the upper district of Clyde. Some years ago a
party of two young men and women, returning from a ball at Lamington,
were upset from a cart in the Clyde,—all were drowned. Some days
after, one of the young couples was found in a deep pot of the Clyde
near Liberton, fast locked in each other's arms.

THE MARTYR'S GRAVE.

I HAVE stood by the martyr's lonely grave,
    Where the flowers of the moorland bloom,
Where bright memorials of nature wave
Sweet perfumes o'er the sleeping brave
    In his moss-clad mountain tomb.

I knelt by the wild and lonely spot
    Where moulders the heart of one
That bled and died, but blanched not
At the tyrant's chain or the soldier's shot,
    Till life's last sands had run.

And the vision of other days came back,
    When the dark and bloody band,
With the might of a living cataract,
Essayed to sweep in their fiery tract
    The godly from the land.

When Zion was far on the mountain's height;
    When the wild was the house of prayer;
Where the eyes of eternal hope grew bright,
O'er the saint arrayed in the warrior's might
    For his God and his country there.

When the barbarous hordes, as they onward rode
    By the wild and rocky glen,
Have heard when away from man's abode
A voice that awed like the voice of God !—
    'Twas the hymn of the fearless men.

For the sunless cave was the martyr's home,
    And the damp cold earth his bed ;
And the thousand lights of the starry home
Were the suns of his path while doomed to roam
    O'er the wilds where his brothers bled.

When the clang of conflict rose on the heath,
    And the watchword of freedom rose,
Like the tones of heaven on the saint's last breath,
Far, far o'er the battle notes of death,
    As he soared to his last repose.

When he stood by the scaffold, the faggot and stake,
    As his earthly heritage ;
Yet welcomed all for his Master's sake,
Whose sword of vengeance yet should awake
    To curb their whirlwind rage.

The vision passed—but the home is mine
    Where the wild bird makes her nest,
On the rocky altar, and mossy shrine,
Where the weeds and flowers of the desert shine
    Round the martyr's bed of rest.

The lovers of freedom can never forget
    The glorious peasant band—
His sires—that on Scotia's mountains met;
Each name like a seal on the heart is set,—
    The pride of his fatherland.

                        H. BROWN.

TO CARNWATH MOAT.

ALL hail !—the lover's hallowed grove,
    Where youths and maids at eve retire,
Where oft the tender vows of love
    Are sworn to last till life expire.

And hail !—the poet's sacred bower—
    When summer suns are sinking low,
And evening's grateful shadows lower,
    Here soft and sweet his numbers flow.

The holy man at morn and even,
    In thee delights to sacrifice ;
To walk and meditate on heaven,
    And happiness beyond the skies.

The village patriot, too, delights
    In thy sequestered shades to roam ;
And think Napoleon closed his eyes,
    An exile 'mid the ocean's foam.

Proud science, too—her favourite walks
    Are round and round thy fairy ring ;
Of causes and effects she talks,
    Then stops to hear thy blackbirds sing.

And many a heart in distant lands,
Remembers thee with fond regret ;
Thy nooks, thy shades, and grassy mound,
Are scenes they never can forget.

The lover's grove, the poet's bower,
The haunt of contemplative sage,
And men that hate tyrannic power—
Thy shades have been from age to age.

There is good reason to believe the *Moat* has been at the bottom of the
etymology of Carnwath. The first time the name appears above-board is
in a Bull from the Pope, authorising *Kurnwood* (that is, the cairn in the
wood) to be erected into a parish distinct from Liberton. The parish of
Carnwath at that time would appear to be almost wholly covered with
wood. The names of many places still confirm this opinion ; thus we
have Woodhead, Woodend, Stabwood, Haywood, Westsidewood, East-
sidewood, Easter Hindsheilwood, Wester Hinchelwood; Cowthalley itself.
in Gaelic, signifies also a wood ; Crosswoodhill, Crosswoodburn, &c., &c.

LORD LAMINTON.

THERE was a lass, as I heard say,
Lived low down in a glen ;
Her name was Catherine Johnstone,
Weel known to mony men.

Down came the Lord o' Laminton,
Down from the south countrie ;
And he is for this bonnie lass,
Her bridegroom for to be.

He's asked her father and mother,
And the chief of a' her kin ;
And then he asked the bonnie lass,
And did her favour win.

Down came an English gentleman,
Down from the English Border ;
And he is for this bonnie lass,
To keep his house in order.

He asked her father and mother,
  As I do hear them say;
But he never asked the lass hersel,
  Till on her wedding-day.

But she has wrote a lang letter,
  And sealed it with her hand,
And sent it to Lord Laminton,
  To let him understand.

The first line o' the letter he read,
  He was baith glad and fain;
But ere he read the letter over,
  He was baith pale and wan.

Then he has sent a messenger,
  And out through all his land;
And four-and-twenty armed men
  Were all at his command.

But he has left his merry men all,
  He left them on the lea,
And he's awa' to the wedding-house,
  To see what he could see.

But when he came to the wedding-house,
  As I do understand,
There were four-and-twenty belted knights
  Sat at a table round.

And they rose up to honour him,
  For he was of high renown;
And they rose all for to welcome him,
  And bade him to sit down.

Oh! meikle was the good red wine
  In silver cups did flow;
But aye she drank to Laminton,
  For with him she would go.

Oh ! meikle was the good red wine,
  In silver cups gaed round ;
At length they began to whisper words—
  None could them understand.

"Oh ! came ye here for sport, young man,
  Or came ye here for play ;
Or came ye here for our bonnie bride,
  On this her wedding-day ?"

"I came not here for sport," he said,
  "Neither did I for play ;
But for one word o' your bonnie bride,
  I'll mount and go away."

They set her maids behind her,
  To hear what they would say ;
But the first question he asked her,
  Was always answered "Nay ;"
The next question he asked her,
  Was "Mount and come away."

It's up the Couden Bank they rode,
  And down the Couden Brae ;
And aye she made the trumpet sound—
  It is a weel-won play.

Oh ! meikle was the blood that was shed
  Upon the Couden Brae ;
And aye she made the trumpet sound—
  It's fair and honest play.

Come all ye English gentlemen,
  That be of England born ;
Come na down here to Scotland,
  For fear ye get the scorn.

They'll feed ye up with flattering words,
  And that nae doubt's foul play ;

And dress you frogs instead of fish,
Just on your wedding-day.

This ballad was first published in the " Border Minstrelsy " under the
title of "The Laird of Laminton." The residence of the lady, and the
scene of the affray at her bridal, is said to have been on the banks of the
Cadder, near to where it joins the Tweed; others say the skirmish was
near Traquair, and the lady's residence was in the glen, about three miles
above Traquair House. The ballad is the original of the song of " Loch-
invar." The Laminton family is of great antiquity, and believed to be
lineally descended from Sir William Wallace and his lady, the heiress of
Laminton; it is now represented by the present Lord Lamington.

CHANGES OF CARNWATH.

WHEN I was a bairn! O when I was a bairn;
What a changed town is our town, since I was a bairn;
The young folks growin' up have a' yet to learn
What a merry town was our town when I was a bairn.

George Mark was then our minister, a very worthy man,
His head was white and hoary, his face was pale and wan;
And the holy truths, frae George, baith young and auld did
    learn—
O, we had a worthy minister when I was a bairn.

And the Lairds o' Carnwath, the auld Lairds o' Carnwath !
O what great mighty men were the Lairds o' Carnwath ;
They were statesmen, and soldiers, and lawyers profound,
There were few, few to match them in Scotland to be found !

And the men o' Carnwath, the auld men o' Carnwath,
O what long-headed men were the men o' Carnwath ;
Johnnie Russell, Johnnie Purdie, and auld James Nairn,
A' were fit to be ministers when I was a bairn !

And the lasses o' Carnwath, the bonnie lasses o' Carnwath,
We had sweet bonnie lasses langsyne in Carnwath ;
The lasses now-a-days, nae doot, are very fine,
But their bonnie grannies were fairer langsyne?

And then in the management of our town's affairs,
We could match any town atween Lunnon and Carstairs ;
Norman Lockhart, Young and Walker, and auld cooper
  Brown—
O their names were the pride and uphold o' the toon !

Ye wad think me a gomeril, ye wad think me a fool,
If ye telt a' the tricks and the pranks o' the schule ;
How we played at the club and the merry foot-ba'—
On the green built great muckle castles o' snaw !

But the days o' langsyne they have melted awa'
Like the day breakin' mists—like our castles o' snaw ;
Our lasses now are grannies, our callans auld men—
O ! the days o' langsyne—they will never come again !

Then dinna set your heart on this fast flittin' scene,
Nor grieve for the days that will never come again ;
Set your heart on the home that is fixed in the sky,
Where auld age never comes, and none ever die !

Rev. Mr. Mark, alluded to in the preceding lines, was the much
respected minister of Carnwath for nearly forty years. He died in 1816.
Many of his pithy sayings were long remembered. Being once asked by
Miss Lockhart—"How old are you, Mr. Mark ? " " Weel, mem, I'm
just exactly the same age as my little finger, ay, and seven years aulder
than my teeth." Another party asking the same question, was answered
—"My age ! hoots man, I'm no sae auld's the Deil, and he's no dead yet !"
His successor, the late Rev. Mr. Walker, breakfasting with him on one
occasion, he observed his visitor fingering at his bread. "What's that
ye're doing, Walker?" "Oh, naething ; just puin' out a hair." He
instantly rang the bell, and the servant appeared, "Hae, Nell, tak'
away that, and bring the hairs on ae plate and the butter on another."
He was much amused by the members of the village library sitting in
judgment and condemning a volume of sermons to be burnt for teaching
heresy. He said the book had been read for thirty years, and nobody
had ever found fault with it but the Carnwath weavers. A young woman
having got herself married to her sweetheart with lines, after being the
mother of a child, waited upon him, and shewed the lines, and told him
she wanted him to break the marriage, for she had ta'en the rue. "Aha !
Peggy, lass," he replied, "If I could lowse marriages, woman, I might
been riding in a coach and six " !

K

LINES ON A DEATH-BED.

On! ye who walk with heedless tread
    The turf with thousands sleeping under,
Softly approach a dying bed,
    And think—whilst soul and body sunder.

Approach the scene, ye gay and young;
    Of fashion, every son and daughter;
How eloquently speaks that tongue
    Which feebly begs a cup of water!

It is a solemn thing to stand
    Beside a death-bed, deeply musing,
And mingle with the weeping band
    While death the silver cord is loosing.

It is a solemn thing to be
    Where life's warm fount is faintly flowing,
Whilst o'er the eye that cannot see
    The shades are thick and thicker growing.

It is a solemn thing to hear
    The parting groan of nature given,
While faith impresses on the ear
    A shriek from hell or shout from heaven.

It is—it is a solemn thing
    To hear, as now I seem to hear it,
The rustle of the angel's wing
    Who bears away the ransomed spirit.

Solemn that mystic veil to view,
    With gentle stir and tremor telling
The soul has made its passage through,
    And found its everlasting dwelling.

Those eyes so dull and rayless now—
Oh! kindly draw the eyelids over;
Now wipe the death damp from the brow,
And let the shroud that body cover.

And in the silence hear the rod,
And deeply grieving o'er your errors;
Oh! hear the solemn voice of God,
When speaking through the King of Terrors!

REV. JAMES PROUDFOOT.

SMOKING SPIRITUALISED.

IN TWO PARTS.—PART I.

THIS Indian weed now withered quite,
Though grown at noon, cut down at night,
Shows thy decay—all flesh is hay:
Thus think and smoke tobacco.

The pipe, so lily-like and weak,
Does thus thy mortal state bespeak;
Thou art e'en such—gone with a touch:
Thus think and smoke tobacco.

And when the smoke ascends on high,
Then thou beholds the vanity
Of worldly stuff—gone with a puff:
Thus think and smoke tobacco.

And when the pipe grows foul within,
Think on thy soul defiled with sin,
For then the fire it does require:
Thus think and smoke tobacco.

And seest the ashes cast away,
Then to thyself thou mayest say,
That to the dust return thou must:
Thus think and smoke tobacco.

PART II

Was this small plant for thee cut down?
So was the Plant of great renown
Which mercy sends for nobler ends :
    Thus think and smoke tobacco.

Does juice medicinal proceed
From such a naughty foreign weed?
Then what's the power of Jesse's Flower?
    Thus think and smoke tobacco.

The promise, like the pipe, inlays,
And by the mouth of faith conveys
What virtue flows from Sharon's Rose :
    Thus think and smoke tobacco.

In vain the unlighted pipe you blow,
Your pains in outward means are so
Till heavenly fire your heart inspire :
    Thus think and smoke tobacco.

The smoke, like burning incense, towers,
So should a praying heart of yours,
With ardent cries surmount the skies :
    Thus think and smoke tobacco.

                                        R. ERSKINE.

For the benefit of the smoker we give a place to these lines, for it is a
great fact, that in spite of King Jamie's Counterblast, and the lectures
of teetotalers, the people of this kingdom invest millions annually upon
the Indian weed !—a great waste of money. Don't smoke, don't smoke,
young friends.   Oh, dear, don't smoke ! it is a desperate waste of money !

THE OLD MAID'S SONG—WAE'S ME FOR NOO.

WAE's me ! for I'm noo thirty-six,
    Though some rather mair wad ca' me,
And ane that's sae auld to get married
    Has little or nae chance ava.

And when that I think upon this,
  Lang sighs frae my bosom I draw;
Oh! is it no awfu' to think
  I'm no to be married ava?

    No to be married ava,
      Ne'er to be married ava;
    Oh! is it no awfu' to think
      I'm ne'er to be married ava?

For ilka young lass that can boast
  That she has a lover or twa,
Will haud out her finger and say,
  Puir body, she's got nane ava!
And then, when they a' get married,
  Their husbands will let them gang braw,
While they laugh at auld maids like mysel,
  For no gettin' married ava.
      No to be married ava, &c.

Some wives are sic wasters o' men,
  Wear dune naething less than their twa;
Now this I wad hold as a crime,
  That ought to be punished by law;
For are they no muckle to blame,
  When thus to themselves they tak a',
Ne'er thinkin' o' mony an auld maiden
  That's no to be married ava?
      No to be married ava, &c.

But as for the men that get married,
  Altho' it were some ayont twa,
I think they should aye be respeckit
  For helpin' sae mony awa.
But as for your auld bachelor bodies,
  Their necks everyane I wad thraw;   .
For what is the use o' their lives,
  If they never get married ava?
      No to be married ava, &c.

Oh ! I wish I could get a bit husband,
  Altho' he were never sae sma' ;
Oh ! be what he like, I wad tak him,
  Though scarce like a mannie ava !
Come souter, come tailor, come tinkler,
  Oh ! come but and tak me awa.
Oh ! gie me a bode ne'er sae little,
  I'll tak it and never say na !
      No to be married ava, &c.

Come deaf, or come dumb, or come cripple,
  Wi' ae leg, or nae leg ava,
Or come ye wi' ae ee, or nae ee,
  I'll tak ye as ready's wi' twa.
Come young, or come auld, or come doited,
  Oh ! come onyane o' ye a',
Far better be married to something
  Than no to be married ava !
      No to be married ava, &c.

Now, lads, an' there's ony amang ye
  Wad like just upon me to ca',
Ye'll fin' me no ill to be courted,
  For shyness I hae flung awa ;
And if ye should want a bit wifie,
  Ye'll ken to what quarter to draw,
And e'en should we no mak a bargain,
  We'll aye get a kissie or twa !
      No to be married ava, &c.

                                    ANON.

THE BRIDAL RING.

Maidens ! list to the song I sing,—
Crosses oft lie in the bridal ring ;
Although it be set with rubies rare,
Although the diamond may sparkle there ;

It may dazzle the eye with its glitt'ring shine,
Its gold may be dug from the richest mine,
Yet true, alas ! is the song I sing—
Crosses oft lie in the bridal ring.

Many a maid may my song deride,
And think all is bliss that belongs to a bride ;
Many now sporting in beauty gay
May deem it a vain and idle lay ;
But ah ! I have seen on the bridal day
As fair and as joyous ones as they,
Who have felt ere now, 'tis the truth I sing—
Crosses oft lie in the bridal ring.

I have seen the bride, in her eye a tear,
When nought but joy should have sparkled there,
Mourn o'er the death-bed of the one
She ever loved and loved alone.
Sad, sad indeed, was that last farewell,
That widow's grief no tongue can tell,
But it proves the truth of the song I sing—
Crosses oft lie in the bridal ring.

I have seen one sit with a hopeless eye
By the dying couch of her cherished boy,
Where day by day, and hour by hour,
She watched him fade like a brief bright flower ;
Oh ! while on his cold green grave she kneels,
With feelings none but a mother feels,
She can tell the truth of the song I sing—
Crosses oft lie in the bridal ring.

I have seen one sit in grief alone,
The rose on her cheeks for ever gone,
Her once fair brow deep lined with care,
And her eye lit up with the maniac's stare,
Counting the hours from night till morn,
Waiting the drunkard's slow return ;
She knows, alas ! 'tis the truth I sing—
Crosses oft lie in the bridal ring.

Many a cheek all wan and pale
Tells a sad and mournful tale;
Many a smile on the lips may glow,
And mock the withering heart below,
And many a sorrow there concealed
That may never to mortals be revealed,
Would prove the truth of the song I sing—
Crosses oft lie in the bridal ring.

ANON.

THE TRYST.

THE gowan glitters on the sward,
  The laverock's in the sky,
And collie on my plaid keeps guard,
  And time is passing by;
    And sad and slow
And lengthened on the ground,
  The shadow of our trysting bush
It wears so slowly round.

The sheep bell tinkles frae the west,
  My lambs are bleating near,
But still the sound that I lo'e best,
  Alake! I canna hear;
    And, sad and slow,
The shadow lingers still;
  And like a lonely ghaist I stand
And croon upon the hill.

I hear below the waters' roar,
  The mill wi' clackin' din,
And Luckie scolding frae her door
  To ca' the bairnies in;
    And, sad and slow,
There are nae sounds for me;
  The shadow of our trysting bush
It creeps sae drearily.

I coft yestreen frae Chapman Tam,
  A snood of bonnie blue,
And promised when our trystin' cam'
  To tie it round her brow ;
    And, sad and slow,
  The mark it winna pass ;
  The shadow of that weary thorn
  Is tethered on the grass.

O now I see her on the way,
  She's past the Witches' Knowe ;
She's climbin' up the Brownies',Brae—
  My heart is in a lowe !
    O no ! 'tisna so,
  'Tis glaumrie I have seen ;
  The shadow of that hawthorn bush
  Will nae move mair till e'en.

The book o' grace I'll try to read,
  Tho' conned wi' little skill ;
When collie barks, I'll raise my head,
  And find her on the hill ;
    And, sad and slow,
  The time will ne'er be gone ;
  The shadow o' the trysting bush
  Is fixed like ony stone !
                    JOANNA BAILLIE.

LAY BY YOUR BAWBEE.

LAY by your bawbee, my Jenny,
  Lay by your bawbee, my dear ;
Do as your ain mother aye did,
  She took gude care o' her gear.

The way young kimmers are drest
  Wise folk are sorry to see ;
Their winnin's a' on their back,
  And that's no the thing that should be.

Work when ye're young and ye're able,
  Be honest and savin' ye're tauld ;
'Twill help when trouble comes on,
  And mak' ye respected when auld.

Lasses and.lads, tak' advice,
  An' dinna ye gang for to woo
Until ye hae gathered the siller,
  An' the weel plenisht kist it is fu'.

Look to Archie an' Peggy,
  They married on naething ava,
An' noo she's gaun beggin' an' greetin',
  And Archie has listed awa' !

                                LADY NAIRN.

A young girl, whose wages had risen from £8 yearly to £16, being
asked if she was not saving siller now, when her wages were doubled,
said—"Oh, no, no." "What do you do wi' your siller, then?" "O, it
just a' gangs for trantles and fal-the-ralls." Young women, beware of
trantles and fal-the-ralls!

THE OPERATIVES' MARCH, MAY, 1831.

BEING AT THE LAST ELECTION BEFORE THE PASSING OF THE FIRST REFORM BILL.

Copies of this song were thrown in great numbers from Sir John
Maxwell's carriage.

March! march ! comrades in freedom now,
  On let us march to the music of order ;
Arms we have none, for no one can need them now ;
  Peace is the word from John o' Groat's to the border.

Long have we wearied and waited to see it,
  Now it is come with its blessing and pride ;
In the hearts of our sons unforgotten shall be it,—
  The king and the country are both on our side.

Our banners are glancing, our sections advancing,
The pipe and the trumpet are pealing above ;
Shout with the voice of men—once again—again !
The Cause and the King that a people can love.
March ! march ! &c.

A cheer for the Queen too, and one be it seen too,
For Sussex, who ne'er was to freedom untrue ;
Shout away ! shout away ! it's for Russell and Grey,
And Lord Harry and all our brave Admiral's crew.
We vow to stand by them, their foes we defy them,
For firmly and bravely they've weathered the storm,
And these were their watchwords, and they'll be our
catchwords—
The Cause of the People, the King, and Reform.
March ! march ! &c.

An immense crowd with music and banners, met the popular candidate, the late Sir John Maxwell of Polloc, at the West Port of Lanark, and drew him in his carriage to Lanark. The election was in the church, and it was a most violent and uproarious scene. The Hon. Charles Douglas was elected, to the great disappointment of the Reformers. When he began to speak, he was only listened to for a few sentences, when the hissing and groaning were such that not a word was audible ; missiles of various kinds were thrown among his supporters, one—a penny—struck the Hon. Member with such violence on the right temple, that the blood ran profusely down his cheek ; at the close, the Whig gentlemen had to act as a body-guard to their opponents on their way through the crowd to the hotel. Such was the last election, under the old system, for the County of Lanark, and it was a rough one. A detachment of the Scots Greys had to be called on, in the evening, to clear the streets of the riotous crowd.

————

YOUNG HYNDFORD.

Young Hyndford was the brawest knicht
That dwelt in fair Scotland ;
But tho' renowned in France and Spain,
He fell by a lady's hand.

And he is to the huntin' gane,
    As fast as he could dri'e;
And he is to his true love gane,
    As fast as he could hie.

His true love forth from her bower came,
    And on her watch-tower stude ;
She thocht she heard a bridle ring,
    The sound it did her gude.

When he cam' to his ladye's bower
    He tirled at the pin,
And wha sae ready as the ladye hersel'
    To open and let him in?

" Ye're welcome, young Lord Hyndford,
    For coal and candle licht,
And so is my young Hyndford
    To stay wi' me the nicht."

" I thank ye for yer licht, ladye,
    I thank ye for yer coal,
But a fairer ladye than ten o' thee
    Waits me at Mungo's Wall."

" A fairer maid than me, Hyndford !
    A fairer maid than me !
A maiden hauf sae fair as me
    Your eyes did never see.

" But if your love be changed, my dear,
    Since better canna be,
At least ye will for auld langsyne
    This ae nicht stay wi' me."

When they were at the supper set,
    And birlin' at the wine;
The ladye's ta'en a sair sickness
    And tae her bed is gane.

Young Hyndford he has followed her,
　　And a dowie man was he;
He found his true love in her bower,
　　And the tear was in his e'e.

He's ta'en her in his armis twa,
　　Wi' mony a kiss and phrase;
A living man he laid him down,
　　But sae he never raise!

"Oh! long, long, is the winter nicht,
　　And slowly dawns the day;
There is a dead man in my bower,
　　I wish he were away."

Then up bespake her bower woman,
　　And she spake up wi' spite,
"If there's a dead man in your bower,
　　It's yoursel' that has the wyte!"

"Oh! heal this dead on me, Catherine,
　　Oh! heal this dead on me,
And the silks that were shapen for me gin Pasche
　　Shall a' be sewed for thee."

Then up and spak' the Popinjay
　　That sat aboon her head,
"Ladye, keep your green cleiden
　　Frae young Lord Hyndford's blude."

"O better I will keep my green cleiden
　　Frae young Lord Hyndford's blude,
Than thou can keep thy clatterin' tongue
　　That trottles in thy head."

She has called upon her bower maidens,
　　She has called them ane by ane;
"There is a knicht in my bower;
　　'Tis time that he were gane."

They booted him, and they spurred him
        As he was wont to ride ;
A hunting horn about his neck,
        A sharp sword by his side.

And they hae ridden along, along,
        All the long summer's tide ;
Until they cam' to Clyde water,
        The deepest place in Clyde.

In the deep, black pot o' Clyde water
        They've placed him safe and soun'
Wi' a stane upon his bonnie breast
        To haud young Hyndford doun.

Syne up then spak' the Popinjay,
        As he sat on a tree—
"And so ye've killed young Hyndford,
        Wha never lo'ed ane but thee."

" Come doun, come doun, my Popinjay,
        Come doun into my hand,
And your cage shall be o' the bonnie beaten gold,
        Where now it is but wand."

" Gae hame, gae hame, ye fause ladye,
        And pay your maids their fee ;
As ye have done to young Hyndford
        Sae wad ye do to me."

" Oh ! had I an arrow in my hand,
        And a bent bow on the string,
I'd shoot a dart at thy proud heart,
        Among the leaves so green."

She hadna crossed a rigg o' land,
        A rigg but barely one,
When she met wi' his auld faither
        Come ridin' all alone.

" Where hae ye been now, ladye fair,
    Where hae ye been so late ? "
" We hae been seekin' young Hyndford,
    But him we canna get."

Neist day cam' seekin' young Hyndford
    Many a lord and knicht ;
Neist day cam' seekin' young Hyndford
    Many a ladye bricht.

" I haena seen him, the young Hyndford,
    Since yesterday at noon ;
He turned his stately steed about
    And hied him thro' the toun.

" But Hyndford kens the fords o' Clyde,
    He'll ride them ane by ane ;
And tho' the nicht was never sae mirk,
    Lord Hyndford will be hame."

It fell upon the very neist day,
    The king was boun' to ride,
And he has missed the young Hyndford,
    Should hae ridden by his side.

The ladye turned her round about
    Wi' meikle mournfu' din ;
" It fears me sair in Clyde's water,
    That he is drowned therein."

Then up bespak' Lord Hyndford's mother,
    And a dowie woman was she —
" There's no a place in a' Clyde's waters,
    But my son wad get thro'."

" Gar dive, gar dive," the king he cried,
    " Gar dive for gold and fee ;
O wha will dive for Hyndford's sake ?
    O wha will dive for me ? "

They dived deep in at ae well head,
    And out aye at the other ;
"We could dive nae mair for Lord Hyndford
    Altho' he were our brother."

It fell that in that ladye's castle
    The king was boun' for bed ;
And then up spak' the Popinjay,
    That flew abune his head.

"Leave aff your divin' on the day,
    And dive upon the nicht;
And where that guileless lord lies slain,
    The candles will burn bricht."

They left the divin' on the day,
    And dived upon the nicht;
And where that guileless lord lay slain
    The candles they burned bricht.

The deepest pot in a' the Clyde
    They found Lord Hyndford in ;
A stone lay on his bonnie breast
    To haud young Hyndford doun.

Then up and spak' the king himsel',
    When he saw the deadly wound—
"O wha has slain my richt-hand man.
    That held my hawk and hound ?"

Then up and spak' the Popinjay—
    "O what needs a' this din ;
His licht-leman, she took his life
    And threw him in the linn."

Then she swore by the grass sae green,
    And she swore by the corn ;
She hadna seen him, Lord Hyndford,
    Since Mononday at morn.

"It has been Kate, my bower woman,
    Oh! ill may her betide;
Wad I hae slain my ain dear love
    And thrown him into Clyde?"

The king he called his hewers all
    To hew baith wood and thorn,
All for to make a strong ball-fire,
    That fair May for to burn.

It wadna tak' upon her cheek,
    Nor yet upon her chin,
Nor yet upon her yellow hair,
    To cleanse the deadly sin.

The maiden touched the clay cold corpse,
    A drap it never bled;
The ladye laid her hand on him,
    And sune the ground was red!

Out they took her, out May Katherine,
    And put her mistress in;
The flame took fast upon her cheek,
    Took fast upon her chin,
Took fast upon her fair bodye;
    She burned like hollins green.

We are not aware of any definite locality in the vicinity of the Clyde being connected by tradition with this ballad. The reader will observe the superstitious beliefs of the olden time in the "candles burning bricht" above the corpse in the Clyde, and the effusion of blood when touched by the murderess. There are half-a-dozen different editions of the ballad in print, under different names. We have given what we believe to be the best. Westraw House, in the Parish of Pettinain, and Carmichael House in the Parish of Carmichael, were the chief seats of the Earls of Hyndford. In consequence of the failure of the male line of that ancient family, at an early period in the present century, the family is now represented by Sir Wyndham Carmichael Anstruther, Bart. There is a pool named the *Black Pot* in the Clyde, a little above the railway bridge.

L

COWDAILY CASTLE.

A BALLAD.

THE snaw had melted on Tintoc so high,
    The ice in Clyde's low vale;
And on Clyde's green banks the flowers bloomed fair,
    And scented the sweet May gale.
The cuckoo sang loud from the Ampherlaw woods,
    The laverock in the sky;
And the lambs skippit licht on the Lampits knowes,
    While the sun shone bright on high.

But the corbie croaked loud on Cowdaily's towers,
    With a harsh and dismal sound;
And the pyets screamed wild with discordant throats,
    On all the trees around;
And the adder was hissing in Loriburn shaw,
    To the fox's angry growl;
While from the greenwood, by the White Loch's flood,
    Came the whoop of the dreamy owl.

Lady Somerville sat in Cowdaily's hie hall,
    She sat all sad and lone,
For her lord had gone, with his merry men all,
    To fight for Queen Mary's throne.
Lady Somerville sat in her hie, hie hall,
    And from the lattice down,
She looked to the east, wi' an aching breast,
    Ower the moss to Carnwath town.

For the bells were ringing in Carnwath kirk,
    With a slow and solemn tone,
And rang in the ear of the lady so fair—
    " Lord Somerville's dead and gone."
" What tidings, what tidings, my warder good,
    From thy tower so steep and high;
What means the knell of that hollow bell,
    That peals along the sky."

" Oh ! the monks are singing, and the bells are ringing
    With a slow and solemn toll ;
For the prayers are prayed, and masses are said,
    For good Lord Thomas' soul—
For Lord Thomas, the founder of Carnwath kirk,
    The builder of Mary's Aisle ;
And aye on this day, for Lord Thomas they pray,
    Who raised the holy pile."

" But what of the war that rages afar,
    Good warder, quickly tell ;
Has our good Queen sped; have the rebels fled;
    Is Lord Somerville safe and well ? "
" No tidings, no tidings, my lady fair,
    But a horseman comes with speed ;
He whips and he spurs ower the knowes and the furze,
    Along the high Woodhead.

" But now as he nearer and nearer comes,
    I think I ken him weel ;
For now as he nearer comes I see
    Bailie Inglis of the Eastshiel."
Bailie Inglis rode up to Cowdaily's yett ;
    His steed was white with foam.
" And what are thy news, my Bailie so true ;
    What news do you bring home ? "

" Oh ! my news are bad, and very, very sad ;
    I come from a field of gore ;
The battle is lost, our Queen is fled,
    Lord Somerville's wounded sore.
Our Lord, who rode forth on a gay gallant steed
    Now comes in a litter home ;
And many a day will pass away
    Ere the fields again he will roam."

And many a day had passed away,
    Many a night of burning pain,

Ere that proud Lord could leave his bed,
   And walk the fields again.

In merry Carnwath, and in Clyde's green strath,
   The swain had left his toil ;
The bells were rung, and the vespers sung,
   In St. Mary's holy aisle.

All was silent and still, and on valley and hill
   The moon shone cold and serene ;
When at dreary midnight, a most fearful sight
   In Cowdaily's towers was seen.
The sound of wassail had ceased in the castle,
   And all asleep were gone ;
All, save the Lord of Cowdaily high halls,
   Who musing sat alone.

He thought of the day when at Langside fray
   He fought for Scotland's Queen ;
For loyal still was the bold Somerville,
   In every trying scene.
He thought of his Queen, and the tears filled his e'en,
   As he looked on the bright gold ring,
Which bade him aye mind the fortunes unkind
   Of the mother and child of a king.

The castle quaked from turret to base,
   Loud thunders pealed on high ;
The lightnings flashed, and a strong wind rushed
   Along the cloudless sky.
The tapers waxed dim, and a spectre so grim
   With eyes of fiery glare
Before him stands, and with upraised hands
   Thus addressed his trembling ear :

" Proud Somerville, hear, and tell it to thine heir,
   And to thine heir alone ;
While that ring they retain, Cowdaily's domain
   Will descend from sire to son.

When the Queen's ring is lost, the fortunes are crossed
Of Cowdaily's barons hie ;
And their lands shall pass to a stranger race,
Their towers in ruins lie."

The noble family who for many centuries possessed the extensive and valuable estates of Carnwath, had their principal residence in Cowthally Castle, built on a small peninsula jutting into the west side of Carnwath Moss, which was surrounded by deep trenches filled with water, and must have been when entire a place of great strength. James, the seventh Lord Somerville, who figures in the foregoing verses, attended the Parliament of 1560, and when an Act was carried to pull down the Romish Church, he, with the Earl of Athole and Lord Borthwick, dissented, saying they would believe only as their fathers had believed. On one occasion he was summoned to attend the General Assembly to assist in purging the religion from Popery, but refused to assist in any such thing. On receiving a letter from Lord Seton, stating that Queen Mary had escaped from Lochleven, he raised all his vassals and retainers, numbering upwards of 300 men, met the Queen at Hamilton, fought at Langside, was carried home to Cowthally, grievously wounded in the face with a dagger and in the thigh with a lance. Somerville of Tarbrax, in the parish of Carnwath, who passed sentence upon and led forth to execution Walter Mill, the last whom the Catholics had the pleasure of burning alive in Scotland for believing the Bible before the Pope, was a cousin of this lord. Queen Mary, when prisoner in England, sent a beautiful gold ring to this nobleman as a mark of her esteem, with the inscription, "Remember my misfortunes." This ring had been lost, and was found early in this century by a person hoeing potatoes. It was as bright and fresh as if come newly from the jeweller's shop, and was believed to be of French manufacture. It is in right of their descent from the lords of Cowthally, that the still flourishing branches of Westsidewood and Ampherlaw inherit their estates.

ON THE POWER OF IMAGINATION.

I LAY in my bedroom in Peebles,
With the window curtains drawn,
While there stole over hills of pasture and pine
The unresplendent dawn.

And in the deep silence I listened,
With a pleased half-waking heed,
To the sound that ran through the ancient town—
The shallow, brawling Tweed.

For the sound was a realization
  Of a dream : and I felt like one
Who first sees the Alps or the Pyramids,
  World-wide, in the setting sun ;

First crossing the purple Campagna,
  Behold the wondrous dome,
Which a thought of Michael Angelo hung
  In the golden air of Rome.

And all through the summer morning
  I felt a joy indeed
To whisper again to myself—
  "This is the voice of the Tweed."

Of Melrose, Neidpath, and Dryburgh,
  Norham Castle, brown and bare,
The merry sun shining on merry Carlisle,
  And the bush aboon Traquair.

I had dreamed,—but more of the river,
  That shining mile on mile
Flowed through my imagination,
  As through Egypt flows the Nile.

Was it absolute truth, or dreaming,
  Which all the wakeful disowns,
That I heard something more in the stream as it ran
  Than water breaking on stones ?

Now the hoofs of a flying mosstrooper,
  Now a bloodhound bay half caught,
The distant sound of a hunting horn,
  The burr of Walter Scott.

Who knows ? but of this I am certain,
  That but for the ballads and wails
That make passionate dead things, stocks and stones ;
  Make piteous woods and dales ;

The Tweed were as poor as the Amazon,
   That for all the years it has rolled,
Can tell but how fair was the morning red,
   How sweet the evening gold.

                                   ALEX. SMITH.

TO MR. JAMES HODGE, FARMER, ARTHUR-SHEIL, LIBERTON.

WITH A MUCKLE CHAIR.

WHEN last I was at Arthursheil
   And saw your household ware,
I saw a thing ye wanted much—
   A roomy muckle chair.
As ye hae got anither tack,
   And dinna need to flit,
As ye hae travelled lang enough
   'Tis now your time to sit.

I haena mony gifts to gie,
   My gang's been rather bare,
But never mind, amang my gudes
   I hae a muckle chair.
And now for auld acquaintance sake,
   Our friendship to renew,
I hae anither for mysel',
   I'll gie this chair to you.

When Tintoc tap puts on his cap,
   Foreboding coming storms,
And murky clouds and hailstones blasts
   December war performs,
Ye'll sit and hear the roaring blast
   Sough o'er the forest bare,
While snugly at your chimney lug
   Ye'll fill your muckle chair.

On Sabbath nichts, as in auld time,
    Wi' a' the family there,
The questions ye'll put round and round
    Out frae the muckle chair.
Youths think thae are a' sae clever noo,
    And fu' o' wit and lair,
Though ignorant o' mony truths
    Taught frae the muckle chair.

Improve the short remaining time
    That you and I may dree,
It canna be that very lang
    Till we be called to dee ;
Instead o' kind and loving friends
    We'll occupy our lairs,
Another race is now come up
    To fill our muckle chairs.

But Jamie, lad, we'll no despond
    Though to the grave we go,
We have a certain confidence
    That death's a vanquished foe ;
And though our case seem lonely now,
    It's no without remeid,
The time is fixed, to us unknown,
    The grave shall yield the deid.

We'll mount into a higher sphere,
    And join the assembled throng,
Wi' harps of gold and waving palms
    We'll swell the heavenly song.
Think not, O man, our life is vain,
    With prospects such as these,
While as eternity shall roll
    We'll sing our Maker's praise.

The lower tribes, who now like us
    Partake a Father's care,
Their little all of life when o'er
    No blessedness they share.

To man alone this hope is lent
Amid his griefs and fears,
He shall a reaping time enjoy,
Though he has sown in tears.

JAMES GRAHAM, CARLUKE.

James Graham was a good specimen of the Scottish workman of the old school, and his friend, James Hodge, another. They were both able, intelligent, well-informed and well-conducted men ; none, I believe, superior in their position. Mr. Graham died at the age of 84, and for the last 16 years of his life had a new New Year's Hymn published in the *Hamilton Advertiser*, expressive of grateful thanks to the Giver of all good. His death was sudden. He gave several lectures to the young men of Carluke on several interesting and important subjects.

LOYAL PETER.

From the GLASGOW HERALD.

Very many in Glasgow and elsewhere who could not appreciate the genius of the late Professor Rankine, one of the most eminent physicists, mathematicians, and engineers of whom his country could boast, knew him as what is called "a social giant." He was fresh, humorous, and innocent as a child ; he was kindly in disposition, so charitable in heart, so sympathetic, so affectionately conservative of all that was lovable in old fashioned ways and things, that he was a universal favourite. His songs are only 19 in number, and some of them are not remarkable. It may be from professional sympathies, but we find few in the volume better than "Loyal Peter," which brings back the memory of dear old Peter Mackenzie of the Glasgow *Reformer's Gazette*. The following verses are both true to their subject, and a fair specimen of Rankine's power.

OUR Peter is a writer bauld,
His style is never muddy, O,
At jobs and quacks he weel can scauld,
His face is round and ruddy, O.
His shape is portly, middle size,
He's sturdy in his walkin', O ;
The sparklin' o' his wits surprise,—
It's fun to hear him talkin', O.

CHORUS—Come Rottenrow and Gallowgate,
Goosedubs and Briggate smeeky, O,
And join in praise o' loyal Pate
Wi' Candleriggs sae reeky, O.

Some quacks sell fusionless peasemeal,
 Pretend it's Revelenta, O,
And brag o' makin' sick folk weel
 In advertisements plenty, O ;
A' crammed wi' lees frae en' to en',
 And balderdash sae weary, O,
When Peter he whips oot his pen
 And dings them tapselteerie, O.

Come Rottenrow, &c.

Some knaves—puir simple folk to rob,
 Get up a scheme called Diddlesex,
But Peter he scents out the job,
 And dings it a' to fiddlesticks.
Our West-end Park will flourish green
 When summer nichts are shorter, O,
Where, but for Peter, would ha'e been
 A park o' bricks and mortar, O.

Come Rottenrow, &c.

Ye rogues o' low and high degree,
 Scamp off wi' fear and quakin', O,
If Peter chance your tricks to see,
 It's then ye'll get a paiken, O.
Ilk honest man and bonnie lass,
 Come brew the toddy sweeter, O,
And drink wi' me a bumper glass
 To the health o' loyal Peter, O.

Come Rottenrow, &c.

THE CONTRAST.

Written under Windsor Terrace, 17th February, 1820, on the death of George III, after a reign of 60 years.

I saw him last on this terrace proud,
 Walking in health and gladness ;
Begirt with his court, and all in the crowd
 Not a single look of sadness.

Bright was the sun, and the leaves were green,
    Blythely the birds were singing ;
The cymbal replied to the tambourine,
    And the bells were merrily ringing.

I have stood by the crowd beside his bier,
    When not a word was spoken,
And every eye was dim with a tear,
    And the silence by sobs was broken.

I have heard the earth on his coffin pour,
    To the muffled drum's deep rolling,
While the minute gun with its solemn roar
    Drowned the death-bell's tolling.

The time when he walked in his glory thus,
    To the grave till I saw him carried,
Was an age of the mightiest change to us,
    But to him a night unvaried.

We have fought the fight,—from his lofty throne
    The foe of our land we have tumbled ;
And it gladdened each eye—save his alone,
    For whom that foe we humbled.

A daughter beloved, a queen, a son,
    And a son's sole child had perished ;
And sad was each heart, save the only one
    By which they were fondest cherished.

For his eyes were sealed, and his mind was dark,
    And he sat in his age's lateness
Like a vision throned, as a solemn mark
    Of the frailty of human greatness.

His silver beard o'er a bosom spread,
    Unvexed by life's commotion,
Like a yearly lengthening snow-drift, shed
    On the calm of a frozen ocean.

Still o'er him oblivion's waters lay,
  Though the stream of life kept flowing;
When they spoke of our king 'twas but to say—
  That the old man's strength was going.

At intervals thus the waves disgorge,
  By weakness rent asunder,
A piece of the wreck of the Royal George,
  For the people's pity and wonder.

He is gone at length, he is laid in the dust,
  Death's hand his slumber breaking;
For the coffined rest of the good and just
  Is a sure and blissful waking.

His people's heart is his funeral urn,
  And should sculptured stone be denied him,.
There will his name be found, when in turn
  We lay our heads beside him.

                                        WOLFE.

MIND AND BODY.

Says mind to body t'other day,
  As on my chin I plied my razor,
" Pray, tell me, does that glass portray
  Your real phiz, or cheat the gazer?

" That youthfu' face, that bloomed as sleek
  As Hebe's, Ganymede's, Apollo's,
Has lost its roses, and your cheek
  Is falling into fearful hollows.

" The crow's fell foot hath set its sign
  Beside that eye which dimly twinkles;
And look! what means that ugly sign?
  Gadsooks, my friend, you're getting wrinkles!

"That form which ladies once could praise,
  Would now inspire them with a panic;
Get Byron's belt, or Worcester's stays,
  Or else you'll soon be aldermanic.

" At sight of that dismantled top
  My very heart, I must confess, aches;
Once famous as a Brutus crop
  You now are balder than Lord Essex.

" Since Wayte's decease your teeth decline,—
  Finding no beautifier near 'em;
Time's tooth has mumbled two of thine,
  Well may them—*edax rerum!*

" Behold! your cheeks are quite bereft,
  Of their two laughter-loving dimples,
And pretty substitutes they've left—
  (Between ourselves) a brace of pimples!

" The fashions which you used to lead,
  So careless are you or so thrifty,
You most neglect when most you need,
  A sad mistake when nearing fifty."

"Stop, stop," cries body, "let us pause
  Before you reckon more offences,
Since you yourself may be the cause
  Of all these dismal consequences.

" The sword, you know, wears out the sheath,
  By steam are brazen vessels scattered;
And when volcanoes rage beneath
  The surface must be torn and scattered.

" Have not your passions, hopes, and fears
  Their tegument of clay out-wearing,
Done infinitely more than years
  To cause the ravage you're declaring?

"If you yourself no symptom show
  Of age—no wrinkles of the spirit;
If still for friends your heart can glow,
  Your purse be shared with starving merit,

"If yet to sordid sins unknown,
  No avarice in your heart has started;
If you have not suspicious grown,
  Sour, garrulous, or narrow-hearted,

"You still are young, and o'er my face
  (Howe'er its features may be shaded)
Shall throw the sunshine of your grace,
  And keep its moral part unfaded.

"Expression is the face's soul,
  The head and heart's joint emanation;
Insensible to time's control,
  Free from the body's devastation.

"If you're still twenty, I'm no more—
  Counting by years, how folk have blundered!
Voltaire was young at eighty-four,
  And Fontenelle at near a hundred!"

ANON.

THE FALLS OF CLYDE.

Oh! I have seen the Falls of Clyde,
  And never can forget them;
For memory, in her hours of pride,
  'Midst gems of thought will set them
With every living thing allied—
  I will not now regret them!

And I have stood by Bonnington
  And watched the sparkling current

Come, like a smiling wood-nymph, on,
  And then a mighty torrent !
With power to rend the cliffs, anon,
  Had they not been before rent.

And I have been in Balfour's cave ?
  But why hath chisel wrought it,
Since he the brutal, but the brave,
  In sore constraining sought it ?
Dark days ! when savage fought with slave—
  Heroically fought it.

And I have hung o'er Burley's leap
  And watched the streams all blending,
As down that chasm so dark and steep
  The torrents were descending ;
How awful is that chaos deep—
  Those rocks so high, impending !

And I have worshipped Corra Linn,
  Clyde's most majestic daughter ;
And those eternal rainbows seen,
  That arch the foaming water ;
And I have owned that lovely queen
  And cheerful fealty brought her.

And I have wandered in the glen
  Where Stonebyres rolls so proudly ;
And watched, and mused, and watched again
  Where cliff, and chasm, and cloud lie,
Listening, while nature's denizen
  Talks to the woods so loudly.

Yes ! I have seen the Falls of Clyde,
  And never can forget them ;
For memory, in her hours of pride,
  'Midst gems of thought will set them
With life's most lovely scenes allied—
  I will not now regret them.
                        Dr. BROWNING.

WALLACE'S CAVE AT CORRA LINN.

LAND of the vale ! astounding flood !
The dullest leaf in all this wood
　　Quakes—conscious of thy power ;
The caves reply with hollow moan ;
And vibrates to its central stone
　　Yon time-cemented tower !

And yet how fair the rural scene !
For thou, O Clyde, hast ever been
　　Beneficent as strong !
Pleased in refreshing dews to steep
The little trembling flowers that peep
　　Thy shelving rocks among.

Hence all that love their country love
To look on thee—delight to rove
　　Where they thy voice can hear ;
And, to the patriot-warrior's shade,
Lord of the vale, to heroes laid
　　In dust, that voice is dear.

Along thy banks at dead of night
Sweeps visibly the Wallace wight ;
　　And stands in warlike rest,
Aloft, beneath the moon's pale beam,
A champion worthy of the stream,
　　Yon grey tower's living crest !

But clouds and envious darkness hide
A form not doubtfully descried :
　　Their transient mission o'er,
Oh ! say to what blind regions flee
These shapes of awful phantasy,
　　To what untrodden shore ?

Less than divine command they spurn ;
But this we from the mountains learn,
   And this the valleys show,
That never will they deign to hold
Communion where the heart is cold
   To human weal or woe.

The man of abject soul in vain
Shall walk the Marathonian plain,
   Or thread the shadowy gloom
That still invests the guardian pass,
Where stood sublime Leonidas,
   Devoted to the tomb.

Nor deem that it can aught avail
For such to glide with oar or sail
   Beneath the piny wood,
Where Tell once drew, by Uri's lake,
His vengeful shafts, prepared to slake
   Their thirst in tyrants' blood !

WORDSWORTH.

Such are the sentiments expressed by two distinguished English poets on viewing the Falls of Clyde. It is well said by another writer, that our noble river altogether, from its sources to its embouchure, is probably, in everything interesting and grand, more opulent than any other river, no matter how boasted of, in all the British Isles !

PENTLAND HILLS.

Airs—" Martyrdom" and " Dundee."

THE pilgrim's feet here oft will tread
   O'er this sequestered scene,
To mark where Scotland's martyrs lie
   In lonely Rullion Green ;
To muse on those who fought and fell—
   All Presbyterians true ;
Who held the League and Covenant—
   Who waved the banner blue !

M

Like partridge to the mountain driven—
  Oh ! long and sorely tried ;
Their cause they deemed the cause of heaven—
  For that they lived and died !
Together here they met and prayed—
  Ah ! ne'er to meet again ;
Their winding-sheet the bloody plaid—
  Their grave lone Rullion's Green.

Oh ! here they sang the holy strain—
  Sweet Martyrs' melody;
When every heart and every voice
  Arose in harmony.
The listening echoes all around
  Gave back their soft reply,
While angels heard the hallowed sound,
  And bore it to the sky.

O faithless king ! hast thou forgot
  Who gave to thee thy crown ?
Hast thou forgot thy solemn oath
  At Holyrood and Scone ?
O fierce Dalziel ! thy ruthless rage
  Wrought langsome misery ;
What Scottish heart could ever give
  A benison to thee !

O Claverhouse ! fell Claverhouse !
  Thou brave but cruel Græme !
Dark deeds like thine will last for aye
  Linked wi' thy blighted name.
Ah ! Pentland hills, sae fair and green
  When in the sunrise gleaming,
Or in the pensive gloamin' hour
  Aneath the moonbeams streaming ;

I love to wander there alone
  Wi' sad and sacred feeling,
While hallowed memories wake the tear
  In waefu' eye oft stealing.

I love the wild sequestered Glen,
Thy bonnie wimplin' burn,
For Scotland's brave and martyred men
Still does it seem to mourn.

LADY NAIRN.

The insurrection quashed at Rullion Bridge originated in Dumfries-shire. Some soldiers there had seized a poor man, and were threatening to *roast* him, when the populace interfered, overcame the soldiers, and rescued the man. Their numbers increased, they went to the west; their numbers still increasing, they resolved to go to Edinburgh. On coming to Douglas the bulk of them lodged one night in the church. At Lanark they renewed the Covenants, and had a guard on the boat over the Clyde, there being no bridge there, and Dalziel with an army was on the other side. They next started on the road for Edinburgh by the villages of Forth and Wilsontown, and were overtaken by a tremendous storm, which thinned their numbers about one-half before they reached Bathgate. Disappointed in their expectations of support at Edinburgh, they kept south of the city, and were overtaken by General Dalziel at Rullion Green at the close of a winter day. After enduring repeated assaults, the Covenants broke and fled to the west. About fifty fell on the field. One man named Ferguson, mounted on a little pony, being unhorsed in the melee, caught a dragoon's horse which was galloping about without a rider. He turned and rode for his home. On crossing the Clyde at Carnwath his own little pony came up to him, so he went home with two horses, being, we believe, the only individual who was richer when he came back than when he went away. One severely wounded called at Blackhill, in the parish of Dunsyre, and asked the shepherd, Adam Sanderson, to bury him on the slope of a rising ground in view of the Ayrshire hills, which was done, he being found dead next day. Some years ago four young men from Carnwath—John French, John Liddle, George Ramsay, and Hugh Black—desirous to test the truth of this tradition, dug up the grave early in the present century, and sure enough the remains of the poor Covenanter were found in a surprising state of preservation, wrapt in what had been a red cloak. In the neck of his coat were two Dutch coins the size of crown pieces. In other respects the stanza in the "Burial of Sir John Moore" was literally descriptive of the scene :—

"No useless coffin enclosed his breast,
Nor in sheet nor in shroud we wound him,
But he lay like a warrior taking his rest,
With his martial cloak around him."

We regret to add that two poor fellows who had found their way to Carnwath were inveigled into the moss by the retainers of the Earl of Carnwath, were there barbarously murdered by them, and buried in the moss. It is told that for some time after a light arose over their graves at night, moved gradually south, and remained suspended above the dwelling of the murderers. Colonel Wallace and the Rev. Wm. Veitch found shelter in a barn at Dunsyre, and many others in other houses in that parish. The Rev. Mr. Veitch at that time tenanted the hills of

Dunsyre, and great efforts were made to seize his person. On one occasion he actually held the reins of the horses of the dragoons while they were searching Anston House for himself, being so thoroughly disguised that they did not recognise him. Shortly after he assisted the Earl of Argyle to escape, and accompanied him to London, both disguised; and a great reward being offered for the apprehension of Argyle, who travelled as servant to Mr. Veitch in England, Mr. Veitch read an advertisement and said, " Here's a fine prize for us, man, if we could get a haud o' Argyle; there's £500 offered to any person who will inform where he is to be found."

BOTHWELL BANK, THOU BLOOMEST FAIR.

On the blythe Beltane, as I went
Be mysel' along the green bent,
When by the crystal waves of Clyde,
Thro' saughs and hanging hazels glyde,
There, sadly sitting on a brae
I heard a damsel speak her say.

Oh ! Bothwell bank, thou bloomest fair,
But, oh ! thou makest my heart fu' sair,
For a' beneath thy holts sae green
My love and I wad sit at een ;
While primroses and daisies, mixt
Wi' blue bells, in my locks he fixt.

But ah ! he left ae dreary day,
And haply now sleeps in the clay,
Without ae sich his dethe to mourn,
Without ae flouir his grave to croun !
Oh ! Bothwell bank, thou bloomest fair,
But, ah, thou makest my heart fu' sair !

Pinkerton first gave these lines to the world in his " Select Scottish Ballads," in 1773, as the old words of the ancient and beautiful air of " Bothwell Bank." Some, however, suspect he was author of these verses himself.

THE VALE OF CLYDE.

ADMIRING nature's simple charms,
   I left my humble home,
Awhile my country's peaceful plains
   With pilgrim steps to roam ;
I marked the leafy summer wave
   On flowing Irvine's side,
But richer far 's the robe she wears
   Within the vale of Clyde.

I roamed the braes of bonnie Doon,
   The winding banks of Ayr,
Where flutters many a small bird gay,
   Blooms many a floweret fair ;
But dearer far to me the stem
   That once was Calder's pride,
And blossoms now, the fairest flower,
   Within the vale of Clyde.

Avaunt, thou life-repressing north !
   Ye withering east winds too ;
But come, thou all-reviving west,
   Breathe soft the genial dew ;
Until at length, in peaceful age,
   This lovely floweret shed
Its last green leaf upon my tomb,
   Within the vale of Clyde.
           JOHN STRUTHERS,
Author of "Poor Man's Sabbath" and "History of Scotland."

SWEET MARY, ADIEU!

SOON, soon the good ship from the Clyde will be starting,
   That wafts me from Scotia, my dear native shore,
And sore bleeds my heart, love, to think we are parting,
   And parting to meet peradventure no more !

Sore bleeds my heart from dear Clydesdale to sally,
  And leave thee behind my departure to rue;
The heartfelt endearments of Clydesdale's sweet valley,
  I sigh to bid these and my Mary adieu!

Yet think not, dear Mary, tho' now we must sever,
  That distance shall wean my affection from thee;
Believe me, as soon Clyde's meandering river
  May alter its course and run back from the sea.
A captive I am, and the chains I lie under,
  Thy charms so engaging around my heart threw,
And love's pleasing fetters I'll ne'er break asunder,
  Tho' I must bid thee, sweet Mary, adieu!

But now we must part, fate forbids me to tarry,
  Forbids our sweet intercourse longer to last,
Yet in my sad breast the remembrance I'll carry,
  The soothing remembrance of days that are past.
And hope softly whispers, tho' now I'm a rover,
  If still, dearest maid, thou art faithful and true,
That yet we shall meet, all our wanderings over,
  No more to be parted—sweet Mary, adieu!

                              REV. W. MILNE, ELLON.

THE DYING MASON.

FAREWEEL to the village, the best on the plain,
The lochs, glens, and green fields I'll ne'er see again,
Adieu to my pleasures, adieu to my care;
My puir auld frail folk, and lasses so fair;
To the kirk where wi' folly I promised to part!
The ane that ensnared me shall die wi' a smart.
But, oh! how the sons of the Lodge can I lea',
And gang to my lang hame—the cauld house o' clay?

Since I was a Mason a sad life I've led,
The auld cantin' crew—everlastingly mad,
That I met wi' the deil in the Lodge they aye said,
But they'll mend gin they miss him, ere a' plays be played.
To Cowan and craftsmen we're punctual and just,
Nae tattlers, nae triflers, nae babblers we trust;
My state may be higher than some wha mair pray,
When I'm in my lang hame—the cauld bed o' clay.

Nae mair will I gang while on this side o' time
Ae step nearer light in the Order sublime;
Nae mair will I meet you, or at night the door bar,
To enter the novice both curious and scaur;
Nae mair to behold you I'll glow with delight,
To see a' the brethren in friendship unite;
I aft hae been wi' you, but soon I maun stay
Confined in my lang hame—the cauld bed o' clay.

Move round, sons of fellowship, yearly move on,
On the lang summer's day make a feast to St. John,
Let love, truth, and justice your actions command,
And shew faith and truth by the waving your hand;
Let virtuous actions the spitefu' defy,
The orphan protect, and the needfu' supply;
Live up, to your principles; oh! that you may
When I'm in my lang hame—the cauld house o' clay.

You'll bury with honour the poor widow's son,
While the crowds from the old wall look curiously on;
With uplifted arms and in silence profound
You'll announce my downfa' as the password goes round.
When lost among nettles, you'll find if you search,
The stone of remembrance is decked wi' an arch :
I'm very low, brethren ; pray wake me to-day,
And then take me hame to my cauld house o' clay.

ANON.

THE MERRY BACHELOR.

WILLIE was a wanton wag,
  The blythest lad that e'er I saw ;
At field and floor he was the brag,
  And carried a' the gree awa'.
And wasna Willie stark and keen
  When he gaed to the weapon-shaw ;
He won the prizes on the green,
  And cheered the feasters in the ha'.

His head was wise, his heart was leal,
  His truth was fair without a flaw,
And aye by every honest chiel
  His word was holden as a law.
And wasna Willie still our pride
  When in his gallant gear arrayed
He won the broose and kissed the bride,
  When pipes the wedding welcome played !

And aye he led the foremost dance
  Wi' winsome maidens buskit braw,
And gave to each a merry glance
  That stole awhile her heart awa' ;
The bride forgot her simple groom,
  And every lass her trysted Joe,
Yet nae man's brow on Will could gloom,
  They liked his rousing blytheness so.

Our good Mess John laughed wi' the lave,
  The dominie, for a' his lair,
Could scarcely like himself behave
  While a' was glee and revel there.
A joyous sight was Willie's face,
  Baith far and near in ilka spot ;
In ha' received wi' kindly grace,
  And welcomed to the lowly cot.

The carlin left her housewife's wark,
  The bairnies shouted Willie's name;
The colley, too, would fidge and bark,
  And wag his tail when Willie came.
But Willie now has crossed the main,
  And he has been sae lang awa';
Oh! would he were returned again
  To drive the doufness frae us a'.

J. BAILLIE.

WOOED AN' MARRIED AN' A'.

THE bride she is winsome and bonnie,
  Her hair it is snooded fu' sleek,
And faithfu' and kind is her Johnny,
  Yet fast fa' the tears on her cheek.
New pearlins are cause o' her sorrow,
  New pearlins and plenishin' too;
The bride that has a' to borrow
  Has e'en right muckle ado.
        Wooed an' married an' a'!
        Wooed an' married an' a'!
        Is na' she very weel aff
          To be wooed and married at a'?

Her mother then hastily spak:
  "The lassie is glaikit wi' pride;
In my pouch I had never a plack
  On the day that I was a bride.
E'en tak to your wheel and be clever,
  And draw out your thread in the sun;
The gear that is gifted, it never
  Will last like the gear that is won."
        Wooed and married and a';
          Wi' havin's and tocher sae sma',
        I think ye are very weel aff
          To be wooed and married at a'.

" Toot, toot ! " quo' the grey-headed faither,
   " She's less o' a bride than a bairn ;
She's taen like a cowte frae the heather,
   Wi' sense and discretion to learn.
Half-husband, I trow, and half-daddy,
   As humour inconstantly leans ;
The chiel maun be patient and steady,
   That yokes wi' a mate in her teens.
      A kerchief sae douce and sae neat,
         O'er her locks that the win' used to blaw ;
      I'm baith like to laugh and to greet,
         When I think o' her married ava."

Then out spak the wily bridegroom,
   Weel waled were his wordies, I ween :
" I'm rich, though my coffer be toom,
   Wi' the blinks o' your bonnie blue e'en,
I'm prouder o' thee by my side,
   Though thy ruffles and ribbons be few,
Than Kate o' the Craft were my bride,
   Wi' purfloes an' pearlins enow.
      Dear, and dearest of ony !
         Ye're dearest and buikit and a' ;
      And do you think scorn o' your Johnny,
         And grieve to be married at a' ? "

She turned, and she blushed, and she smiled,
   And she lookit sae bashfully doon ;
The pride o' heart was beguiled,
   And she played wi' the sleeves o' her gown ;
She twirled the tag o' her lace,
   And she nippit her boddice sae blue,
Syne blinkit sae sweet in his face,
   And aff like a maukin she flew.
      Wooed and married an' a',
         Wi' Johnny to roose her an' a' ;
      She thinks hersel very weel aff,
         To be wooed and married an' a' !

                              JOANNA BAILLIE.

DAYLIGHT WOOIN'.

IT was on a morn when we were thrang,
  The kirn it crooned, the cheese was making,
  And bannocks on the girdle baking,
When ane at the door chappit loud and lang.
Yet the auld gudewife and her Mays sae tight,
  Of a' this bauld din took sma' notice, I ween ;
For a chap at the door, in braid daylight,
  Is no like a chap that's heard at e'en.

But the jocky auld laird of the Warlock Glen,
  Wha waited without, half-blate, half-cheery,
  And langed for a sight o' his winsome deary,
Raised up the latch, and cam crously ben.
His coat it was new, and his o'erlay white,
  His mittens and hose were cosy and bein ;
But a wooer that comes in braid daylight,
  Is no like a wooer that comes at e'en.

He greeted the carline and lasses sae braw,
  And his bare lyart pow sae smoothly he straiket,
  And he lookit about, like a body half glaiket,
On bonny sweet Nanny, the youngest o' a'.
" Ha, laird ! " quo the carline, " and look ye that way ?
  Fy, let nae sic fancies bewilder ye clean ;
An elderly man, in the noon o' the day,
  Should be wiser than youngsters that come at e'en."

" Na, na," quo the pawky auld wife, " I trow
  You'll no fash your head wi' a youthfu' gilly
  As wild and as skeigh as a muirland filly;
Black Madge is far better and fitter for you."
He humm'd and haw'd, and he drew in his mouth,
  And he sqeezed the blue bonnet his twa hands between,
For a wooer that comes when the sun's i' the south
  Is mair landward than wooers that come at e'en.

"Black Madge is sae carefu'."   "What's that to me?"
"She's sober and eident, has sense in her noddle;
She's douce and respeckit"—"I care no a boddle—
Love winna be guided, and fancy's free."
Madge tossed back her head wi' a saucy slight,
    And Nancy loud laughing ran out to the green,
For a wooer that comes when the sun is bright
    Is no like a wooer that comes at e'en.

Then awa' flung the laird, and loud muttered he:
    "A' the daughters of Eve, between Orkney and Tweed O,
    Black or fair, young or auld, dame or damsel or widow,
May gang in their pride to the deil for me!"
But the auld gudewife and her Mays sae tight
    Cared little for a' his stour banning, I ween,
For a wooer that comes in braid daylight
    Is no like a wooer that comes at e'en.

                                        J. BAILLIE.

THE AULD BEGGAR MAN.

THE auld cripple beggar cam jumpin', jumpin',
Hech! how the bodie was stumpin', stumpin',
His wee wooden leggie was dumpin', dumpin';
    Saw ye e'er sic a queer auld man?

And aye he hirpled and hoastit, hoastit,
Aye he stampit his foot and he boastit,
Ilka woman and maid he accostit;
    Saw ye e'er sic a queer auld man?

The auld wives cam hirplin' in scores frae the clachan,
The young wives cam rinnin', a' gigglin' an' lauchin',
The bairnies cam toddlin', a' jinkin' an' daffin,
    An' pookit the tails o' the queer auld man.

Out cam the young widows, a' blinkin' fu' meekly,
Out cam the young lasses, a' smirkin' fu' sweetly,
Out cam the auld maidens, a' bobbin' discreetly,
    An' got a bit smack frae the queer auld man.

Out cam the big blacksmith, a' smeekit an' duddy,
Out cam the fat butcher, a' greasy an' bloody,
Out cam the auld cartwright, the wee drucken bodie,
    And swore they would slaughter the queer auld man.

Out cam the lang weaver, wi' his biggest shuttle,
Out cam the short snab, wi' his sharp cutty whittle,
Out cam the young herd, wi' a big tattie beetle,
    An' swore they would batter the queer auld man.

The beggar he coost aff his wee wooden peg,
An' he showed them a brawny, sturdy leg;
I wat but the carle was strappin' an' gleg;
    Saw ye e'er sic a brisk auld man?

He thumpit the blacksmith hame to his wife;
He dumpit the butcher, wha ran for his life;
He chased the wee wright, wi' the butcher's sharp knife;
    Saw ye e'er sic a brave auld man?

He puffed on the weaver, he ran to his loom;
He shankit the snab hame to cobble his shoon;
He skelpit the herd, on his bog reed to croon;
    Saw ye e'er sic a strong auld man?

The wives o' the toun then a' gathered about him,
An' loudly an' blythely the bairnies did shout him,
An' hooted the loons wha had threatened to clout him;
    Kenn'd ye e'er sic a lucky auld man?

                                        BALLANTYNE.

TIBBIE FOWLER.

TIBBIE FOWLER o' the Glen,
   There's owre mony wooin' at her;
Tibbie Fowler o' the Glen,
   There's owre mony wooin' at her.
Wooin' at her, pu'in' at her,
   Courtin' at her, canna get her;
Filthy elf, it's a' for pelf
   That a' the lads are wooin' at her.

Ten cam east, and ten cam west,
   Ten cam rowin' owre the water,
Twa cam doun the lang dyke side;
   There's twa-and-thirty wooin' at her.
There's seven but, and seven ben,
   Seven in the pantry wi' her;
Twenty head about the door;
   There's ane-and-forty wooin' at her.

She's got pendles in her lugs;
   Cockle shells wad set her better!
High heel'd shoon and siller tags,
   And a' the lads are wooin' at her.

Altho' a lass was ne'er sae black,
   If she hae the penny siller,
Set her on a Tintock Tap,
   The win' will blaw a man till her!
But tho' a lass were ne'er sae fair,
   If she want the penny siller,
She may stand for evermair,
   Ere there come a man till her!

There are different opinions respecting the age and the authorship of
this song. It first appeared in 1787 in Johnson's "Museum;" a fragment
was published by Herd in 1776. R. Chambers, finding a Tibbie Fowler
married to young Logan of Restalrig in the 16th century, concludes she

is the Tibbie of the song. It may be so, but the pointed reference to
Tinto shows the writer was acquainted with Clydesdale. There is a
tradition that a minister of Carnwath was the writer, which is not
unlikely.

SAE WILL WE YET.

COME sit down, my cronies, and gie us yer crack,
Let the win' tak the cares o' this life on its back,
Our hearts to despondency we never will submit,
For we've aye been provided for and sae will we yet.
                    And sae will we yet, &c.

Let the miser delight in the hoarding of pelf,
Since he has not the saul to enjoy it himself:
Since the bounty of Providence is new every day,
As we journey thro' life let us live by the way.
                    Let us live by the way, &c.

Success to the farmer, and prosper his plough,
Rewarding his eident toils a' the year through !
Our seed-time and harvest we ever will get,
For we've lippened aye to Providence, and sae will we yet.
                    And sae will we yet, &c.

Long live the Queen, and happy may she be,
And success to her forces by land and by sea !
Our enemies to conquer her we never will permit,
For we've aye been victorious, and sae will we yet.
                    And sae will we yet, &c.

                              WALTER WATSON.

Walter Watson was a weaver in Chryston; died in 1854, in his 75th
year.

TRANENT WEDDING.

IT was at a wedding at Tranent,
Where scores an' scores on fun were bent,
An' to ride the broose wi' full intent
    Was either nine or ten, jo !

    Then aff they a' set gallopin', gallopin' !
    Legs an' arms a' wallopin', wallopin' ;
    Shame tak' the hindmost, quo Duncan M'Callopin,
    Laird o' Tullyben, jo.

The souter he was fidgin' fain,
An' stuck like rozet till the mane,
Till smash like auld boots in a drain,
    He nearly reached his end, jo !
            Yet still they a' gaed, &c.

The miller's mare flew owre the souter,
An' syne began to glower about her ;
Cries Hab, " I'll gie you double mouter,
    Gin ye'll ding Tullyben, jo ! "
            Then still they gaed, &c.

Now Will, the weaver, rade sae kittle,
Ye'd thought he was a flying shuttle,
His doup it daddet like a bittle,
    But wafted till the end, jo ?
            Yet still they a' gaed, &c.

The tailor had an awkward beast,
It funket first, and syne did reest,
Then threw poor snipe an ell at least,
    Like auld breeks owre the mane, jo !
            Yet a' the rest gaed, &c.

The blacksmith's beast was last o' a',
Its sides like bellowses did blaw,
Till he an' it got sic a fa',
    An' bruises nine or ten, jo !
        An' still the lave gaed, &c.

Now Duncan's mare she flew like drift,
An' aye sae fast her feet did lift,
Between ilk stenn she gae a rift
    Out frae her hinder end, jo !
        Yet aff they a' gaed, &c.

Now Duncan's mare did bang them a',
To rin wi' him they maunna fa' ;
Then up his grey mare he did draw—
    The broose it was his ain, jo !

    Nae mair wi' him they'll gallop, they'll gallop,
    Nae mair wi' him they'll wallop, they'll wallop,
    Or they may chance to get some jallop,
    Frae the Laird o' Tullyben, jo !

PETER FORBES.

Peter Forbes was a gardener at Dalkeith. The "Tranent Wedding"
is a spirited and graphic picture of a custom at marriages in the country
districts in Scotland, which we do not recollect being noticed anywhere
except in Scottish Song. As soon as the minister utters the emphatic
words—"*I declare you married persons*," those who mean to run, or ride
the *broose*, start as hard as their feet or their horses can carry them, to the
house of the bridegroom : the first there announces the marriage ; gets
a bottle and returns to meet the bridal party, when all are treated with
a glass to drink the health and happiness of the new married couple.
After this ceremony, the brooseman throws the bottle from him as far as
he can, although it should not be half emptied, and the glass after it.
Such is the custom of country weddings in Clydesdale.

N

BABITY BOWSTER.

"Wha learned you to dance, Babity Bowster, Babity
  Bowster,
Wha learned you to dance, caperin' Betsy Ben, O ?"
"Oh ! my mother learned me to dance, Babity Bowster,
  Babity Bowster ;
My mother learned me to dance, and that richt weel ye
  ken, jo."

"But wha gied you the keys to keep, Babity Bowster,
  Babity Bowster ;
Wha gied you the keys to keep, caperin' Betsy Ben, O ?"
"Oh ! my mother gied me the keys to keep, the keys to keep,
My mother gied me the keys to keep, and that richt weel
  ye ken, jo.   As Sung in Upper Clydesdale.

GLASGOW FAIR.

Oh ! the sun frae the eastward was peeping,
    And braid through the winnocks did stare,
When Willie cried—"Tam, are you sleeping ?
    Make haste, man, and rise to the fair ;
For the lads and the lasses are thranging,
    And a' body's noo in a steer ;
Fy, haste and let us be ganging,
    Or faith we'll be langsome, I fear." .
                    Lilt te turan an uran, &c.

Then Tam he got up in a hurry,
    And wow but he made himsel' snod,
And a pint o' milk brose he did worry,
    To make him mair teugh for the road ;
On his head his blue bonnet he slippet,
    His whip owre his shouther he flang,
And a clumsy oak cudgel he gruppet
    On purpose the loons for to bang.
                    Lilt te turan an uran, &c.

Now Willock had trystet wi' Jenny,
    For she was a braw canty queen,
Word gaed that she had a gay penny,
    For which Willie fondly did green.
Now Tam he was blaming the liquor,
    Yae nicht he had got himsel' fu',
And trysted gleed Maggy M'Vicar,
    And faith he thocht shame for to rue.
            Lilt te turan an uran, &c.

The carles, fu' cadgie, sat cracking
    Upon their white nags and their brown,
Wi' snuffing and laughing and joking,
    They soon cantered into the town ;
And there was the funning and sporting—
    Eh, me ! what a swarm o' braw folk—
Rowly-powly, wild beasts, wheel o' fortune,
    Sweety stan's, Maister Punch, an' Black Jock.
            Lilt te turan an uran, &c.

Now Willock and Tam, gay an' bousie,
    By this time had met wi' their joes,
Consented wi' Gibbie and Susie
    To gang awa' down to the shows ;
And there was the fiddling and drumming,
    Sic a crowd they could scarcely get through,
Fiddles, trumpets, and organs a bumming—
    Oh, sirs ! what a hullabaloo !
            Lilt te turan an uran, &c.

Then hie to the tents at the paling,
    Weel thacket wi' blankets and mats,
And deals seated round like a tap-room,
    Supported on stanes and on pats ;
The whisky like water they're selling,
    And porter as sma' as their yill,
And aye as you're pouring they're telling,
    " Troth, dear, it's just sixpence the gill."
            Lilt te turan an uran, &c.

Says Meg, " See yon beast wi' the claes on't,
    Wi' the face o't as black as the soot,
Preserve's ! it has fingers and taes on't—
    Eh, lass, it's an unco like brute !"
" O woman, but ye are a gomeral,
    To mak sic a wonder at that,
D'ye na ken, you daft gowk, that's a mongrel
    That's bred 'twixt a dog and a cat."
                Lilt te turan an uran, &c.

"See yon supple jade how she's dancing,
    Wi' the white ruffled breeks and red shoon,
Frae the tap to the toe she's a' glancing
    Wi' gowd, and a feather aboon.
My troth, she's a braw decent kimmer
    As I have yet seen in the fair."
" Her decent," quo' Meg ; " she's a limmer,
    Or faith she would never be there."
                Lilt te turan an uran, &c.

Now Gibbie was wantin' a toothfu :
    Says he, " I'm richt tired o' the fun,
D'ye think we'd be waur o' a mouthfu'
    O' gude nappy yill and a bun ?"
" Wi' a' my heart," says Tam, " I'm willing ;
    It's best to water the corn.
By jing ! I've a bonnie white shilling,
    And a saxpence that ne'er saw the morn."
                Lilt te turan an uran, &c.

Before they got out o' the bustle,
    Puir Tam got his fairing, I trow,
For a stick at the gingebread played whistle,
    And knocked him doon like a cow.
Says Tam, " Wha did that, deil confoond him ;
    Fair play, let me win at the loon."
And he whirled his stick round and round him,
    And swore like a very dragoon.
                Lilt te turan an uran, &c.

Then next for a house they gaed glowering,
  Where they might get wetting their mou,
Says Meg, " Here's a house keeps a pouring,
  Wi' the sign o' the Muckle Black Cow."
" A cow," quo Jenny, " ye gawkie !
  Preserve us but ye've little skill ;
Did ye e'er see a hawkie like that ?
  Look again and ye'll see its a bill ! "
          Lilt te turan an uran, &c.

But just as they darkened the entry,
  Says Willie, " We're now far enough,
I see it's a house for the gentry—
  Let's gang to the sign o' the Pleugh."
" Na faith," then says Gibbie, " we'se rather
  Gae daunner to auld Luckie Gun's,
For there I'm to meet wi' my faither,
  And auld uncle John o' the Whins."
          Lilt te turan an uran, &c.

Now they a' in Luckie's had landed,
  Twa rounds o' the bicker to try ;
The whisky and yill round was handed,
  And baps in great bannocks did lie.
Blind Aleck the fiddler was trysted,
  And he was to handle the bow :
On a big barrel head he was hoisted,
  To keep himsel' out o' the row.
          Lilt te turan an uran, &c.

Had ye seen sic a din and guffawing,
  Sic hooching and dancing was there ;
Sic rugging, and riving, and drawing
  Was ne'er seen before at a fair ;
For Tam he wi' Maggie was wheeling,
  And he gied sic a terrible loup
That his head came a thump on the ceiling,
  And down wi' a dump on his doup !
          Lilt te turan an uran, &c.

Now they ate and they drank till their bellies
   Were bent like the head o' a drum ;
Syne they raise and they capered like fillies
   Whene'er that the fiddle played bum.
Wi' dancing they now were grown weary,
   And scarcely were able to stan',
So they took to the road a' fu' cheery,
   As day was beginning to dawn.
                  Lilt te turan an uran, &c.

Glasgow, 1820.   JOHN BRECKENRIDGE, COMPOSITOR.

I'LL GAR OUR GUIDMAN TROW.

I'LL gar our guidman trow
   That I'll sell the ladle,
If he winna buy to me
   A bonnie side saddle
To ride to kirk and bridal—to ride to kirk and bridal
   And round about the town—
Then stand about, ye fisher jauds,
   And gie my gown room !

And I'll gar our guidman trow,
   I'll tak' the fling strings,
If he winna buy to me
   Twal bonnie goud rings ;
I'll ane for ilka finger—I'll ane for ilka finger,
   Ay, and twa for ilka thoom—
Stand round about, ye fisher jauds,
   And gie my gown room !

And I'll gar our guidman trow
   That I'm gaun to dee,
If he winna hire to me
   Valets two or three,
To bear my train up frae the dirt—to bear my train up
   frae the dirt
      And ush me through the town—
Then stand about, ye fisher jauds,
   And gie my braws room !

And I'll gar our guidman trow
That I'll tak the pet,
If he winna buy to me
A braw beaver hat,
Wi' gold about the edges o't—wi' gold about the edges o't,
And a feather in the croon—
Then stand around, ye fisher jauds,
And gie my braws room !

FIRST PUBLISHED IN 1824.

ADDRESS TO WILLIAM BERTRAM, Esq.,

ON AGAIN TAKING POSSESSION OF THE PATERNAL MANSION AFTER
AN ABSENCE OF FIVE YEARS.

Clydesdale people have no sympathy with the Landlord Shooting
Disease which afflicts the people of the Green Island.

SCION of a noble race,
Who never feared their foes to face,
Welcome to your natal place—
       Welcome home to Kersewell !

Welcome to fair Kersewell's towers,
Welcome to its peaceful bowers,
Wecome as the summer flowers,
       Welcome home to Kersewell !

The lambkin's bleatin' on the lea,   ⸢
The wee bird's singin' on the tree,
The gentle humming of the bee
       Is welcome home to Kersewell.

Long, long we did thy absence mourn ;
Sair, sair our hearts with grief were torn ;
With joy we now hail thy return,
       And welcome thee to Kersewell !

Come and make the orphans smile,
Come and make cauld care resile,
Come and cheer the sons of toil,
       And welcome to fair Kersewell !

The widow now has ceased to wail,
And hearts, once sick, are now quite hale,
And cheeks are bright which once were pale,
     Since ye came home to Kersewell?

Blessings on thy lady fair !
Blessings on thy son and heir !
And on all thy children rare !
     Blessings on fair Kersewell !

May every virtue, every grace,
Adorn bold Bertram's honoured race ;
Accept Carnwath's sincere embrace,
     And welcome home to Kersewell!

                                   W. G.

This gentleman is the descendant and representative of Guilelmes de
Bertram, who came into Britain with William the Conqueror.

———

The people of Clydesdale are not wanting in respect to their superiors,
as the following lines, no less than the preceding, will shew.

WELCOME FOR LORD AND LADY DOUGLAS
TO BOTHWELLL CASTLE.

THIS happy hour makes rich amends
     For many a silent year,
Through which fair Bothwell's noble halls
     Deserted did appear.

No joyous mirth, no revelry,
     As once full sway held there ;
And high born dames, with gallant knights,
     That revelry did share.

Yet ofttimes in my youthful days,
     Glad birth-days I have seen,
When old and young assembled were
     And danced upon the green.

And all abundantly supplied
  With bounteous good cheer ;
The Douglas birthdays were a talk
  To all both far and near.

Then raise aloud the welcome shout,
  All hearts beat wild with joy !
This day be one of pure delight,
  Unmixed without alloy.

For Home's young lord brings home his bride
  To Bothwell's fair domains ;
Long life and happiness attend
  Those names, so dear to fame.

And she has come, a sweet young bride,
  In artless loveliness ;
And all those gentler virtues has
  That make a fireside blest.

And oh ! that he may long be spared
  To grace the name he bears,
And cherish tenderly his bride
  Through many happy years.

May richest blessings rest upon
  Douglas's happy choice,
And Bothwell Castle be the home
  Of pure domestic joys.

And may their much-loved, honoured name
  Still flourish and increase,
And may their lives be lives of love,
  Their end, be one of peace.

                              M. C., UDDINGSTON.

COVINGTON MILL.

Lives there a man, who all unmoved can tread
Above the dust of the immortal dead ?
Who this historic land can travel round
Nor find one spot of consecrated ground.
Oh ! let not such a heartless piece of stone
Set foot upon the soil of Covington ;
For there, at northern base of Tinto hill,
Was dragged to death the godly, good Cargill.

Still stands the house wherein the man of God,
That fatal day, had found his last abode ;
All lonesome now these sad and silent walls—
And yet their sight such memories recalls,
That house from me more reverence demands
Than proudest palace built by human hands.

My native land, this praise to thee is due,
Thy chosen heroes never have been few.
I speak not of her kings, who, as a race,
Have done the royal sceptre no disgrace ;
Nor of our nobles, who may proudly stand
Comparison with chivalry of any land—
I speak of men employed in daily toil,
Artificers, and tenants of the soil.

Men of the Covenant, all good and true—
When friends to Christ were faithless, faint, and few—
Who, viewed as metals, were the genuine gold,
Old Roman valour cast in Christian mould ;
Loving their Lord as the apostles loved,
And, like the twelve, in front of death unmoved.

Some call them traitors ; 'tis with scorn denied—
To their oppressors be the term applied ;
True to their God, nor to their king untrue,
Their hearts were breaking whilst their swords they drew.

Some call them rebels; we the slander fling
Back on their profligate and perjured king,
Who, had he but one spark of honour shown,
Had found in them the pillars of his throne!

Ye noble souls! yours was the rising tide
The winds might ruffle but not turn aside;
Defeated oft, ye saw the battle plain
Drenched with your blood, and cumbered with the slain;
Their severed heads to gibbet-irons consigned,
To black and wither in the tainted wind.
Ye saw the weak down-trodden by the strong,
Unheard the cry, "How long, O Lord, how long?"
Till for a time, it seemed the Righteous One
Had ceased to reign, or slumbered on His throne.

Beneath this baptism of fire and blood,
Erect and unsubdued the martyrs stood,
With front defiant to the spoilers turned
Godwards—content to be the bush that burned.
Ah! may the mighty God raise up such men,
Should He in judgment send such times again.

REV. JAMES PROUDFOOT.

Donald Cargill was apprehended at Covington Mill, by Irving of
Bonshaw; and was executed at Edinburgh.

CARNWATH BRASS BAND.

CARNWATH Brass Band, Carnwath Brass Band;
O I never saw a band like Carnwath Brass Band:
Frae Orkney to Gretna, seek thro' a' the land
And ye'll never find a band like Carnwath Brass Band.

Carnwath Brass Band, a' are strappin' young men;
Some are six feet six, some are five feet ten;
Little Johnie is the crute, and Jamie wants a hand.
Yet, ye'll never find a band like Carnwath Brass Band!

When the band gaed to Biggar, a' the lasses were surprised,
To see a band o' men o' such wondroùs size,
In uniform so fine, and in stature so grand ;
O they never saw a band like Carnwath Brass Band !

Their music loud and strong, re-echoed to the skies,
The very hares and foxes were filled wi' surprise ;
Some little hills micht dance, but auld Tintoc made a stand,
Astonished at the strains o' Carnwath Brass Band !

At Biggar and Carluke they behaved unco weel ;
Did their duty and cam' hame without servin' the Deil ;
And when they were at Linton, astonished a' the land,[1]
Wi' the nimble footed powers o' Carnwath Brass Band.

But O ! the last St. John's day they got an unco' fa' ;
Altho' it was winter, it was neither frost nor snaw ;
Yet they drank themselves so drunk, that some could scarcely
    stand !
And wasna' that a shame to Carnwath Brass Band ?

The laddie wi' the red cap, that thumps the muckle drum,
Was so very fou, he could hardly gar't play *bum ;*
And Johnnie roared "The Ewie," when he wasna' fit to stand,
And wasna' that a shame to Carnwath Brass Band ?

Lang Jock's been often ill, but never was seen worse,
He was so doiled and dwabble, that he couldna' clean his horse,
But lay as he'd been shot at Sebastopol so grand—
And wasna' that a shame to Carnwath Brass Band ?

Lazy, leein' dirty Dan, got himsel' so clatty fou,
He was carried thro' the toon like a newly stickit sow !
In the smiddy lay in state, like a Satan's firebrand—
And wasna' that a shame to Carnwath Brass Band ?

---

[1] Of eight prizes for races at Linton, the Band brought seven to
Carnwath.

Young men o' the band, tak' an auld friend's advice,
Beware o' whisky drinking if ye wad be wise;
Carry on as ye've begun, and a bairn may understand,
Ye'll no very lang be Carnwath Brass Band!

BOTHWELL BRIG.

" O Billie, Billie, bonnie Billie !
   Will ye gang to the wood wi' me ?
We'll ca' our horse hame masterless,
   An' gar them trow slain men are we."

" Oh, no ! oh, no !" says Earlston,
   " For that's the thing that manna' be;
For I am sworn to Bothwell Hill,
   Where I maun either gae or dee."

So, in the morning Earlston rose,
   An' mounted up by break o' day;
An' he has joined oor Scottish lads,
   As they were marching out the way.

" Now, fareweel, father, and fareweel, mother,
   An' fareweel my sisters three ;
An' fareweel, my Earlston,
   For thee again I'll never see."

So they're awa' to Bothwell Hill,
   And waly they rode bonnily ;
When the Duke o' Monmouth saw them comin',
   He went to view their company.

" Ye're welcome, lads," then Monmouth said ;
   " Ye're welcome, brave Scots lads, to me ;
And sae, are ye brave Earlston,
   The foremost o' your company ?

"But yield your weapons, one and a';
  Oh, yield your weapons, lads, to me;
For gin ye'll yield your weapons up,
  Ye'll a' gae hame to your ain countree."

But, up then spak' a Lennox lad,
  And waly but he spoke bonnilee;
"I winna yield my weapons up
  To you, nor onie man I see."

Then he set up the flag o' red,
  A' set about wi' bonnie blue:
"Since ye'll no cease, and be at peace,
  See that ye stand by ither true."

They stelled their cannons on the height,
  And showered their shot down in the howe,
An' beat our Scots lads even down,
  Thick they lay slain on every knowe.

As ever ye saw the rain down fa',
  Or yet the arrow frae the bow,
Sae our Scots lads fell even down,
  An' they lay slain on every knowe.

"Oh, hold your hand," then Monmouth cried;
  "Gie quarters to your men for me!"
But wicked Clavers swore an oath,
  His cornet's death revenged s'ud be.

"Oh, hold your hand," then Monmouth cried;
  "If ony thing you'll do for me,
Hold up your hand, you cursed Græme,
  Or rebel to our king you'll be."

The wicked Clavers turned about,
  I wot an angry man was he;
And he has lifted up his hat,
  And cried, "God bless his Majesty."

Then he's awa to London town ;
Ay, e'en as fast as he can dree;
Fause witnesses he has wi' him taen,
An' taen Monmouth's head frae his bodie.

Along the brae, beyond the brig,
Mony brave men lye cauld an' still;
But lang we'll mind, and sair we'll rue
The bloody battle of Bothwell Hill.

THE DOUGLAS TRAGEDY.

The Ballad of the Douglas Tragedy is one of the few to which popular tradition has ascribed a complete locality. The town of Blackhouse, in Selkirkshire, is said to have been the scene of this melancholy event.

"Rise up, rise up, now !" Lord Douglas, she says,
"And put on your armour so bright,
Let it never be said that a daughter of thine
Was married to a lowlander knight.

"Rise up, rise up, my seven bold sons,
And put on your armour so bright,
And take better care of youngest sister
For your eldest's awa' the last night."

He's mounted her on a milk-white steed,
And himself on a dapple gray,
With a bright horn hung down by his side,
And lightly they rode away.

Lord William lookit o'er his left shoulder
To see what he could see,
And there he spied her seven brethren bold
Come riding o'er the lea.

"Light down ! light down ! Lady Margaret," he said,
    "And hold my steed in hand,
Until that against your seven brethren bold
    And your father I make stand !"

She held his steed in her milk-white hand,
    And never shed one tear,
Until that she saw her brethren fa',
    And her father hard fighting, wha loved her so dear.

"Oh ! hold your hand, Lord William," she said,
    "For your strokes they are wondrous sair ;
True lovers I can get many a' one,
    But a father I can never get mair."

Oh ! she has taen out her handkerchief,
    It was o' the holland sae fine,
And she dighted her father's bloody wounds
    That were redder than the wine.

"Oh chuse ! oh chuse ! Lady Margaret," he said ;
    "Oh, whether will ye gang or bide ? "
"I'll gang, I'll gang, Lord William," she said,
    "For ye have left me no other guide."

He's lifted her on a milk-white steed,
    And himself on a dapple gray,
With a bright horn hung down by his side,
    And slowly they baith rode away.

On, they rode on, and on they rode,
    And a' by the light o' the moon,
Until they cam' to yon wan water,
    And there they lighted down.

They lighted down to tak' a drink
    Of the spring that ran so clear ;
And down the stream ran his gude heart's blude,
    And sair she 'gan to fear.

" Hold up, hold up! Lord William," she says,
  " For I fear that you are slain ! "
" 'Tis naething but the shadow of my scarlet cloak
  That shines on the water sae plain."

Oh! on they rade, and they rade on,
  And a' by the licht o' the moon,
Until they cam' to his mother's ha' door,
  And there they lighted down.

"Get up, get up! Lady Mother," he says,
  "Get up and let me in!
Get up, get up! Lady Mother," he says,
  For this night my fair Lady I've won.

" Oh! mak' my bed, Lady Mother," he says,
  " Oh mak' it braid and deep!
And lay Lady Margaret close at my back,
  And the sounder I will sleep."

Lord William was dead long ere midnight—
  Lady Margaret ere the day ;
And all true lovers that go thegither,
  May they have mair good luck than they !

Lord William was buried in St. Marie's Kirk,
  Lady Margaret in Marie's Choir ;
Out o' the lady's grave grew a bonnie red rose,
  And out o' the knight's a brier.

And the twa met, and the twa plat,
  And fain they wad be near ;
And a' the world might ken right weel
  They were twa lovers dear.

And by and by rade the black Douglas,
  And wow but he was rough ;
For he pulled up the bonnie red brier,
  And flang't in St. Marie's Loch.

o

ADIEU TO CLYDESDALE.

A COLD December's wintry sun
   Had ushered in a cheerless day,
When I to leave my native land,
   Reluctantly was called away.

Deep lay the snow, like winding sheet,
   O'er level lawn and distant hill ;
And silence had the murmurs hushed
   Of river and of distant rill.

And when each cairn and mountain top
   Receded slowly from the view,
They seemed like loving, lingering friends,
   All loath to take a last adieu.

But oh ! to pass the cherished spot,
   My home, my Eden, and my pride ;
Where I so long had happy been,
   Within the murmurs of the Clyde.

Sweet are the landscapes on the Clyde,
   But none of them can e'er excel
The lovely dale that lies between
   Great Tinto Hill and Coulter Fell.

Could I my life live o'er again,
   And dearest wishes all fulfil,
My choice would still be on the Clyde,
   My dwelling would be near Cornhill.

And yet, that river were a waste,
   And that fair vale no more were fair
Without the presence of the friends
   Who have their home and dwelling there.

Long, long be it their happy home,
Their cares and sorrows be but few ;
Long may they live to walk with God,
When I have bid them all adieu.

These lines are believed to be the last lines written by the Rev. James Proudfoot, the late much respected Free Church minister of Coulter, on leaving his home, to which, alas! he never returned.   He died at Lower Norwood, London, on the 15th November, 1876, in the 50th year of his ministry, 16 of which were spent in the Established, and 33 in the Free Church.   His friends will not do justice to his memory if they do not gather together, for publication, his poetical and literary productions, which were of a very superior order.

RICHIE STORRIE.

The Earl of Wigton, who died in 1665, by his lady, Jane Drummond, a daughter of the Earl of Perth, had five sons and three daughters. Lilias, the second daughter, fell in love with one of her father's servants, named Richard Storrie, eloped, and succeeded in forming with him a matrimonial union. The family afterwards obtained for Storrie a situation in the Custom-house. The marriage of this pair made a great noise at the time, and gave rise to the following ballad :—

THE Erle o' Wigton had daughters three,
O braw wallie, they were bonnie ;
The youngest o' them, an' the bonniest too,
Has fa'en in love wi' Richie Storrie.

" Here's a letter for you, fair lady," he said ;
" Here's a letter for you, my lady ;
The Erle o' Home wad fain presume
To be a suitor to you, my lady."

" I'll hae nane o' your letters, Richie," she said ;
" I'll hae nane o' that letter frae you ;
For I hae made a vow, and I'll keep it true,
That I will marry nane but you."

"O do not say so, fair lady," he said !
"O do not say so, my lady so true ;
For I've neither castles, nor land, nor rent,
    In health and comfort to keep you.

"And ye maun wear ribbons, and pearlins, and rings,
    And silks and satins so fine, lady,
And laces around your bonnie white neck,
    O' the goud that shines so fine, lady."

"I'll lie 'yont a dyke, dear Richie," she said ;
"Wi' you I would lie 'yont a dyke,
And I'll aye be obedient to your command
    And bide wi' you whaur ye like.

"Fair Powmoodie is mine, dear Richie,
    And goud and pearlins too ;
Gin ye'll consent to be mine, dear Richie,
    I will gie them a' to you."

O he's gone away on the braid, braid road,
    And she's gane thro' the broom so bonnie ;
Her silken robes flowed down to her heels,
    And she's awa wi' Richie Storrie.

The lady gaed up the Parliament stairs,
    Wi' pendles in her lugs so bonnie ;
Many a lord lifted his hat frae his hair,
    But never dreamed she was Richie's lady.

Up then spak' the Erle o' Home's lady—
    "O Lily ! warna ye richt sorrie
To leave the lands o' bonnie Cumbernauld
    And follow on wi' Richie Storrie ? "

"O what need I be sorrie, Ladie Home ;
    O what need I be sorrie ?
For I've gotten the lad that I like best, Ladie Home,
    And that's my ain dear Richie Storrie.

" And I've gotten the lad was ordained for me,
　And that's my ain dear Richie Storrie,
　And I wadna' gie him for your proud, proud lord,
　To change, indeed, I wad be sorrie ! "

Boghall Castle, Biggar, was for many centuries the residence of the
Earls of Wigton.

CLYDESDALE FOLK.

On Yarrow braes and Ettrick shaws beat leal, leal hearts
　and warm,
In men, and dames, and lovely maids, that cheer alike and
　charm ;
But lealer hearts and fairer forms are no in Scotland wide,
Than those that trace and sweetly grace the bonnie banks o'
　Clyde.

The Tweed rows down his water far along yon mountain
　glen,
Where lovely rills and lofty hills are round the hames o'
　men ;
But Tintock rears a prouder crest, and guards a fairer tide,
In casting his broad shadow o'er the valleys o' the Clyde.

Where glow the hearths as erst they glowed, wi' them we
　left behind ;
Where love and worth combined to bless the kindest of the
　kind,
And bright intelligence lits up the fare, they freely there
　provide,
When couthily they crack within the happy hames o' Clyde.

May peace and plenty dwell wi' them, who still are dwellers
　there ;
May love the sunny ringlets wreathe, and wit the hoary
　hair ;

And sympathies that aye are young immingles life's ain tide,
While harps are strung, and songs are sung, on the bonnie
banks o' Clyde.

H. SCOTT RIDDELL.

DOLLERIE MILLS.

Dollerie Mills! Dollerie Mills!
I'll ne'er forget Dollerie Mills!
My bosom swells, my e'e it fills,
When I think on Dollerie Mills.

Oh! there I spent life's early days,
In sporting on Dollerie's braes;
And bathed my feet in Turret's rills,
Swift gliding by Dollerie Mills.

And when I think on dear Dalvreck,
What it was once, now what a wreck!
Again the briny tear distils
For it, and dear Dollerie Mills.

My father and my mother dear,
My brothers and my sisters fair,
Your pictures still my memory fills
When I think on Dollerie Mills.

Dollerie! what a lovely scene!
Dollerie's woods are fresh and green;
Her evening song the mavis trills
So sweetly at Dollerie Mills.

Though short my span of life has been,
Yet many changes I have seen,
And many hearts the cold grave fills
That loved me at Dollerie Mills.

Our uncle James, and uncle John,
Aunt Isabell, they all are gone ;
The thought my heart with sorrow fills,
They'll ne'er see more Dollerie Mills.

But we'll meet again in the heavens high
Above yon stars, and above yon sky,
Where rapture every bosom fills—
Far, far, from dear Dollerie Mills.

JOHN M'EWAN.

In memoriam of James, John, and Isabell M'Owen, all most respectable people of Dalvreck and Crieff, whose remains repose in the churchyard of Monzie, near Crieff.

THE WESTPORT TREE.

THE old tree ! the good old tree ! and is it down at last ?
Full many a winter it hath stood each rude tempestuous blast;
Through the summer time of beauty, verdant clad for many
    a year,
It hath reared its giant timbers, to an old age grey and sere.

Oh, would that tree had language ! what might it not unfold,
Of scenes in which it bore a part, far in the days of old ?
Race after race have sprung since then, and fallen to decay,
Unmoved there stood that aged trunk, with aspect cold and
    grey.

Wallace the brave !—in Scottish hearts so fondly yet en-
    shrined—
Rode past with silken banners gaily floating in the wind ;
His little band of followers, so trusty, tried, and true,
Clinging round with deep devotion—it had them all in view.

That tree hath been the centre place of many a joyous game,
In happy childhood's blythesome hours, as sorrows went and
    came ;

Tiny feet and sunny faces, young hearts yet full of glee,
Have danced in boist'rous merriment around the Westport
tree.

Where are those merry children now ?   Some, scattered far
and wide,
Have left for lands across the sea their native vale of Clyde ;
Yet still in memory they will trace the merry days of yore,
And grieve to hear the Westport tree is standing now no
more.

LANARK.

WANT O' SILLER.

Oh, the weary want o' siller !
Oh, the waefu' want o' siller !
It maks na what be in your pow,
If your pouch be bare o' siller.

It's waur than a' the woes o' life,
And sair benumb a bodie's noddle,
For wit and lair without the pelf
Is never reckoned worth a bodle.
Oh, the weary want o' siller, &c.

I've written books, baith prose an' verse,
With mony a roosin' dedication ;
But nane wad tent the puir baugh chiel—
There's nought for me but black starvation.
Oh, the weary want o' siller, &c.

I've been in love out owre the lugs,
As mony a chiel has been afore me,
But 'cause my mailen was sae sma',
The saucy limmers did abhor me.
Oh, the weary want o' siller, &c.

An' oh, but my ain shanks be sma',
My nose is sharp as ony filler;
Grim death will soon hae me awa';
Ohone! ohone! the want o' siller!
    Oh, the weary want o' siller, &c.

ANON.

THE DEATH OF DR. LIVINGSTONE.

" BUILD me a hut to die in,
    'Tis all I ask of man;
A little place to lie in,
    And end life's weary span.
Thence shall my weary spirit ·
    · Fly up to Jesus' breast,
And through His grace inherit
    An everlasting rest!"

They built a hut, and laid him
    Upon his lowly bed;
Then tenderly did aid him,
    Till the weary spirit fled.
His precious dust—they bore it
    O'er mountain, stream, and plain;
And yon ship did restore it
    To Britain's coast again.

Put on thy mourning, London,
    And take with tears the trust;
From sunrise until sundown,
    Gaze on his glorious dust:
Then open wide the Abbey,
    Reserved for famous men—
The warrior and the rabbi,
    Made great by sword and pen.

"Prepare the traveller's mansion,"
   I hear them say in heaven;
" Let it have a wide expansion,
   No stinted space be given.
Small was the Afric shieling
   In which he breathed his last;
But splendid be his dwelling,
   When all his toils are past."

I see him 'mid the glory,
   With his father and his wife,
Recounting all the story
   Of his eventful life.
And, hark! there come faint traces
   Of the great man's heavenly words :
What are they? " Afric's races
   Shall soon become the Lord's."

Recited by the Rev. Fergus Ferguson at the soiree of Hamiltonians at
Glasgow on 12th February, 1875. On the eve of one of his great battles
Nelson said, "Now for a peerage or Westminster Abbey." It is certainly a notable fact, that a Clydesdale cotton-spinner should have a
grave in that splendid mausoleum; and we have no hesitation in saying
that few there, if any, were better entitled to such an honour.

WISHAW GILL.

'MANG scenes of grandeur tho' I rove,
   By glen or tow'ring hill,
There's nought seems so enchanting
   To me as Wishaw Gill.
Oh! there I spent life's sunny days,
   Ere care my heart did fill,
And dear to me is that auld road
   That winds thro' Wishaw Gill.

And that wee burn o' Temple Ha'—
   It's music mak's me thrill,
It sings a cheering welcome aye
   To me in Wishaw Gill.

I often sit and ponder now,
    Down by Coltness auld mill,
And those that sleep in yon kirkyard
    Seem with me in the Gill.

Fond brothers seem to live again,
    And wander there at will;
Ance more I dream we're gathered a'
    And singin' in the Gill,
Or joining with the grand old band
    The echoing woods to fill;
Those strains seem floating still around
    The banks o' Wishaw Gill.

Thus memory reads a glowing page
    I love to think of still,
Again I feel that happiness
    O' langsyne in the Gill;
But like a dream they pass away,
    And all again is still,
And mournfully I sit and sigh
    Alone in Wishaw Gill.

                                    ANON.

JACOBITE SONG.

Tune—" Auld Langsyne."

O Caledon ! O Caledon ! how wretched is thy fate,
I, thy St. Andrew, do lament your poor unhappy state ;
O Caledon ! O Caledon ! how grieved am I to think,
Your sad story written is—with blood instead of ink.

In days of yore you were renowned, conspicuous was your
    fame,
All nations did your valour praise and loyalty proclaim ;
Your ancient rights you did maintain, and liberty defend,
And scorned to have it thought that you on England did
    depend.

Unto your kings you did adhere, stood by the royal race,
And with them honours great did gain, and paths of glory
    trace;
With royal Stuart at your head, all enemies did oppose,
And, like your brave heroic clans, in pieces cut your foes.

Your kings did justice then dispense, and led you on to fight,
And your stupendous courage was, like their example, bright;
A happy people then you were, with plenty did abound,
And your undaunted loyalty with blessings great was crowned.

But oh, alas! the case is changed, you're wretched and forlorn,
The hardships now imposed on you, by slaves are only borne;
Your ancient rights, which you so long did with your blood
    maintain,
Are meanly sold and given up, and you dare scarce complain.

Justice now has left the land, with taxes you're opprest,
And every little prattling wretch may freely you molest;
The choicest of your noble blood are banished far away,
And such as do remain at home must truckle and obey.

Your martial spirit's quite decayed, you're poor contented
    slaves,
You're kicked and cuffed, oppressed, harassed, by scoundrels,
    fools, and knaves;
Against your king you did rebel, abjured the royal race,
For which just heaven did punish you, with woe, contempt,
    disgrace.

This prince alone the crown should wear, and royal sceptre sway,
To him alone you should submit, and your allegiance pay;
A prince endowed with virtues rare, so pious and so great,
That were it not to punish you, he'd have a better fate.

Your reputation thus you may, thus only can, retrieve,
And till you justice do to him, you need not think to thrive;
Oh! may the Almighty King of kings His sovereign power
    extend,
And his anointed precious life from perils all defend.

Oh ! may just heaven assert his right, him to his own restore,
And may the Scottish nation shine illustrious as before ;
O Caledon ! O Caledon ! how joyful would I be,
To see the king upon his throne, and you from chains set free.

GEORGE LOCKHART, Esq.,
The Jacobite Laird of Carnwath; died in 1732.

This gentleman was the eldest son of Lord President Lockhart, and the second Lockhart of Carnwath. He was a Commissioner for the Union, M.P. of the first British Parliament, engaged in all the intrigues for the restoration of the Stuarts, in 1715 was for a time imprisoned in Edinburgh Castle on suspicion, raised a troop of horse for the service of the Pretender, and narrowly escaped losing both life and fortune for his devotion to that cause ; but with a Scotsman Archbishop of Canterbury, and another wielding the rod of the British Empire, at present (1882), Scotland has no reason to complain of the Union.

DOWN THE WATER.

WHEN worn and fagged with care and trouble,
We sigh for breeze of wave and stubble,
And see the dark prospective smash—
Oh ! waft us down to fair Lamlash.

When trade is dull and looms are still,
And silent stands the idle mill,
And hopes prove vain that found on *jute*,
We'll seek the smiling shores of Bute.

Killarney's lakes are fair to view
When sparkling bright 'neath waves of blue,
But sweeter far with thee, my own,
To bill and coo at sunny Strone ;

Or, dreaming in some shady dell,
To watch dim mists creep down Goatfell,
Or hear thy loved voice tune a stanza
To murmuring wave in wild Lochranza ;

Or when the yellow harvest moon
Sheds tender brightness o'er Dunoon,
To hear the maidens in their glee
In music float from Hunter's Quay.

Let burning Sappho waft her strain
In music o'er the Ægean main !
We've heard a strain that's dearer far
Steal o'er the loch at Arrochar.

JOHN TWIG.

IN MEMORIAM OF A. WALKINSHAW,

BEREFT OF LIFE AT LEGGANFOOT RAILWAY CROSSING, NEAR THANKERTON, CLYDESDALE, 1877, AGED 17 YEARS.

HE is gone in his early manhood days
From the hearts who held him dear,
He is gone from his mother's anxious gaze,
And she mourns him with many a tear.

Swift came the message, short was the warning,
And plain is the lesson to all :
At life's busy noontide, at evening or morning,
Be ready, the Master may call.

His mother, alas ! will miss her son,
No other can fill his place ;
God grant her strength life's race to run,
And give her comfort and grace.

There are others, too, who weep for a friend
Who loved them with fervour and truth ;
Ah ! little they thought that the friendship would end
Ere he passed o'er the threshhold of youth.

Like the meteor's flash, with relentless power
Came the engine with fiery breath,
And bore him down as a fragile flower,
And he soon was still in death.

He has gone from all life's pleasure and pain,
    Its hours of toil and rest,
And we hope that to him to die was gain,
    And that now he is fully blest.

JOHN BLACK.

PEDEN AT THE GRAVE OF CAMERON.

To this spot did Peden, one of Cameron's dearest friends, repair, and harassed and vexed with personal sufferings, he sat down by the grave, and meekly raising his eyes to heaven, prayed, "Oh, to be wi' Richie!"

A SOUND of conflict in the moss! but that hath passed away,
And through a stormy noon and eve the dead unburied lay;
But when the sun a second time his fitful splendours gave,
One slant ray rested, like a hope, on Cameron's new-made grave.

There had been watchers in the night,—strange watchers, gaunt and grim,
And wearily, with faint, lean hands, they toiled a grave for him;
But ere they laid the headless limbs unto their mangled rest,
As orphaned children sat they down and wept upon his breast.

Oh! dreary, dreary was the lot of Scotland's true ones then—
A famine-stricken remnant, wearing scarce the guise of men;
They burrowed far and lonely 'mid the chill, dark mountain caves,
For those who once had sheltered them were in their martyr graves.

A sword had rested on the land! it did not pass away;
Long had they watched and waited, but there dawned no brighter day;
And many had gone back from them who owned the truth of old,
Because of much iniquity their love was waxen cold!

There came a worn and weary man to Cameron's place of rest,
He cast him down upon the sod, he smote upon his breast ;
He wept as only strong men weep when they must weep or die,
And "Oh, to be wi' thee, Richie !" was still his bitter cry.

" My brother ! oh, my brother ! thou hast passed before thy
    time,
And thy blood it cries for vengeance from this purple land
    of crime.
Who now shall break the bread of life unto the faithful
    band ?
Who now upraise the standard that is shattered in thine
    hand ?

" Alas, alas, for Scotland ! the once beloved of heaven !
The crown is fallen from her head, her holy garment riven ;
The ashes of her Covenant are scattered far and near,
And the voice speaks loud in judgment which in love she
    would not hear.

" Alas, alas, for Scotland ! for her mighty ones are gone ;
Thou, brother, thou art taken—I am left almost alone ;
And my heart is faint within me, and my strength is dried
    and lost—
A feeble and an aged man alone against a host !

" Oh ! pleasant was it, Richie, when we two could counsel
    take,
And strengthen one another to be valiant for His sake ;
Now seems it as the sap were dried from the old blasted tree,
And the homeless and the friendless would fain lie down
    with thee."

It was an hour of weakness as the old man bent his head,
And a bitter anguish rent him as he communed with the dead ;
It was an hour of conflict, and he groaned beneath the rod,
But the burden rolled from off him as he communed with
    his God.

"My Father! O my Father! shall I pray the Tishbite's
    prayer,
And weary in the wilderness whilst Thou would have me
    there ;
And shall I fear the coward fear of standing all alone,
To testify for Zion's King and the glory of His throne ?

"O Jesus ! blessed Jesus ! I am poor and frail and weak,
Let me not utter of my own, for idle words I speak ;
But give grace to wrestle now, and prompt my faltering
    tongue,
And breathe Thy name into my soul, and so I shall be strong.

"I bless Thee for the quiet rest Thy servant taketh now,
I bless Thee for his blessedness and for his crowned brow,
For every weary step he trod in faithful following Thee,
And for the good fight foughten well and closed right
    valiantly.

"I bless Thee for the hidden ones who yet uphold Thy name,
Who yet for Zion's King and Crown shall dare the death of
    shame ;
I bless Thee for the light that dawns even now upon my soul,[1]
And brightens all the narrow way with glory from the goal.

"The hour and power of darkness is fleeting fast away :
Light shall arise on Scotland—a glorious, glorious gospel day ;
Woe, woe to the oppressors ! they shall shrivel in His
    hand ;
Thy King shall yet return to thee, thou covenanted land.

"I see a time of respite, but the people will not bow ;
I see a time of judgment, even a darker time than now !
Then, Lord, uphold Thy faithful ones, as now Thou dost
    uphold,
And feed them as Thou still hast fed Thy chosen flock of old.

---

[1] Peden was believed to possess the spirit of prophecy.

P

"The glory! oh, the glory! it is bursting on my sight;
Lord, Thy poor vessel is too frail for all this blinding light!
Now let Thy good word be fulfilled, and let Thy kingdom
    come,
And, Lord, even in Thine own best time, take Thy poor
    servant home."

Upon the wild and lone Airmoss down sank the twilight grey,
In storm and cloud the evening closed upon that cheerless
    day;
But Peden went his way refreshed, for peace and joy were
    given,   .
And Cameron's grave had proved to him the very gate of
    heaven!

P.

LINES ON THE SCOTTISH MARTYRS.

I said my harp should sleep for aye--flung by--a useless
    thing;
I said that thou, my joyous muse, must curb thy eager wing;
I said that I must onward press, my pilgrim path along,
Nor cheer me as in days gone by with the glad voice of song.

Vain thought for him who strays alone o'er this wild, martyr
    land;
I feel a spell upon me here I may not understand.
If on these scenes that stretch around mine eye unmoved
    should look,
The murmuring streams would speak to me with sadly mild
    rebuke.

For still they seem to whisper, as they sweep their pebbled
    bed,
The names of those who here of old for Jesus lived and bled;
And still they seem to image, in their pure and peaceful flow,
The holy lives of those who dwelt beside them long ago.

Each rock and cave, each woody holm, preserves their memory
    still;
There stands for them a monument in every rugged hill;
And yet along the mountain side a lingering echo floats,
Where oft of old their song of praise sent up its joyful notes.

The old familiar voices upon the breezes come;
And while all nature speaks aloud, shall man alone be dumb?
Ah, no! nor is his voice unheard; the same rejoicing strain
That gladdened once the wilderness is thrilling there again.

'Tis heard by Renwick's simple tomb, amid the green Glen-
    cairn;
'Tis heard amid the heathy wilds of lone and drear Carsphairn;
'Tis heard beside the silvery Ken, and by the banks of Ayr,
Where Welch and Guthrie raised of old the voice of praise
    and prayer.

'Tis heard where lie the bones of him[1] who lived to preach
    and pray,
And died with prayer upon his lips amid the bloody fray;
'Tis heard where pours the winding Nith, and sweeps the
    placid Dee;
It mingles with the voice of streams, and with the sounding
    sea.

'Tis heard beside the rude gray stones,[2] where oft, in days of
    old,
The holy convocation met the sacred feast to hold;
Green Anwoth's heights have heard afar the same triumphant
    song,
And all the echoing rocks around the hallowed strain prolong.

'Tis heard where'er the memory lives of those whose blood
    was shed
Like water in the glorious cause of Christ, their living head;

[1] Cameron, who lived preaching and praying, and died praying and
fighting.
[2] Communion stones at Irongray.

'Tis heard where'er a Christian's heart to Christ's high call
    responds,
And shakes from off his fearless soul the world's debasing
    bonds.

'Tis heard from thousand voices now, of steadfast men and
    true,
Where once the scattered remnant met, the faithful but the
    few;
And still more loud that strain shall swell, tho' hand should
    join in hand,
From moor to hill, from hill to shore, to drive the dauntless
    band.

Vain thought, that they whose breasts are warmed with
    blood of martyred sires,
Whose songs of praise unsilenced rose, 'mid tortures, chains,
    and fires,
Should shrink because the tempest gloom hangs lowering o'er
    their path,
Or quail before the ruder storm of man's relentless wrath!

Vain thought, that they whose eyes are fixed in confidence
    and love
On Him who deigned to leave for them His glorious home
    above,
And for the joy before Him set, such bitter anguish bore,
Should fear to tread the roughest way which he has trod
    before.

Ah! no; where'er the shepherd leads the trusting sheep
    will go;
Rejoicing still to follow him, because his voice they know;
And pleasant is the path to them, tho' rugged oft it be,
Where yet the footsteps of the flock are traced along the
    lea.

                                    REV. JAMES G. SMALL.

POOR DAFT JAMIE.

ATTENDANCE give whilst I relate
How poor daft Jamie met his fate;
'Twill make your hair stand on your head
As I unfold the horrid deed.

That hellish monster, William Burke,
Like Reynard, sneaking on the lurk,
Coyducked his prey into his den,
And then the woeful work began.

" Come, Jamie, drink a glass wi' me,
And I'll gang wi' ye in a wee,
To seek your mother i' the town—
Come, drink, man, drink, and sit ye down."

" Na, na! I'll no drink wi' thee the noo,
For if I do 'twill mak' me fou;"
"Tuts man! a wee, wee drap will do you guid,
'Twill cheer your heart and warm your bluid."

At last he took the fatal glass,
Not dreaming what would come to pass;
When once he drank he wanted more,
Till he fell drunk upon the floor.

Burke cast himself on Jamie's face,
And clasped him in his foul embrace;
But Jamie waking in surprise,
Writhed in an agony to rise.

At last, with nerves unstrung before,
He threw the villain on the floor;
And though alarmed, and weakened too,
He would have soon o'ercome the foe.

230

But help was near, for it Burke cried,
And soon his friend was at his side;
Hare tripped up Jamie's heels, and o'er
He fell, alas! to rise no more.

Now both these bloodhounds him engage
As hungry tigers filled with rage;
Nor did they handle axe or knife
To take away poor Jamie's life.

No sooner done, than in a chest
They crammed this lately welcomed guest
And bore him into Surgeons' Square—
A victim fresh, a subject rare!

And soon he's on the table laid,
Exposed to the dissecting blade,
But where his members now may lay
Is not for me, nor you, to say.

But this I'll say—"Some thoughts did rise;"
It filled the students with surprise
That so short time should intervene
Since Jamie on the streets was seen.

But though his body is destroyed,
His soul can never be decoyed
From that celestial state of rest
Where he, I trust, is with the blest.

WRITTEN BY J. B.

Above is a copy of a broadside sung on the streets of Edinburgh after the execution of the murderer, Burke, and is a graphic account of the popular belief of the manner in which Daft Jamie was murdered. He was a poor harmless imbecile, well known on the streets of Edinburgh; usually bare-headed, bare-footed, and walked about with his hands clasped together, and may be said to have inaugurated the *Beard Movement*, for at that time, if not the only, he was almost the only person to be seen unshaven upon the streets. No case ever struck the public heart or imagination with greater horror than the West Port murders. The young women of Edinburgh, when they went out after sunset, kept their hands and aprons upon their mouths lest they should be suffocated with a plaster. Burke and Hare were well known at Carnwath, having on the previous harvest been employed at Carlindean. It was believed they murdered a poor hawker woman on that farm the night before they left; at anyrate, she was never seen there again. It was only for one that Burke was executed, but the actual number perpetrated was confessed to be at least 16 murders! When he appeared on the scaffold in company with the hangman, he was saluted with a hurra! as loud as George IV. received when he first alighted at Holyrood. I heard them both. "Choke him, Hangie! choke him!" was loudly and repeatedly vociferated.

THE BURNHOUSE KIRN.

WHEN the win's o' November blaw cauld owre the plain,
An' this hairst has been a hairst o' never ceasin' rain,
Tho' the Austrians and the Turks at ilk ither stand an' girn,
Yet we'll dance and be merry at the Burnhouse Kirn.

I've been in the crowded city among thousands o' men,
And on Tintoc's lonely summit where no fox wad mak' his
    den ;
Yet frae the crowded city to the mountain's lonely cairn,
Oh! there's naething can compare to the Burnhouse Kirn!

When Johnnie wi' his fiddle sets us a' dancin' mad,
An' the wee bit drap o' toddy mak's us a' singin' glad,
For a' our toils and troubles we dinna care a pirn,
When dancin' a' so merry at the Burnhouse Kirn.

There are some holy men, wi' faces ever sad,
Wad hae us to believe it's a sin to be glad ;
O ye stupid ignoramuses! gang to Moses an' learn—
The very Bible says, "Rejoice when ye celebrate the Kirn!"

Miss Wilson is as smart a lass as ever met the e'e,
And Maggie's cheeks, they are as sweet as apple pies to me ;
I rede ye a', baith great an' sma', tak' tent or ye may learn
That your hearts have got a scowther at the Burnhouse Kirn.

Sweet sings the laverock frae the cloud, the mavis frae the
    tree,
But there's a bonnie, bonnie bird that's sweeter far to me ;
Young men, beware! I fear, I fear, some hearts will get a
  ˙ birn!
Frae some bonnie witchin' een, at the Burnhouse Kirn.

Burnhouse is a farm at Carnwath where the feast of "Ingathering"
was duly observed for many years.—Exodus xxiii. 16, and Leviticus
xxiii. 39-41.

THE FLOWER OF WESTRAW.

O THERE blooms a bonnie lily in the woods o' Westraw,
A sweet an' bonnie lily in the woods o' Westraw,
An' monie a ane wad fain wile the bonnie flower awa'
Frae its sweet native bowers in the woods o' Westraw.

Oh ! pure are the streams of meandering Clyde,
An' sweet an' fair the bonnie flowers that deck the river-side,
But purer far, an' fairer, an' sweeter than them a'
Is the bonnie flower that blooms in the woods o' Westraw !

The merry lads o' Covinton may boast o' lasses fair,
An' Pettinain the praises o' his hinnie-lippit dear ;
But Covinton or Pettinain have none amang them a'
To match the bonnie lily in the woods o' Westraw !

In Carnwath toun, the gallant lads, so merry, brisk, an' fair,
A' wear their bonnets on their heads wi' sic a jaunty air,
That the hearts o' the lasses ane wad think was at their ca',
But they maunna try the bonnie flower that blooms at Westraw.

Young Johnnie was as blythe a lad as ever trod the plain,
An' thocht to win the bonnie flower, he was so spruce an' vain,
But she bade him try some muirlan' Meg at Wingate or
    Skylaw,
For he couldna please the bonnie flower that blooms at
    Westraw.

I ask not fame or fortune, high station, rank, or power,
But health and peace, contentment, and Westraw's bonnie
    flower;
Gie ithers India's diamond mines, and a' California,
But gie me the bonnie lily in the woods o' Westraw!

AYE WORK AWA'.

HELP yoursel' where'er ye gang, aye work awa'!
'Mang the summer's sunshine, an' the cheerless winter's snaw,
Never lippen till your frien's tho' they may loudly blaw—
Help yoursel' where'er ye gang, aye work awa'!

Fortune favours them wha work aye wi' a busy hand,
Folk never will win forrit if they at the fire-en' stan';
Look before ye loup, baith in meikle things an' sma'—
Tak' a' things in a canna way, an' aye work awa.

If ye canna speak a kindly word about the folk ye ken,
Oh! never let a bitter ane anither's ear gae ben;
For they're lifeless that are faultless, there's nane without
    a flaw,
Speak kindly o' your neebours then, an' aye work awa!

Keep ye a caum sough as ye dauner up an' doun,
Empty barrels aye are sure to gie the loudest soun';
An' when ye hear o' ithers' quarrels while they scrape an'
    craw,
Let your word among them be't—aye work awa'!

This life o' oors is just a fecht frae the cradle to the grave,
But the promise o' a better ane is given to the brave;
So let us fecht wi' faithfu' hearts, an' we'll win owre it a'—
Help yoursel' where'er ye gang, aye work awa'.

                    JOSEPH WRIGHT, COATBRIDGE.

GLAISCA WHISKY.

COME all ye folks who weary are
  O' life, its cares and trouble,
Who anything will do and dare
  So you may burst the bubble ;
I have a plan within my head
  That's new and nothing risky,
Whene'er you want to nick the thread,
  Just try oor Glaisca whisky.

CHORUS—Try oor Glaisca whisky ;
      Try oor Glaisca whisky ;
    It gies us pleasure wi' our death,
    So hey for Glaisca whisky !

A plunge in Clyde's no jist the thing ;
  But people who are dreary
May into it themselves gae fling,
  But I'm for something cheery.
The knife—the name o't gars me grue,
  An' mak's my face look dusky ;
But I prefer the barley broo,
  An' stick to Glaisca whisky.
      Try the Glaisca whisky, &c.

Death by the rape—weel, I'm no sure
  But I'd prefer't to mony ;
But then, my frien's, a dance in air
  Is onything but bonny ;
So they may hang themselves wha will,
  But I'm for something frisky—
Hey, landlord, fetch anither gill
  O' hame-made Glaisca whisky.
      Try the Glaisca whisky, &c.

The pooshin stuffs the doctors sell
  You scarcely can get ony,
But Glaisca whisky bears the bell,
  It's flavoured wi' sae mony ;

An' pooshin sellin's sae fenced roun',
To buy it is but risky;
But ye may cut throats, hang, or droon,
When primed wi' Glaisca whisky!
Try the Glaisca whisky, &c.

J. LIVINGSTON.

Written after reading the analysis of the Glaisca whisky in the *Mail*.

THE BAD WIFE.

I wi' an ill wife am perplexed,
I'm grieved, heart broken and sad,
Frae mornin' till e'en I'm sae vexed,
In truth I am like to go mad.

I try still to mak' her contented
By lettin' her carry the purse,
If I seek but a bawbee, demented,
She stampin' and ragin' doth curse.

And when even I try to be jolly,
Or to syne down care tak' a drap,
Enraged, she ca's it a folly,
Nor fails to lay sair on my tap.

And when, too, she wi' her kimmers
Do happen for to disagree,
She ca's them a' strumpets and limmers,
And a' the blame comes upon me.

Fie, Death, come quick, dinna tarry,
And freely I'll gie you my wife,
And again never mair would I marry,
To lead such a sorrowful life.

JAMES SMITH.

James Smith, we are proud to say, was a native of Carnwath, and
hailed from that large section of the parish "where heather blooms and
moorcocks craw." Tom Campbell asks—

"In joyous youth what heart hath never known
Thought, feeling, taste, harmonious as its own ?
Who hath not owned, with rapture smitten frame,
The power of grace, the magic of a name ? "

Certainly not Jamie Smith, for there was a bonnie lassie at the Skylaw
who had so completely enthralled the heart of honest Jamie, that, to use
a common but not very dignified expression, he could hardly tell what
end o' him was uppermost. He had good reason to be happy. Jessie,
with her ruddy cheeks and smiling countenance, always seemed glad to
see him, and joked and ridiculed those whom he supposed to be his rivals.
But alas! alas! one Sunday he was at Carnwath church, and had taken
his seat in the front of Wilsontown gallery, with the Skylaw shepherd and
his large dog beside him. But who can express his surprise, his rage and
indignation, when the precentor rose, and with loud tone and deliberate
voice proclaimed for marriage the lady whom he adored with his hated
rival! "Frailty, thy name is woman." Only last Friday she had pledged
her love to Jamie, and this was the manner in which she had kept her
vows. Being quite beside himself, in his passion he seized the shepherd's
dog by tail and neck, and hurled the unoffending animal at the head of
the precentor. That functionary screamed with terror, Bawty yelled and
howled, and the whole congregation was in uproar. After performing
this feat Jamie stalked down stairs, and left the astonished kirk folk to
compose themselves at their leisure ; he had enough to do to compose his
own mind. There is another incident in the experience of Jamie which
we have no doubt many of our readers will think strikingly corroborative
of Shakespeare's assertion that the lover, the lunatic, and the poet
are all akin to each other.

One fine summer Sunday morning Jamie had breakfasted on a couple
of salt herrings before going to church. The day was warm, the road
was long, the church was crowded, the very passages were filled with
people who could not get seats, and Jamie was in a pouring sweat and
suffering under a most intolerable thirst. The heat, the crowded church,
the long walk, and the herring breakfast, all combined had raised his
craving for water to a condition almost maddening. He would have left
the church, but the passage was impracticable. At length a bright idea
flashed upon his mind ; relief was within reach. He saw from the cloth
on the pulpit railing that a baptism was contemplated ; he rose from his
seat, walked to the pulpit stair, ascended half way up. The people were
astonished—alarmed. Did he mean to lay violent hands on the minister?
The minister's countenance changed, the minister's voice changed—at
length became silent altogether. Half-a-minute of painful suspense followed. He lifted both his arms—Was it to assault the minister? No,
but to grasp with eager and trembling hands the basin with the water for
dispensing the holy sacrament of baptism ; and in three or four long
pulls, with a goodly pause, and a hem and a hearty smack of his lips
between each draught, half-emptied, then replaced the sacred vessel, and
quietly resumed his seat, to the great relief of both minister and congregation. Jamie, on being questioned and remonstrated with on the
impropriety of drinking the baptism water, pled the example of David
eating the shewbread when he was hungry, which it was not lawful for
any to eat but the priests, while no such peculiar sanctity attached to
the baptism water, and was he to die for thirst and water in the house?
not likely !

THE BATTLE OF WATERLOO.

ON the sixteenth day of June, my boys,
    In Flanders where we lay,
The bugle did the alarm sound
    Before the break of day;
The British, Belgians, Brunswickers,
    And Hanoverians too,
They Brussels left that morning bold,
    For the plains of Waterloo.

Napoleon to his men did say
    Before that they began,
"My heroes, if we lose the day,
    Our nation is undone;
The Prussians we've already beat,
    We'll beat the British too,
And display victorious eagles
    On the plains of Waterloo."

Then soon the battle did begin
    And cannons loud did roar,
We being short of cavalry,
    They pressed on us full sore;
Three British cheers we gave them then,
    And volleys not a few,
We made them wish they were in France
And far from Waterloo.

For full four hours and longer
    We sustained the bloody fray,
And through the dark and dreary night
    Upon our arms we lay;
The orders of our General bold
    Next day we did pursue,
And retired in files for six long miles,
    To the plains of Waterloo.

On the eighteenth, in the morning grey,
  Both armies did advance,
On this side stood brave Britain's sons,
  On that the pride of France ;
The fate of Europe in his hand,
  Each man his sabre drew,
And death or victory was the word
  On the plains of Waterloo.

Upon the right they did begin,
  Prince Jerome led the van,
Imperial guards and cuirassiers
  Thought none could them withstand ;
But British steel soon made them yield
  Though our numbers were but few,
We prisoners made, though more lay dead
  On the plains of Waterloo.

Upon our left they bent their course
  With disappointed rage,
The Belgian line stood for a time,
  But could not stand the charge ;
Then Caledon struck up her drone,
  And loud her chanter blew,
Played Marshal Ney a new strathspey
  To the tune of Waterloo.

Lord Wellington's a hero bold,
  His courage aye was true,
Both skill and valour he displayed
  That day at Waterloo.
Two years were added to our time,
  For pay and pension too,
And now we are recorded all
  As men of Waterloo !

Two of our greatest modern poets, Scott and Byron, have sung of
Waterloo. The above lines are the production of a common soldier who
was personally engaged in that terrible struggle. There were five men
from Carnwath on that eventful day. John Dymock, who had been

with Abercrombie in Egypt, with Sir John Moore at Corunna, and with Wellington all through the Peninsular War, and except a slight wound on the foot with a spent ball, never received a scratch, although in several engagements he saw his comrades fall on his right hand and on his left. George M'Call of Carnwath, in the Greys, had his head taken off by a cannon ball. One man in the same regiment, known to his comrades as Wee Craig, had a similar fate ; but instead of falling, he instantly grasped with both hands the cloak in front of the saddle, and kept his seat, with the blood streaming on his comrades. When this happened they were retreating, by advancing one hundred yards and retreating two, and the horse kept its place with its headless rider upon his back while the regiment performed this manœuvre three times, then the one on his left cut the girth with his sabre and the man fell to the ground. When fighting, the sword of one broke at the hilt, and turning to his neighbour, he said, "O Jock ! what will I do now ; " he had scarcely spoken when his head was cloven to the teeth. Another had his head cut quite through. Thomas Finnie, at an early stage, was disabled by a wound in the arm. Dixon Vallance, near the close, had an eye blown out by a musket ball ; he had at the time accidentally turned his head, or the ball would have gone through it altogether. Robert Andrew was in a regiment of foot formed in hollow square ; he was in front, kneeling on one knee ; a regiment of French dragoons walked leisurely round to see if they could not find a gap to spring in among them ; one of them brandished his sword to cleave Rob's head, but Rob was all alive, and seeing what was coming, drew the trigger of his musket and sent a ball into the trooper, accompanied with the message, "Take you that, my lad." He immediately fell to the ground. Such is a short note of Carnwath's experiences at Waterloo. Vallance, Dymock, Andrew, and Finnie survived many years after. At this terrible battle it was computed that 40,000 men were killed and disabled, besides horses unnumbered.

BY MEDWIN'S STREAMS.

Air—Rocks of Gibraltar.

By sweet Medwin's streams at e'en
I've rambled oft unseen,
To meet wi' the lassie I lo'e dearly, O !
Where the burnie gurgling plays
'Neath its verdant, flowery braes,
As down the glen it wimples clearly, O !

Pearly dew the flowerets kissed
As they hung their blooming crest,
And perfumed the e'enin' gales that gently fanned them, O !

And the hares were sporting seen
On the Spittal knowes sae green,
As the gloamin flung her mantle all around them, O !

Beauteous scenes inspired my breast,
As I onward lightly pressed,
And beheld in them sweet emblems of my dearie, O !
Till the loveliest of all forms
I enfolded in my arms,
And with boundless joy embraced my dearie, O !

Oh ! how swift the moments flew,   .
As we trod the sparkling dew
Beneath the lady moon, that beamed so kindly, O !
Oh the joys felt when we met,
And our vows I'll ne'er forget
As each parting pledge we sealed with kisses fondly, O !

T. D.

MY MOTHER.

I LOVE to visit the lone churchyard
    Where the dead are soundly sleeping,
And there to sit on my mother's grave,
    And ease my heart with weeping.
To weep in secret silence there,
    O'er all to life that bound me,
And think of nought but the spirits of light
    That invisible hover around me.

I love to visit the lone churchyard,
    For there my mother's resemblance
Appears like a seraph reflected bright,
    In the tears of a sad remembrance.
While busy memory early scenes
    Of youth and joy is tracing,
So bright the picture grows, I think
    My presence she still is gracing.

I love to visit the lone churchyard,
  When the shades of eve are coming ;
When the wind sends forth its fitful gusts,
  And the gloomy trees are humming.
Sounds ! how unlike my mother's voice,
  The voice of heavenly gladness ;
That oft my soul with rapture filled
  But now is lost in sadness.

                                    ANON.

A MOTHER'S DIRGE.

BRING me flowers all young and sweet,
That I may strew the winding sheet,
Where calm thou sleepest, baby fair,
With roseless cheek and auburn hair.

Bring cypress from some sunless spot,
Bring me the blue forget-me-not,
That I may strew them o'er thy bier
With long-drawn sigh and gushing tear.

Oh ! what on earth can ever prove
So constant as a mother's love !
Oh ! what on earth can give relief
Or solace to a mother's grief !

No more, my baby, shalt thou lie
With drowsy smile and half-shut eye,
Pillowed upon my fostering breast,
Serenely sinking into rest.

The grave must be thy cradle now ;
The wild flowers o'er thy breast shall grow,
While still my heart is full of thee
In widowed solitude shall be.

                  Q

Yea! from mine arms thy soul hath flown
Above, and found the heavenly throne,
To join that blest angelic ring
That aye around the altar sing.

Methought, when years had rolled away,
That thou wouldst be mine age's stay;
And often have I dreamt to see
The boy—the youth—the man in thee

But thou art gone! forever gone!
And left me childless and alone,
To pour the bitter, bitter tear,
Without a hope of comfort here!

Farewell, my child! the dews shall fall
At morn and evening o'er thy pall;
And daisies, when the vernal year
Revives, upon thy turf appear.

Farewell, my child! if life were long
This would be even a heavier song:
But years like phantoms quickly pass,
Then look to us from memory's glass.

Soon on death's couch shall I recline :
Soon shall my head be laid with thine;
And we in rapture meet above,
To live for evermore in love.

These lines contain a complaint more than usually mournful and
pathetic; it is no less than the wailings of a broken heart—the language
in which we give vent to our feelings on beholding the ruin of our best-
formed and proudest hopes. What a consolation it is to the bereaved the
hope of meeting again, and for ever, in a happy eternity.

THE LAIRDS O' CARNWATH.

THE Lairds o' Carnwath! O the Lairds o' Carnwath!
I sing to the praise o' the Lairds o' Carnwath;
Frae the east to the west, frae the Tweed to Cape Wrath,
Ye'll find nae sic Lairds as the Lairds o' Carnwath!

When the good and the great King Robert was gone,
Wha settled for ever our auld Scottish throne,
Sir Simon of Lee had the glorious part
To lay in the grave—not his head—but his heart.

In the dark and the dreary Covenant days,
When our faithers were hunted, like hares on the bracs,
By Claverhouse' troopers, owre mountain and strath,
They had aye a gude friend in Sir George o' Carnwath.

When bonnie Prince Charlie cam' over the main,
To fight for the crowns which he thought were his ain,
In a' the great dangers attendin' his path,
He had nae truer friend than the Laird o' Carnwath!

And now, gentle comrades, before I sit down,
One bumper I crave yet, I beg as a boon,
May a' sort of happiness wait on the path
Of Lockhart of Lee and the Laird o' Carnwath!
Nov., 1869.

Sung at the dinner in honour of the majority of the late Sir N. M.
Lockhart. Only five years after, this talented, accomplished, and amiable
young gentleman was called away from this sublunary state of things.
His death was reckoned a great misfortune to a wide district, as he lived
long enough to shew that he felt a deep interest in the welfare and
prosperity of the numerous population upon his extensive estates. "But
the ways o' heaven are aboon a' ken."

OLD SCOTCH TUNES.

IMMORTAL tunes! immortal!
    How many a man and maid
Have brightened at your stirring strains,
    Have wept when you were played,
Who now are sleeping, far and wide,
    Deep in the silent shade.

        But ye live on for ever,   .
            For ever fresh and new,
        Unshadowed by a touch of age,
            No halt in your measure true.

Free as the breezy air of heaven
    Still wings "The Braes o' Mar,"
"Kind Robin lo'es," as erst he did,
    And "Gillie Callum's War,"
"The Brig o' Perth," and "Monymusk,"
    Still as ye were—ye are.

But we drop out and perish :
    Our partners of old years,
Far in the dark I see them,
    Half blinded by my tears.
Give o'er ! O tunes, give o'er !
    Ye raise the dead for me ;
They come from every bracken bush,
    From every hazel tree.

Nay, sound once more—ye raise them
    And bring them back to life
Crowned with a strength immortal,
    Victorious after strife !
All that was earth hath left them ;
    All that was heaven remains :
The god-like in the human soul,
    Divested of its stains.

Are they, as I am, conscious
  That thus we meet again?
Once more beside each other
  Recalled by music's strain.

May not the angelic harmony
  Which is to raise the dead,
Thus steal upon the sleeping soul
  From which this life hath fled?
The last trump of the angel,
  Which wakes the sleeping spheres,
What is it but the harmony
  Returning of past years—
The life and love of which the sound
  Awakes the soul that hears?

But oh! ye tunes! however that may be,
Ye are not more, but less, than we;
The lost whom ye recall to earth
Are they who gave you first their birth.
You cannot live and they be dead,
Your presence here is in their stead.

                    BISHOP EWING OF ARGYLE.

WHEN SHALL WE MEET AGAIN?

WHEN shall we all meet again?
Oft shall glowing hope expire,
Oft shall wearied love retire,
Oft shall death and sorrow reign
Ere we all shall meet again.

Though in distant lands we sigh
Beneath a far—a foreign sky,
Though the deep between us rolls,
Friendship still unites our souls,

And in fancy's wide domain
Oft we all shall meet again.

When the dreams of life are fled
And its wasted lamp is dead,
When in cold oblivion's shade
Beauty, wealth, and fame are laid,
Where immortal spirits reign,
There may we all meet again !

GOING HOME.

WE said that the days were evil,
  We felt that they might be few,
For low was our fortune's level
  And heavy the winters grew ;
But one who had no possession
  Looked up to the azure dome,
And said, in his simple fashion—
  " Dear friends, we are going home.

" This world is the same dull market
  That wearied its earliest sage ;
The times to the wise are dark yet,
  But so hath been many an age ;
And rich grow the toiling nations,
  And red grow the battle's spears,
And dreary with desolations
  Roll onward the laden years.

" Oh ! what need of the changeless story
  Which time hath so often told,
Of the spectre that follows glory,
  The canker that comes with gold ;—
That wisdom, and strength, and honour
  Must fade like the far sea foam,
And death is the only winner—
  But, friends, we are going home.

" The homes we had hoped to rest in
 Were open to sin and strife,
The dreams that our youth was blest in
 Were not for the wear of life;
For care can darken the cottage
 As well as the palace hearth,
And birthrights are sold for pottage,
 But never redeemed on earth.

" The springs have gone by in sorrow,
 The summers were grieved away,
· And ever we feared to-morrow,
 And ever we blamed to-day.
In depths which the searcher sounded,
 On hills which the high heart clomb,
Have trouble and toil abounded—
 But, friends, we are going home.

" Our faith was the bravest builder,
 But found not a stone of trust;
Our love was the fairest gilder,
 But lavished its wealth on dust;
And time hath the fabric shaken,
 And fortune the clay hath shewn,
For much they have changed and taken,
 But nothing that was our own.

" The light that to us made baser
 The paths which so many choose,
The gifts there were found no place for,
 The riches we could not use;
The heart that when life was wintry,
 . Found summer in strain and tome,
With these to our kin and country,—
 Dear friends, we are going home!"

                    FRANCIS BROWN.

www.ingramcontent.com/pod-product-compliance
Lightning Source LLC
Chambersburg PA
CBHW020101030726

47498CB00006B/1887